The
HOUSE
at
MERMAID'S
COVE

D0956974

ALSO BY LINDSAY JAYNE ASHFORD

The Snow Gypsy
Whisper of the Moon Moth
The Woman on the Orient Express
The Color of Secrets
The Mysterious Death of Miss Jane Austen
Frozen
Strange Blood
Where Death Lies
The Killer Inside
The Rubber Woman

The
HOUSE
at
MERMAID'S
COVE

LINDSAY JAYNE ASHFORD

LAKE UNION
PUBLISHING

Text copyright © 2020 by Lindsay Jayne Ashford
All rights reserved.

Published by Lake Union Publishing, Seattle

www.apub.com

Amazon, the Amazon logo, and Lake Union Publishing are trademarks of Amazon.com, Inc., or its affiliates.

ISBN-13: 9781542006354
ISBN-10: 154200635X

Cover design by David Drummond

Printed in the United States of America

In memory of my great-aunt Amelia Groom,
in whose house I believed a fox hid behind the cactus
pattern on the wallpaper—my earliest memory of the
awesome power of imagination.

Chapter 1

Cornwall, England: April 1943

I thought the sea would take me, but it spat me out as the sky was turning pink. I drifted in like flotsam, washed up in a sandy hollow among weed-strewn rocks. I lay there, numb with cold, broken shells prickling my cheeks. Why could I feel my face but not the gashes on my feet?

I must have been slipping into unconsciousness when the banshee wail of a gull pierced the fog inside my head. As I gulped for breath, a gush of water stung my nose and tongue. It tasted like Dublin Bay oysters. How strange, when my life was hanging by a thread, to remember something I hadn't eaten for a dozen years.

It was a dog that found me. If it hadn't been for him, I might have lain for hours in that hidden place, until the tide came creeping in to pull me back to where I'd come from. He'd been rooting about in the trees above the cove and gone tearing off when he scented something more interesting on the beach. Not me. A rotting gannet, I found out later.

I heard the barking over the lapping of the waves and the cries of the seabirds. Then I caught the sound of someone singing. A man's voice, deep and clear. The words were in Latin. For a moment I thought I really had died. It was the sort of thing I'd always imagined angels singing. But then the dog came bounding over, snuffling in my ear and pawing the bare skin of my shoulder.

The singing stopped. I felt the thud of feet on the sand as the man ran to see what his animal had found. A pitiful, shameful sight I must have been—naked but for the chemise, which had ripped when the waves carried me through the spiked ribs of the metal barrier at the mouth of the cove.

I heard him catch his breath as he dropped down beside me. I felt the heat of his hand on my head, his fingers raking cropped hair wet and slick with salt, like the fur of a seal. Then he must have spotted what was stitched into the neck of the chemise, because he said it aloud.

Nine-three-seven.

That was the first clue to where I was: my number, spoken in English. His hand traced one of the threadlike scars that crisscrossed my back. Then his fingers were on my wrist, feeling for a pulse.

"Can you hear me?" He turned my head sideways. He scraped sand from around my nose. The smarting sensation brought a muffled whimper from somewhere inside me. Then I felt the weight of his body pressing down on my back. Seawater gushed from my mouth. I spluttered, retched. The dog barked at me. I could smell his breath, rancid with dead meat.

"Be quiet, Brock!" He grasped my shoulders. "Can you sit up?" He turned me over so that I was half sitting, half lying, on the sand. Through a blur of salt water, I saw that the chemise had ridden indecently up my thighs. The shock of that brought the wrong language to my lips.

"Ne me regardez pas!" My hands went to the frayed hem of the fabric, tugging uselessly.

"You're French?"

As my vision cleared, I saw flecks of amber and gold in his irises. Black lashes and eyebrows. A face not much older than mine. "Not French. Irish," I croaked back. The sea had burned my throat.

He tilted his head, an intense look in his eyes as if he were trying to see through mine to catch a glimpse of what lay inside.

I tried to stand up. But when the soles of my feet met the sand, I crumpled.

"You're bleeding!" He took a large white handkerchief from his pocket and wrapped it around my right foot. As I watched him, I realized that blood was oozing from my left ankle, too. When he saw it, he pulled off his sweater and unbuttoned his shirt, which he bound around my other leg. I caught the scent of his skin as he bent over me. It made me think of the men I'd seen sunbathing on the deck of the ship as we'd headed up the coast of Africa and into the Mediterranean. I watched his hands, mesmerized, wondering if any of those men were still alive.

"You need a doctor." He wrapped his sweater around my shoulders like a shawl. Then he lifted me as if I weighed no more than his dog. One of his hands was under my thigh. Somewhere in my fogged brain a voice cried out. But I hadn't the strength to make him put me down.

He carried me across the beach to a low building sheltered by the trees that fringed the cove. The morning sun lit up walls of pale gray stone with sky-blue painted shutters over the windows. I wondered where I was. My throat stung too much to ask. He held me with one arm as he dug in his pocket for a bunch of keys.

It was as dark as night inside. There was a faint smell of fish and woodsmoke. He set me down on a pile of something that rustled as I settled into it. When he struck a match to light a kerosene lamp, I saw rods propped against the wall in front of me and nets hanging from the rafters. I was sitting on a great heap of sailcloth, my injured feet resting on a coil of rope. The dog was beside me, making a bed for himself in the crook of my arm. I hugged him to me like a furry hot-water bottle.

"I'm going to light a fire—get you warmed up a bit." He was crouching in front of a potbellied iron stove, tossing in kindling and logs from a willow basket. "Can you get out of that wet undershirt? I'll fetch you a blanket."

I glanced across at him as he went back to the stove, afraid that he would turn around and see even more than he'd already seen. But he was pouring water from a big metal canister into a kettle, which he set on top of the stove. It was hard to wriggle out of the chemise. The sea had molded it to my body like a second skin. He kept his back to me until I'd covered myself up.

"Take a drop of this while the kettle boils." He handed me a silver flask.

I hesitated as I brought it up to my mouth. The shiny metal reflected the lamp, throwing a glimmer of gold across his bare chest.

"It's brandy," he said.

I shuddered as it went down. It sent fire into my stomach, like the wine they give you at Mass. But I didn't like the taste of it as much. I passed the flask back to him.

I suppose I should have been afraid, sitting there naked and crippled under a blanket. But he was looking at me the way you'd look at a rare insect in a glass jar. I could almost hear him sizing me up: the shorn hair, the scars, the number, the foreign language. Prisoner of war? Escaped convict? Spy?

"The only other thing I have down here is tea," he said. "Will you take it black? There's no milk or sugar—but I think there might be some honey."

The hot, sweet tea revived me. But as warmth spread through my body, my feet began to throb. He saw me wince as I shifted them off the coil of rope. The dog raised his head and licked my chin.

"I'm going to telephone the doctor," he said. "And I'll bring you some clothes."

"Thank you—you're . . ." I faltered, unable to look at him. His eyes unnerved me. "You're very kind. But I don't need a doctor. I can dress the cuts—if you have bandages and iodine." I was still looking at my feet. "I'm a nurse," I said. Not a lie. But not the whole truth.

"An Irish nurse—who speaks French." He said it softly, almost to himself.

"I was working in Africa—the Belgian Congo," I said. "Everyone at the hospital spoke in French. I was on my way back to Ireland. The ship was hit."

His eyes narrowed. "What ship?"

"The *Brabantia.*"

"Where were you?"

I closed my eyes. "I'm not sure. Somewhere in the English Channel. It was the middle of the night." A jumble of images surged out of the darkness, like the seawater that had come gushing from my mouth and nose. *All those people.*

"Was it a mine or a torpedo?"

"I . . . I don't know." All I remembered was standing on the deck, looking at the stars, thinking how impossible it seemed that a war was going on. And then the rail I'd been holding on to was blown clean away. I could recall the shock of the icy water, the muffled shouts and screams as I fought my way to the surface. The smell of the smoke drifting across the water. And then the awful silence as I drifted away, clinging to a splintered raft that had once been a dining table.

"Who were you traveling with?"

"No one." That was the truth. The woman who was sharing my cabin had left the ship at Marseille, thank God. But if I'd told him that, he might have asked who she was. And the temptation had already taken hold of me. The dawning realization that, to this man, I could be anyone; I could shed my old identity like the clothes that had gone down with the ship.

He stopped to pick up my chemise, which was lying in a damp heap on the floor. "I'll get this washed and mended for you." It was inside out—the number clearly visible. I thought he was going to ask me what it signified, but he didn't.

"I won't be long. I'll bring you some clothes and something to eat. Come here, Brock!" The dog jumped off me.

"Thank you, Mr. . . ."

"Trewella. Jack Trewella. Forgive me—what's your name?"

I opened my mouth but all that emerged was air. I coughed and put out my hand, pretending that the seawater had brought on a choking fit.

"It's all right—you can tell me later." He disappeared. I heard the key turn in the lock.

Chapter 2

I wondered why my rescuer had bothered to lock the door when he knew that I couldn't walk. I hoped he'd done it as an act of protection—not because he thought I was a spy pretending to be disabled by a few cuts. Perhaps he would come back with a gang of policemen. I told myself that if he really thought I was a threat, he wouldn't have shown me such gentle kindness. Naïve of me, I suppose. But for all my adult life I'd been living in a bubble where there was little room for pretense.

I pictured him climbing a path through the trees with my torn underwear tucked under his arm. He'd said he was going to get it washed and mended. Something in the way he'd spoken suggested servants, not a wife. I asked myself what kind of Englishman would be singing in Latin while walking his dog. Could he be a priest? If he was, he would probably try to make me go back. And that was something I had already decided I couldn't do.

I must have fallen asleep while I waited for him to return. I dreamed that I was on board a ship. Not the *Brabantia*, but the liner that had taken me out to Africa in '34. In the dream it was our first night out of port, and I was dancing. It was an odd thing to dream about because for me that floating ballroom was out-of-bounds. We had to be in our cabin by eight thirty, with lights-out at nine. My roommate would always be snoring gently a few minutes later. But not me. The life of the ship was just starting at that time of the evening. I would catch drifts of music: the notes of melodies I remembered from my teens. It brought back the faces of boys who had waltzed me round the dance halls of Dublin. Boys whose lips had hovered dangerously close to mine, smelling of cigarettes and ginger ale.

From the age of eighteen I had been kept away from all this. For three years I'd lived behind high walls, deprived of all the pleasures I'd taken for granted as a girl. But on board the ship the world I had left behind was there—just yards away. I was permitted to walk around the decks during daylight hours, but not to join in the games of tennis and quoits the other passengers were enjoying. I could go to the library for the service of worship that was held there, but I couldn't take any of the books from the shelves. I remember stopping in front of a billboard advertising films that were being shown on the voyage. I'd stared at the faces of Clark Gable and Jean Harlow, longing to see *Saratoga*. It had been easier when I was shut in not to miss such things.

Lying awake in my cabin I would hear the clink of ice as waiters pushed buckets of champagne along the corridor; waves of laughter as the doors to the saloon opened and closed; and later, when the band had stopped playing, I saw shadowy profiles outside my window— lovers kissing in the dark.

One night, when sleep refused to come, I crept out of the cabin sometime after midnight with a shawl draped over my head and shoulders. Even though it was dark, I was afraid of being recognized. On my daytime walks I had sometimes caught male passengers following me with their eyes. It seemed that for some men, a woman like me presented a peculiar attraction. A special challenge. To be seen prowling the decks in the early hours of the morning would, I feared, encourage that sort of man.

I'd settled myself into a deck chair, gazing at a vast starlit sky, watching a banana moon slip out of the waves. I must have fallen into a sort of trance as I imagined myself suspended between its yellow horns as if

I were lying in a hammock. As it climbed higher, I was looking down at the houses of the people on the coasts bordering the sea. But they were dream houses and had no roofs. I could see couples side by side in bed, children cuddling toys as they slept. It had felt like a glimpse of the life I could have had.

The sound of something rattling overhead brought me out of that deep sleep—that dream of a dream. I sat up, startled, wondering where on earth I was. My brain took a while to make sense of the shadowy shapes of the boathouse, to work out that the noise I could hear was a gull hopping about on the roof.

Perhaps I shouldn't have been surprised that on my first day of freedom—in this place whose name I didn't yet know—I'd dreamed about dancing and marriage and children. For all the years of trying, I'd never really managed to bury the yearnings that had surfaced on that voyage to Africa. Nine years on, I was as far from suppressing that side of my nature as I'd been at twenty-one. Further, perhaps—because heading back to Europe on the *Brabantia*, I had prayed for a way out. And three days later the ship had been hit.

All those people.

Your fault. You willed it.

Better if you had died, too.

The damning voice inside my head was silenced by the creak of the door opening.

"I've brought the first aid kit you asked for. And something for you to wear."

His voice was muffled by the pile of things he was carrying in his arms. I could see only the top half of his face. There was no sound of Brock, the dog. He must have left him at home—wherever that was.

"There's bread and some eggs, too. Sorry I can't offer you bacon—our pigs are feeding half the county these days."

A farmer, then, I thought, *not a priest.* I wondered if I had imagined that otherworldly singing.

He laid the bundle down beside me.

"Thank you, Mr. Trewella."

"Please—call me Jack." He pulled a metal skillet from a bag slung across his shoulders. While he busied himself at the stove, I examined the clothes he'd brought me. On top of the pile was a shamrock-green scarf of the softest wool. I thought it might be cashmere. I wasn't certain, as I'd never owned anything like that. There was a cream silk blouse, still wrapped in tissue paper as if it had never been worn. Underwear of the same fabric slid out from another swathe of tissue paper. I felt blood surge into my cheeks as I held up a lace-trimmed camisole. Whose clothes were these? What woman would lend garments like this to a total stranger?

"I hope they'll fit you." He was breaking an egg into the pan.

"I think they will." I had the camisole on now. It felt wrong, wearing something so luxurious next to my skin. I slipped my arms into the sleeves of the blouse and began fastening the tiny pearl buttons. "They're lovely—whose are they?"

Fat sizzled in the pan, drowning out the first words of his reply. "Left them behind before the war. They're not too old fashioned, are they?"

"Not at all." I wondered what he would say if I told him what kind of clothes I usually wore. I spotted a label inside the heather-colored woolen skirt he'd brought for me. *Lanvin of Paris*. That sounded as expensive as the silk underwear. It wasn't easy wriggling into it while lying down, but I managed somehow. There was a cardigan—mauve, like the skirt. I felt much warmer when I put it on. Finally, I knotted the scarf around my neck. My legs would have to remain bare until the wounds had healed. I undid the handkerchief and shirt Jack had bound round them. The white cotton was covered in bloodstains.

"I'm sorry I've made such a mess of your things," I said.

"Don't be," he called over his shoulder. "Your need was greater than mine."

"Well, it was very good of you." I started dabbing iodine onto the torn flesh. The sting of it made me wince.

He brought the eggs to me as I was fastening a bandage around my right foot. He made a table from an upturned wooden crate and set the plate on it. "Sorry it's rather primitive. I would have taken you to the house, but it's a steep climb through the woods. It would have been tricky, carrying you."

"Thank you." I was suddenly famished. But I hesitated. Eating alone, without the ritual that had accompanied every meal, was something I never did.

"Go on—don't let it go cold."

I tore the bread in half and jabbed it into one of the eggs.

He dropped into a squatting position so that his head was level with mine. "What happened to your hair?"

My free hand went to my head. The short tufts had dried into salt-encrusted spikes. I wondered if that was why he'd brought me a scarf—so I could cover it up. I stared at a trickle of egg yolk oozing over what was left of the bread.

"I'm sorry," he said again. "You don't have to tell me—not if it's painful for you. But can I know your name?"

I heard the piercing cry of a seagull and the scratch of its claws as it landed on the roof. Jack was waiting for an answer. I knew without looking at his face that he thought I was working out some lie. But it wasn't that. I had surrendered my name, along with everything else I possessed, twelve years ago. I had been given another one—not of my choosing. A man's name. A saint's name. From the very start, it mocked me. I felt I would never be able to live up to it.

"My name is . . . Alice." The word felt strange, like a pebble in my mouth.

"Alice." He said it with a smile in his voice, as if he were coaxing a child. "Alice what?"

I was afraid to tell him. It would give him power over me. The power to send me back.

"If I don't know your surname, I won't be able to contact your family," he said. "You'll want them to know you're all right."

"I have no family. My parents are dead. There's no one else."

I took another mouthful. It tasted like the breakfasts I remembered from Ireland. There had been eggs on the ship, but they had been pale and insipid compared to these. And I had heard passengers say that in England people were having to eat powdered eggs brought in from America.

"But there must be someone who's expecting you?" He was looking at my hands. At the silver band on my ring finger.

"These eggs are very good," I said. "Do you keep chickens?"

"Yes. And cows. Although there's barely enough grass for them now, with all the wheat we're having to grow." His eyes searched my face. "I want to help you, Alice. But you must understand: This country is at war. I have to know that you're not—"

"I know what you're thinking," I said quickly. "I'm not an enemy. I'm not an escaped convict, either." I stared at the empty plate in front of me. If it hadn't been for my feet, I could have tried to get away, broken out next time he left me and taken my chances in whatever place this was. But my injuries weren't going to heal overnight. I was his prisoner. I was going to have to tell him some of it, at least. I took a breath. "You saw the number on my chemise?"

He nodded.

"I was given that number when I joined the order."

His forehead creased into neat furrows. "Order?" From the look in his eyes, he was imagining something secret and sinister.

"The Sisters of Mary the Virgin."

"You're a *nun*?"

"I was." I'd used the past tense. It felt terrifying. I half expected a bolt of lightning to pierce the wooden ceiling and strike me dead on the spot.

Chapter 3

I don't think Jack believed me at first. He was quite clever about it—appearing to accept what I'd said but throwing in the odd comment or question to test me out. He asked me about my work in Africa. He wanted to know why I'd left the Congo to return to Ireland.

"It wasn't my choice," I replied, "but the first rule of the convent is obedience. Sister Clare—the nun in charge of the mission hospital—said they were sending me back to the motherhouse for what they call spiritual refreshment." I shook my head. "It sounds disloyal, I know, but I couldn't bear the thought of being back inside those walls, cut off from life."

"Not disloyal." He shrugged. "Understandable." He told me then that he didn't really go along with organized religion. Singing in the church choir was the limit of his involvement. "We're rehearsing a Gregorian chant for the Easter service," he said. "'*Regina*' something—I can never remember the title."

"'*Regina Caeli*'—'The Queen of Heaven.'"

His eyes crinkled at the edges. It almost looked like a smile. "Devil of a job, memorizing Latin," he said. "But I suppose I shouldn't really say that in front of a nun."

I thought I'd passed the test. Then, without missing a beat, he said: "I couldn't help noticing those scars on your back. Who did that to you?"

I looked away. "No one."

"No one?" There was more than an edge of disbelief in his voice.

"I did it to myself. They call it mortification of the flesh. It was part of what we had to do. Every Wednesday and Friday after lights-out."

"My God," he murmured. "No wonder you wanted to leave." He stood up and went to throw more wood into the stove. Then he asked me what I planned to do if I wasn't going back to the convent.

"I don't have a plan," I said. I paused. All I wanted was to escape my old life. But I had no idea how I would live outside of the order. I was afraid to ask yet more from this man who had already done so much for me, but with no money and nowhere to go, I had to summon up the courage. "Could I stay for a while? Do you need help on the farm? I could work in return for food and a place to sleep."

I still had no idea where in England I was. That was something else I wanted to ask, but I was afraid of blowing a hole in the fragile web of trust we had begun to weave. I feared it might make him doubt me, make him think I really was a spy.

"Well, there's plenty of work. But finding you a bed . . ." He trailed off with a shake of his head. "The house is packed to the rafters. It's been taken over by the government—for military training. They've commandeered every room—including mine. And we have a group of children—evacuees—living in the servants' quarters."

Servants' quarters. That sounded quite grand—nothing like the farmhouses I had known as a child. I glanced at the fishing nets hanging from the rafters, at the long black shadows of rods and oars cast by the glow of the hurricane lamp. "Couldn't I stay here?"

"Here?" His eyes widened. "With the stink of fish and mildew? What would you sleep on?"

I patted the heap of sailcloth. "I can make a bed of this."

"Really?"

I smiled. "Believe me, it won't be any less comfortable than a convent mattress."

"But wouldn't you be frightened, all alone down here at night?"

I almost laughed. "You know, one of the worst things about being a nun is that you never get to be alone. Your cell is a space in a dormitory divided by nothing more than curtains. When you're not working, praying, eating, or sleeping, you're expected to sit with the other nuns, sewing or knitting. The number of times I've longed to curl up in a quiet corner with a book . . ." I drew in a breath and huffed it out. "It would be sheer bliss to have a place all to myself."

"Well, all right." He stood up. "I can bring you sheets and a couple more blankets. You'll need a nightgown, soap—that sort of thing." He looked at his feet, as if the thought of what a woman might need embarrassed him.

"Soap—yes, please. And something to brush my teeth with, if possible," I said.

"What about a mirror?" He glanced around the room. "There's no mirror in here."

I couldn't help smiling at that. "Nuns aren't allowed mirrors. Even the one in the cabin on the ship had to be unscrewed before I came on board. I haven't looked at myself since I took my vows." That wasn't quite true. As a novice, the urge to see my own face had often got the better of me. I would glance at myself as I passed the large window at the end of the dormitory on the way to vespers, when the darkening sky gave the glass a reflective quality. The same temptation came when I was polishing my shoes, or the brass inkwells in the writing desks. I used to wonder whether the ban on mirrors was really about vanity, or if it was to stop you from looking too deep inside yourself, wondering if you really belonged.

"I didn't know that," he said. "I can bring one, if you want."

"Well . . ." My hand went to my hair. To fit into this new world, I was going to have to make myself look presentable. "Perhaps a small one would be useful."

He nodded. "I'll fetch more wood for the stove, too. It can be cold down here at night. And I'll bring whatever food I can lay my hands on. As I said, things are very tight. Everything's rationed. We're luckier than most, with the farm, but it's a struggle to feed everyone."

"Please—I don't want anyone going short on my account. You say there are children living with you?"

He nodded, frowning.

"I couldn't bear the thought of taking food that they might need."

"But you have to eat."

"What you've just given me will keep me going until tomorrow."

"Seriously?"

I gave him a wry look. "It's Lent. I've been keeping a daytime fast for the past three weeks."

"But you don't have to do that anymore."

"I suppose I don't." I shrugged. "But soon I'll be hobbling around. I can go collecting whelks and limpets from rock pools. We used to make soup with them in Ireland."

"Please don't—not until you're stronger. The rocks are treacherous when they're wet. When you can walk properly, I'll take you up to the farm to help with the milking. There's always some of that to spare. We have potatoes, onions, apples—and plenty of eggs." He looked over his shoulder as he reached the door. "Is there anything else you need for tonight?"

"Could I have something to read?"

"A Bible?"

I hesitated. I didn't want him to think that I was turning away from all that. But the Bible was all I'd been permitted to read. I longed for something else. Something unfamiliar. "That would make me feel very much at home," I said, "but could I have some other book, too? Anything you have—it doesn't matter what."

This time, when he left me, he didn't lock the door. While he was gone, I slithered off the heap of sailcloth and got myself into a kneeling position, which allowed me to fashion the jumble of fabric into something resembling a bed. When I'd finished, I glanced at the cobweb-frosted window above my head, wishing I could get outside to open the shutters and let in some light. Was this morning or afternoon? I had no idea how many hours had elapsed since he'd found me. There was no bell to tell me the time.

In Africa my days had been regulated by the mission bell. It began with matins. I never really got used to being torn from sleep when it was still dark, to dress and go to chapel. Then, at daybreak, came the act of praise called lauds. The Divine Office continued at regular intervals until lunchtime, with prime, terce, and sext. At three the bell rang for none—afternoon prayers. Vespers came at five, and the final bell, for the anthem to the Virgin, was at eight o'clock. Whatever you were doing, when the bell rang you had to stop. Often it made me seethe inside. How could God want me to run off to the chapel when I was holding the hand of a patient who was dying?

I wondered what my days were going to be like now, without the rhythm and ritual of the religious life. I wasn't turning my back on God. I couldn't imagine giving up those daily prayers—but there would be nothing and nobody telling me to offer them up at a certain time, in a certain place. Obedience was the thing I'd struggled with more than anything. That vow was broken. But what about the others? Poverty? Chastity?

I knew nothing about money: how much things cost, how much I would need to earn to live independently. Men were another matter. Sister Clare had warned me on my first day at the mission hospital that a nun's habit wouldn't stop men from being interested in me. I'd worked with them, taken care of them. Belgian doctors, Congolese nursing assistants, patients from the villages, the mines in Katanga, and the government offices. I wasn't immune to the surreptitious glances I sometimes attracted. But I'd always had the starched white wings of my wimple to hide behind. What would it be like to go out into the world without that protective armor?

I dropped onto all fours and began crawling across the room in a bid to distract myself from the bewildering chatter inside my head. There was a row of shelves between the windows. They were filled with all kinds of fishing paraphernalia: reels, hooks, knives, floats. But as I paused to look, something else caught my eye. Tucked in a shadowy corner of the middle shelf were five small, slim books. By stretching up I was just able to reach them. I pulled one out, angling the cover to the light cast by the lamp. *Tide Tables for Falmouth and South Cornwall 1938*. Cornwall. The finger of England that pointed west, to America. So that was where the sea had brought me.

The other four books were the same, but for different years. Each gave the times and heights of the local tides for every day of the year, along with the times of sunrise and sunset and the phases of the moon. There were blank pages at the end of each of the books, some of which had been written on. There were dates with the names of different fish alongside them: sardines, mullet, bass. I wondered if this was Jack's handwriting.

I put the books back and crawled on, to a door to what turned out to be a toilet. There was a bucket of water beside it and strips of newspaper threaded onto a loop of string that hung from a hook on the wall. I wondered how I was going to be able to get myself onto the seat. I glanced behind me. Perhaps I could fashion a crutch from something. The fishing rods looked too flimsy. And the oars were too long. I shuffled my way to the stove and rummaged through the sticks on the floor.

"Alice."

I hadn't heard him come in. It was so odd, hearing him call my name—as if it were another woman he was addressing, not me. Alice had been left behind with my hair, my watch, and the photo of my parents the day I became Sister Anthony. As I battled to become that new person, it had often felt as if I were standing outside my body, watching myself wrestle with a stranger. A girl with fierce eyes and wild hair whose stubborn traits I was trying to subdue.

"Alice—are you all right?"

"Yes . . . I . . . I was looking for a stick. To help me get around."

"I should have thought of that." He put down the sack he was carrying and went back outside, returning with an ax in his hand. He reached for one of the half dozen oars propped against the wall. In a deft movement he chopped it in half. Then he emptied the sack and wrapped it around the broad end of the broken oar, securing it with a piece of string. "It's not ideal," he said, as he brought it to show me. "But hopefully it'll do the job."

I practiced hobbling around while he stoked up the fire. The ball of my right foot was very painful, but the left one was only sore around the ankle. I found that I could hop with that foot if I leaned on the improvised crutch. There was a pair of Wellingtons near the door, and I asked him if I could borrow them.

"They'll be very big on you."

"It doesn't matter—it's just to stop the bandages getting dirty." When I'd done a circuit of the room, I asked him if I could go outside and open one of the window shutters to let in a little light.

"I'll do that." He straightened up.

"Please, let me try," I said.

He nodded, watching me as I made my way to the door. I managed to open it without losing my balance. The air felt cool and fresh, with a lemony tang of seaweed. I saw that the tide had come right up the beach. The place where Jack had found me had disappeared. Only the tops of the rocks were visible. I could see a row of thin metal spikes protruding from the surface of the water. It stretched right across the cove—a barrier to stop enemy boats from landing. I realized how lucky I had been not to get trapped in it. If my chemise hadn't ripped, I would probably have drowned.

The water was very calm—tiny waves breaking on the shingle. But the thought of being in it or on it made my stomach flip over. I doubted I would ever be able to set foot in a boat again.

The cove curved in a wide semicircle. Beyond the rocks, farther along the shoreline, I glimpsed a huddle of cottages that reminded me of the fishing villages along the coast of Ireland. Above the houses were sloping fields dotted with cows.

Jack came outside as I was opening the shutters. "Make sure you close them before it gets dark," he said. "We have blackout at night here—no light allowed to be visible from any window. I don't want to scare you, but we get enemy planes on bombing raids along this coast."

"Yes, of course." After what had happened to the *Brabantia*, I was only too aware of how close the Germans were.

"Are you sure you'll be all right down here on your own?" His eyes met mine. "I have to go now, I'm afraid—there's a lot happening up at the house." He looked away, toward the tumbling waves, as if he had been about to say more but had thought better of it.

"Does anyone know that I'm here?"

"Not yet." He let out a breath. "I thought it best to keep quiet about you, for now. People around here are very touchy about strangers."

"When will you tell them?"

"When you're well enough to come up to the farm."

"You won't say that I'm a nun, will you?"

He cast me a puzzled look. "Not if you don't want me to."

"It's just . . ." I faltered.

"I think I understand," he said. "You don't want to be typecast. You want to be yourself."

I nodded. But the voice inside my head hissed his words back at me. *Be yourself?* I'd been a nun for all my adult life. What kind of person would be left, with all that stripped away?

"I'll be back first thing in the morning." He reached out as if to take my arm. His hand hovered briefly in the air. Was he afraid to touch me? Or did he think I'd be offended if he tried to help me back inside the boathouse? He tilted his palm, turning the gesture into a sort of wave. Then he headed toward the trees, his boots leaving a trail of prints in the pale sand. I followed him with my eyes until he disappeared.

Chapter 4

Jack had left a saucepan of water warming on the stove, and I used it to rinse the salt out of my hair. It was a difficult balancing act, getting the saucepan onto the floor, but I managed it. I knelt and dunked my whole head in. When I had toweled it dry, I picked up the small circular mirror Jack had brought. Looking at my reflection made blood surge to my cheeks. Beneath the tufts of dark auburn hair were darker eyebrows. Eyes of moss green stared back at me, wary as a cornered fox. I raised my left hand to my face, touching the sprinkling of freckles on my cheekbones. I didn't remember those. Had the African sun caused them, beating down day after day, year after year, on the few square inches of my body that weren't covered up?

My pointed chin and spiky hair gave me the look of an inquisitive elf. I heard the echo of a voice from long ago. Dan—the boy I had loved in Dublin—used to call me "pixie face." That was when my hair hung halfway down my back and was almost impossible to tame. On bicycle rides with Dan the wind would tug it from the army of pins required to fashion it into a bun. Could it grow long again, after all these years of being cropped? It had been growing during the sea voyage, but the longest wisps were no more than a couple of inches. The rule was that it must be shaved every two months. I would have been due for a cut the day I was supposed to arrive in Dublin.

The reflection in the mirror blurred as I relived the shock of being bald that first time. The ritual was performed in the laundry room of the convent. The novices were seated in a row on a wooden bench. Three nuns, armed with clippers and shears, shaved our heads as bare as billiard balls. The floor was a mess of chestnut, blond, and black locks. The shoes of the barber nuns bristled with the clippings, like a small army of furry animals.

As I fluffed up the damp wisps on my forehead, the silver ring on my hand caught the light. I set the mirror down and splayed out my fingers. I was no longer a bride of Christ. No longer entitled to wear this wedding band. With some difficulty I pulled it off. The skin was white where it had been.

It felt as if I'd amputated part of my body. To distract myself, I picked up the book Jack had bought me. The title and the author were unfamiliar: *Frenchman's Creek* by Daphne du Maurier. I wondered if the writer was French and the book a translation. Opening it, a handwritten note dropped out.

"I hope this is suitable—one of our visitors left it behind. It's set in this part of the world, and the author lives in Cornwall. The river she describes is our river."

It was the same well-shaped, sloping script I had seen in the tide tables on the shelf: Jack's handwriting.

The note had been tucked into the front of the book. I saw that *Frenchman's Creek* had been published quite recently—in 1941—and that the author had written several other novels, two of which had been made into films. I read the first paragraph—a bewitching description of the sea wind blowing into the Helford River estuary as gulls and wading birds skimmed the surface of the water.

I turned back to the synopsis on the dust jacket. It said the novel was the story of a wealthy married woman of the seventeenth century who flees her superficial life in London, looking for peace of mind amid the hidden creeks and woodlands of Cornwall, and finds the passion her spirit craves with a dangerous pirate. I smiled, wondering what Sister Clare would think of such a book.

I'd read four chapters when I realized it was getting dark outside. With the help of Jack's makeshift crutch, I heaved myself upright and went out to close the shutters. The tide was on its way out again. The receding water had exposed the ugly metal barrier designed to stop enemy craft from landing on the beach. It was a crisscross of spiked metal poles, wrapped with barbed wire. It marred what would otherwise have been a perfect vista. A couple of red-legged oystercatchers were picking at shells near the water's edge. A ridge of clouds hung low on the western horizon, tinged scarlet by the dying rays of the sun. The water was very still.

The river she describes is our river.

Jack's words came back to me as I lingered in the doorway, listening to the sweet, haunting cries of the oystercatchers. I knew now that what I was looking at was not the sea but an estuary. The wide mouth of the Helford River. As I turned to go back inside, I caught a glimpse of the moon in a cleft in the clouds on the eastern edge of the water. I stood a little longer, watching it rise, pale yellow, its ghostly reflection shimmering on the water. The wading birds suddenly took flight, as if something had startled them. There was no sign of anyone or anything in the cove. Then I heard a distant drone as if a swarm of bees was heading in from the sea. Looking up, I saw a plane silhouetted against the moon. Two planes. Then a third. Was this the enemy? Was it one of the bombing raids Jack had talked about? With a shiver of fear, I hobbled back inside.

I lay awake, listening, well into the night. But all I could hear were the waves and, later, the patter of rain on the window. I closed my eyes, inhaling the smell of woodsmoke tinged with the rancid odor of fish. This place was very different from the nuns' dormitory in Africa, where I would listen for the rustle of lizards in the thatched roof, breathe in the scent of mimosa through the window screens, and hear the slap of banana leaves when the wind blew.

Faces began to appear, like an old school photograph being unrolled in my mind's eye. I said a prayer for each of them: the young African men I'd trained to assist me in the hospital—Boula, Rutshuru, Kalulu, and Batembo—who had decorated my compartment in the train with swathes of flowers and clusters of fruit the day I left the mission hospital for the long journey back to Ireland. Then there were the nuns I'd lived and worked with—some of whom had been truly sad to see me go; others, like Sister Clare, had eyes that flashed their disappointment in me as they waved goodbye. And two other faces, too young to understand why the woman who gathered them up in her arms was wetting their skin with her tears. *Dear God, keep them safe.* As I drifted into sleep, I managed one last prayer: *You've brought me to this place. Please—let me do some good.*

Waking the next morning, I immediately rolled off the bed, onto my knees. I was halfway through the first Ave Maria before I remembered where I was, and that I no longer needed to do this unless I wanted to.

Did I want to? To drop this daily ritual would feel as strange to me as not brushing my teeth. It was part of waking up, repeating the salutation to the Virgin Mary. It brought my dozing brain to life. And yet it was something I had often chafed against. *Hail Mary, full of grace, the Lord is with you. Blessed are you among women, and blessed is the fruit of your womb, Jesus. Holy Mary, Mother of God, pray for us sinners now and at the hour of our death. Amen.* Saying it over and over—fifty times in the rosary prayer alone—made it feel like a magic spell: the sort of thing I'd seen witch doctors perform when they went into a trance.

And yet it was the Ave that I'd clung to as I drifted in the black, icy water of the English Channel. *Pray for us sinners now and at the hour of our death.* Muttering the words through my chattering teeth had somehow shut out the terrifying reality that I was close to drowning.

My rosary beads had gone down with the *Brabantia*. But I had been using them for so long that I didn't really need the physical beads to remember the meditations on the events of Christ's life and the prayers that punctuated them. I would miss the feel of them, though. Perhaps I could make my own version with pebbles and shells from the beach—a simpler rosary for the new person I wanted to be.

I reached for the cardigan Jack had given me, lifting it up until the soft wool touched my mouth. That was another reflex action. Every morning as a nun, I'd had to kiss my veil and my scapular—the long tabard I wore belted over my robe—before putting them on. At eighteen, I'd naïvely believed that when I put on the clothing of a nun and gave up my worldly possessions, I'd be transformed, almost instantly. I didn't realize that I was embarking on a never-ending struggle to attain the humility the religious life required.

The item of clothing I'd most detested was the skullcap. It clasped the head closely and had drawstrings on it. I'd stood in the laundry room of the convent in Dublin, my head newly shorn, listening to the Mistress of Postulants as she instructed us in the way to put the cap on. I could still hear that voice—the exact words—as if it had happened only yesterday: *The tighter you draw those strings, the better you will restrain the imagination. God doesn't want you wasting your time with daydreaming.*

I shook the memory from my mind. But the instruction was as pertinent now as it had been then. I mustn't waste time with daydreaming. The crack of light coming through the shutters told me that the sun was up. I wanted to make myself respectable by the time Jack arrived with breakfast. Show him that it wouldn't be long until I was able to make myself useful.

I reached for the rest of the new clothes. I couldn't yet think of them as *my* underwear or *my* blouse: having owned nothing for so many years, the idea of anything being mine was hard to grasp. As I fastened the tiny pearl buttons, a distant bark told me Jack was coming. Seconds later Brock was at the door, paws scrabbling against the wood. I heard Jack call him. Then there came two short knocks.

"Can I come in?" The morning sun lit up his face as he stood in the doorway. His black hair was tousled, and stubble shadowed his jaw. One wing of the collar of his shirt was tucked into his sweater while the other stuck out. He looked as if he'd been up all night. "Off you go, Brock—go and chase some seagulls!" He shut the door behind him.

I went to haul myself up, but he was beside me before I had maneuvered the crutch into position.

"Let me help you." He hooked one arm around my back.

"No, really," I said, shifting my body sideways. "Thank you for offering, but I need to get used to doing it myself."

"Of course." He stepped back as if he'd trodden on a snake. "How did you get on last night?"

"Quite well, I think. It took me a while to get off to sleep—I saw planes flying over the sea when I went out to close the shutters."

He nodded. "Falmouth took a direct hit last night. It's only a few miles from here. It's a major port—and the Germans are aware of that—but they often miss, and it's the poor devils who live close by that take the brunt of it."

"Were people killed?"

He looked away. "We don't know what the casualties are yet. But it's pretty certain there will have been fatalities."

I thought of how tranquil this place had seemed when I was standing outside, looking up at the moon, before the planes had appeared. The thought of people watching that same scene and moments later being annihilated was unimaginably awful. It seemed so random, so unfair. And yet I had seen something very similar firsthand, when the ship was blown up. Why had I been saved when so many others had lost their lives?

"Has there been any news of the *Brabantia*?" I held my breath, almost wishing I hadn't asked.

He nodded. "There was a piece in the *Times* this morning. There were more than a hundred survivors—picked up by a Royal Navy patrol vessel."

More than a hundred. But there had been more than three hundred of us on board. I wondered if Jack could sense the guilt I felt.

"I brought you some more clothes." He put the bulging sack he was carrying down beside the bed. "These are a bit more practical than what I gave you yesterday—the sort of things you'll need if you're going to work on the farm." He pulled out a pair of khaki-colored trousers with a bib attached and held them up. "This is what the Land Girls wear—dungarees. Not very flattering, I'm afraid."

"Land Girls?"

"It's what they call the women who've been drafted in to work on farms in place of the men who've gone off to fight. They're not *girls*, not really—well, a few of them are quite young, I suppose, but some of them are old enough to be grandmothers." He laid the dungarees down on my bed. "I suppose you're wondering why *I'm* still here, not in uniform?"

I shook my head. It should have occurred to me, but it hadn't—that a man of his age would be required to fight.

"It's because food production is so vital to our ability to defeat the enemy. They think I'm of more use here than chasing Hitler."

"Well, I'm looking forward to helping you." I was glad to think that what I'd be doing was something essential to the war effort. I smiled at the thought of wearing dungarees. I'd never worn trousers. I wondered what else was in the sack. It would be strange having different sets of clothes to choose from. I hadn't had to make such choices for years.

"Oh—I brought this back, too." He dug in the sack and produced my chemise, which had been washed and mended.

"Thank you." I wondered who had sewn the fine, almost invisible stitches—and how he had explained who the chemise belonged to. But before I could ask, he said: "I've had to tell people there's someone living here. One of the fishermen from the village round the bay saw the smoke from the stove last night. He came to find me—thought there might have been an intruder. I told him that you were my cousin Alice from Ireland."

My eyes widened.

"People are terrible gossips around here," he went on. "I thought it would be easier if I said you were a member of the family. I described you as my father's cousin's daughter, who was living and working in a London hospital that was destroyed in a bombing raid. I said you were wearing this—hospital issue—when the bomb fell." He laid the chemise on my makeshift bed, next to the dungarees. "You'll remember that, won't you?"

"Er, yes. Your father's cousin's daughter . . ." I raked my tufty hair, filled with panic at the thought of putting on an act. And ashamed that the lies I was going to have to tell were the result of my own selfish decision to cast off the past. I ought to have realized that this cover story he'd come up with was unexpectedly elaborate, that he had gone to extraordinary lengths to help me—and that there had to be an ulterior motive. But I was so overwhelmed by the speed at which my life was changing I didn't question it.

"If you get into conversation with anyone, you'd better refer to me as Cousin Jack." He drew in a breath. "One other thing, I need to know your surname. You'll need an identity card. Everyone has one. You have to carry it with you at all times."

I hesitated, wondering fleetingly if I should make something up. Perhaps it would be easier to play the role he had cast me in if I went under a different name. But that felt dishonest. Jack had done so much for me. I felt I owed him the truth. "It's McBride."

He took a pencil and notebook from the pocket of his shirt and scribbled it down. "And your date of birth?"

"The twenty-third of January 1913."

He glanced up from writing, eyebrows raised. "You're thirty?"

"Yes."

"You don't look a day over twenty-one." He grunted a laugh. "They should patent the religious life as an elixir of youth. What age were you when you became a nun?"

"I was eighteen when I entered the convent. Twenty when I took my perpetual vows."

"How long were you out in Africa?"

"Nine years. I went to Belgium first, to the order's sister convent in Brussels. I studied for eight months at the Institute of Tropical Medicine there. That was my passport to Africa—to what I longed to do."

An image flashed into my mind of my nine-year-old self in a classroom at St. Brigid's school in Dublin. I was listening intently to a nun reading aloud from a book with a cover of red and gold. It was the story of Mary Moffat, whose nursing skills saved the life of the explorer David Livingstone when he was savaged by a lion. She married him and spent her life teaching native children and ministering to the sick. That was the beginning of my fascination with Africa.

Jack was writing in his notebook again. "Is that where you learnt French," he said, "in Belgium?"

"I learnt it at school, but I wasn't very good. It came more easily living among people who spoke it all the time."

He went over to the stove and opened the creaky metal door, throwing wood onto the glimmering embers. "I've brought more eggs," he said. "There's a loaf of bread, some cheese, and some milk. Oh, and apples—they're a bit shriveled, but they're nice and sweet." He took the food from a knapsack on his back. Then he wiped the frying pan with a piece of rag.

"Please . . ." I hobbled across the room. "You don't have to cook for me—I'm sure I can manage."

He glanced at me over his shoulder. "I can't have you frying eggs while standing on one leg—you might end up setting fire to the place."

"Oh . . . I . . ." I looked down, embarrassed.

"You thought I was being kind." His voice was matter-of-fact. He *was* being kind, but there was an air of detachment about him. As if compassion were something to be despised. "I should sit down if I were you—rest that foot. You'll be of use to neither man nor beast until it heals."

I couldn't argue with that. I lowered myself onto the pile of sailcloth and watched him make breakfast.

"Do you always sit like that?" He cast me a curious look over his shoulder.

"Like what?"

"With the tips of your fingers tucked inside the cuffs of your cardigan."

I glanced down, suddenly self-conscious. I'd done it without thinking. "It's a habit—pardon the pun." I smiled. "At the convent, it was ingrained in us that our hands must learn to stay still and out of sight except when needed. They used to be hidden by the sleeves of my robe."

He laughed. "I don't suppose you're any good at bell ringing, are you?"

Now it was my turn to look puzzled. "Well, I did take my turn at it in Africa. Why?"

He flipped the eggs onto a plate. "We're going to be ringing the church bells on Easter Sunday—for the first time since the war started. Churchill announced it on the radio this morning." He carved a hunk of bread, holding the loaf in the crook of his arm as he took the knife to it. "Up to now, they were only supposed to be rung to warn of an invasion."

"Does that mean the war's nearly over?"

"I wish it did. Things are looking better now the Americans are in—but the Germans aren't going to give up easily." He shrugged. "It's a gesture, I think. Today is Hitler's birthday, apparently, and the bells thing is Churchill sticking two fingers up at him. Anyway, we don't have any bell ringers. All the men who used to do it have gone off to fight.

31

I wondered if you could give me some tips—and maybe help if you're feeling better by Sunday?"

"I'd like that." I smiled my thanks as he set the plate in front of me. "My father was a bell ringer."

"What did he do? For work, I mean."

"He was a doctor. He died while I was in the Congo. A car accident." The saliva that had trickled into my mouth at the sight of food dried up. I felt tears prickle the backs of my eyes. Why had I let that out? Nuns weren't supposed to talk about their families. In the hour of recreation at the mission hospital, it was a strict rule that the past must never be mentioned.

Jack must have seen my face change. "I'm sorry, I shouldn't have asked. I'll leave you in peace to eat your breakfast. You don't want an audience, I'm sure."

I swallowed the tears down. "Please don't go. Not if you don't have to, I mean. I'm not used to eating alone. Won't you share this with me?"

He said he'd eaten already, but I wasn't certain he was telling the truth. I told him I wouldn't be able to manage the whole loaf before it went stale. When I said that, he cut himself a slice and spread it with a dollop of honey. For a while we both ate in silence.

"No second thoughts," he said between mouthfuls, "about going back to the convent?"

"No."

"I thought perhaps you'd change your mind—that you were too traumatized yesterday to think straight."

I shook my head, staring at the flames burning blue and gold behind the soot-smeared glass in the door of the stove. The memories of those terrifying hours in the English Channel seared my brain, too harrowing to put into words. I could still hear the faint, forlorn cries of those who, like me, were clinging to broken hunks of wreckage, fighting for life. A child calling for its mother, the voice growing fainter as I kicked out, powerless against the swell, unable to reach it. And when all human sounds had faded away, and I was utterly alone in the icy water, my mind began to play tricks. I thought I heard another voice, somewhere above my head, telling me I'd been saved because I had work to do. Was it delirium? Or an angel? If I tried to explain it to Jack, he'd probably think I was unhinged.

"When you think you're going to die, it makes you question what your life has been, and what it could be if you only had the chance to live," I murmured, still staring into the fire. "All I've ever wanted to do was to please God. I want to do some good in the world, in whatever way I can. But I've lost the conviction that doing it as a nun is the only way."

"But how do you know you'd please God more in the world than if you stayed with the order?"

"Because I don't believe God approves of hypocrites," I replied. "And that's what I'd be if I went back to live under a holy rule I only pretend to obey." I held his gaze. He had that curious look in his eyes again—the same expression I'd noticed yesterday—as if I were a laboratory specimen he was observing. "I had no idea how bad the war was until I got on the boat," I went on. "Newspapers were not permitted to us, but passengers sometimes left them on the deck. I began to grasp the scale of what was going on. And then, at Freetown, a new passenger joined the ship. Lieutenant Commander Roland Hill, of the Royal Navy, on his way to a new posting in Gibraltar. He was put at our table, and one evening, when I mentioned what I'd read in the papers, he told me about the death camps in Poland."

"What did he say?"

"That the Nazis have killed more than a million Jews; that they're being taken away from their homes to these labor camps, where they work until they drop or are deliberately killed in mass executions. Hundreds of thousands of entirely innocent men, women, and children."

Jack drew in a breath. "We've known about them since the end of last year, but I don't think most people here can comprehend it. It's . . . unimaginable evil."

"I couldn't sleep the night I heard about it. It made me feel so useless, on my way to be shut up inside the walls of a convent. I couldn't believe God would want me to do that at a time when there was so much need. So, you see, I'd already decided—before the ship was hit—that I couldn't carry on as I was."

"What about the sisters at the convent in Dublin? Are you sure about not letting them know you survived?"

I nodded. "I realize it might sound like a cowardly decision, but there's a good reason behind it. If they knew I was alive, they'd have to repay the dowry my father gave to the convent when I took my vows."

"But don't you want that money?" Jack tilted his head, regarding me in that curious way again. "It would allow you to set yourself up in whatever new life you want."

I stared at my hands, at the pale band of flesh where my silver ring had been. "I'd rather make my own way. They deserve to keep it. It makes me feel less guilty for quitting."

"Couldn't you just refuse to take it?"

"I could, I suppose. But it's so much simpler this way. If I'm honest, I just don't want to have to face them, to explain myself. You can't just leave a convent. You have to be given permission to leave."

"But what's to stop you just walking out?"

"Can you imagine what that would be like? Walking out in the middle of Dublin, with no clothes, no money? What would I do? Where would I go?" I shook my head. "I'd have to wait. Stay inside the convent until all the proper procedures had been followed. The Mother Superior would have to petition Rome for letters of release. It would take months. And in the meantime, they'd do everything in their power to convince me to stay—it reflects badly on the order when a nun renounces her vows." I ran my finger over the ribbed cuff of my cardigan. "I couldn't bear that. I want to be out in the world, doing something to help end this war, not kicking my heels waiting for endless paperwork."

"Hmm." He went over to the door and opened it. Brock, who had been waiting patiently outside, came bounding in and jumped up to lick my chin. "I have to go now." Jack clipped a leash onto the dog's collar. "Come on, old boy—leave her alone." He gave the leash a gentle tug. "Get some rest," he said. "We'll see how you are tomorrow. When you're well enough I'll take you up to the farm and show you the ropes." He turned back as he reached the door. "Is there anything else you need? Anything you want to ask?"

"What's this place called?" I angled my head toward the shelves that held the tide tables. "I know that we're in south Cornwall, and that we're near the mouth of the Helford River—but does this little bay have a name?"

"It has a Cornish name. *Porthmorvoren.* In English, it's Mermaid's Cove."

Jack had left a pile of logs outside the boathouse. By laying a folded blanket on top of it, I made a comfortable seat. It was pure pleasure spending a whole day doing nothing but reading a novel and watching the comings and goings of the seabirds.

The cove was deserted. As far as I could tell from the limited movement my injured foot allowed me, the only human tracks in the smooth, sea-washed sand were Jack's. I spotted a couple of small fishing boats—they looked very much like the ones I remembered from the old days in Dublin. I wondered if the people on board could see me, and whether they'd heard Jack's story about me being his cousin. I quailed at the thought of them coming ashore. How could I keep up the pretense of being a relative of Jack's when I knew so little about him?

But the day passed without anyone else setting foot in Mermaid's Cove. The only living creature I saw, apart from the gulls wheeling overhead, was a robin who flew down from its perch among the clumps of pink sea thrift that clung to the rocks. It seemed unafraid of me—and when I threw crumbs of bread onto the sand, it came closer and closer, until I could have reached out and touched it.

As darkness fell, I went to get undressed. My old chemise had fallen onto the floor when I'd pulled the blanket from under it. I bent to pick it up. It felt stiff and coarse compared to the silk nightdress Jack had given me. Looking at it made me think of a snake that had shed its skin. The scales of my old life had fallen away—and now I had this new, shiny skin that felt soft and strange and would take time to get used to.

I turned back the collar of the chemise, looking at the number stitched inside the neck. Nine-three-seven. If I lived to be a hundred, I doubted I would ever forget that number. As a novice in Dublin, I was told that it had previously belonged to a missionary nun who was murdered while serving in the same part of Africa that I would eventually be sent to. I'd seen the face of this nun, Sister Marie-Louise, in the convent's magazine. Over the years I'd often wondered what she would have thought of me. I felt I could never live up to a woman who had paid the ultimate price for her commitment to serving God. Every time I thought of her, I felt like a traitor.

Was I truly called? That question was on my mind so often in Africa. It wasn't when I was with a patient or traveling to the clinics out in the bush—it was when I was on my knees in the chapel, my mind on the case the bell had dragged me away from instead of the words of the prayers I was mechanically reciting. How could I know the answer to that question when the self I was seeking to be true to had been left behind in Ireland, buried in the walls of the convent?

Now, as I clambered into my sailcloth bed, I thought about the life I'd left behind. I stared at the shadows thrown onto the ceiling of the boathouse by the glow of the stove. The roof of the building where

I'd slept in Africa wasn't slate like this one. It was made of galvanized iron lined with timber. Lizards and snakes were able to climb into the gap between the two layers. I used to listen to them rustling around, hoping they wouldn't drop onto my head in the middle of the night. It had happened once—not when I was asleep but when I was sitting up, writing in bed. A boa constrictor—just a baby, luckily—had landed on my shoulder. The shriek I'd let out had brought my twenty-three bald-headed, bleary-eyed roommates leaping to the rescue.

I remember thinking, after it happened, that the snake had been a sign. I'd been jotting down the mea culpa when it dropped on me. This was the twice-daily self-examination that had to be written in notebooks in pencil. It meant "I accuse myself." That evening I'd been writing about temptation. Of wanting to take more of the delicious, ice-cool mango that Kalulu had brought me when I came out of the operating theater, of wishing I could join two of the doctors who had been invited to a weekend house party at the home of a mineowner upriver, of thinking of excuses to visit the orphanage attached to the hospital—for my own reasons, not the medical needs of the children. The snake was like the devil on my shoulder, hissing contempt at my miserable failings.

I turned over in my boathouse bed, trying not to catch the bandages on my feet as I did so. What would I have written about today, I wondered. *I accuse myself of looking in a mirror, of not saying grace before eating, of reading a forbidden book, of failing to notify the convent that I'm alive, of planning to lie about my past . . .* The list went on and on. I imagined reading out that catalog of imperfections to Sister Margarita, the Mistress of Postulants in Dublin. As a novice, I used to break into a sweat just thinking about revealing my shortcomings. My faults seemed to repeat themselves week after week. *You master one imperfection and ten others sprout like dragons' teeth.* I could picture Sister Margarita shaking her head, hear her sucking in her breath.

I used to wonder what Jesus would make of all the rules the convent imposed on those within its walls. There was nothing in the Gospels about not looking in mirrors, not making friends, or taking a vow of celibacy. I closed my eyes and turned over, pulling the sheet up over my head. What I wanted was to lead the kind of life he would approve of, without all the restrictions of the order. It was all well and good telling Jack that I was ready to leave the order. But could I really do it? Was I strong enough?

Unable to shut out the babble in my head, I got up and lit the lantern. Its yellow rays glimmered on the shiny black cover of the Bible Jack had brought me. It was on the upturned apple box I was using as a bedside table. It sat there, accusingly. I hadn't been able to bring myself to open it. I limped over to the shelves under the window. An idea had come to me—something I had done as a girl of sixteen but hadn't been permitted to do as a nun. I would start a journal. A record of this new life I was embarking on. The only source of paper in the boathouse was the blank pages of the tide tables. They were all out of date, so I didn't think Jack would need them.

I took one of them from the shelf, flicking through to the back. There were a few lines of handwritten notes about a fishing trip, dated March 1938. His writing was very neat and meticulous compared to my own scrappy script. A few of the letters had a dramatic flourish. The capital S of the word *sardine* looked like a curled serpent about to strike, and the lowercase *d* had a tall, looped back. There was another word, *Firefly*, that was a forest of loops at the end. Was that the name of a boat? His boat?

Turning the page, I noticed something else. A name. Morwenna. Was this another boat? Or a woman? There was nothing to give any clue. Just a date in April 1938. Exactly five years ago. There was no more writing. Just blank pages after that.

Chapter 5

The next morning, I woke suddenly, gasping for breath, my heart beating fast. What my sleeping mind had conjured up was so vivid it took me several seconds to grasp where I was. In the dream I had been on a boat—not the *Brabantia*, but one of the small wooden craft, called pirogues, that were the main means of travel for the native people of the Congo. We were gliding along misty rivers banked by dense forests looped with lianas. The young black men who poled the boat along were singing a ballad with a strange repetitive rhythm. Then I heard cries coming from the forest. The screams of children. I tried to make the boatmen stop, but they wouldn't listen. I scrambled up and tried to jump out. Then I was in the water. I was fighting the current, trying to get to the children.

I felt a hard, biting sensation in my chest. The faces of the children hovered in front of me. It was as if, wide awake, I could still hear them calling out to me. It took me a while to realize that the voices were real. There were people outside the boathouse—on the beach.

I struggled into my clothes. In my haste I forgot to use the crutch to help me up, only realizing when I reached the door that my right foot wasn't hurting anymore. I slipped my legs into the Wellingtons and opened the door just a crack. The sunlight was dazzling. I shaded my eyes with my hands.

Four children were darting in and out of the waves. The eldest was a girl about nine or ten years old with blond braids streaming out behind her in the breeze. She and another girl were running away from two boys. The bigger boy was throwing water from a pail, and the smaller one was stumbling along in a gas mask, his arms outstretched and his fingers clawing the air as if he were pretending to be a monster.

There was a woman chasing after them, shouting at the boy with the pail. She had the same blond hair as the older girl, held up in a bun, which began to slip down her head as she picked up speed. As I watched, three of the children disappeared behind some rocks. The woman went after them. The smallest boy, left behind, started spinning round and round, until he toppled onto the sand. The gas mask must have banged against him as he fell because he let out a yell and clutched his head. His mother seemed not to have heard him. I could hear her giving the other children a piece of her mind behind the rocks. I wanted to run to the little boy and gather him up. But I dithered on the doorstep, afraid of interfering.

Soon the woman reappeared. "Oh, Ned! What have you done!" She scooped the child up. She undid his gas mask and tilted his head to examine it. "Let's kiss it better!" She buried her face in his golden-brown curls. As she straightened up, she caught sight of me and waved. Hoisting him onto her hip, she came across the sand.

"Hello," she said, holding out her free hand. "I'm Merle." She pronounced the name the French way, not rhyming it with "pearl" the way English and Irish people would. But her accent wasn't French. Her voice had a lilting quality, softer than Jack's. "I'm from the house." She nodded toward the trees above the beach. "Are you the cousin? From Ireland?" The way she said it was tentative, almost reverential. As if she were addressing someone terribly important.

"Yes, I . . . I'm Alice." Her hand felt warm. I could feel grains of sand on her palm. Smile lines crinkled at the corners of her eyes, which were the same pale blue as the water behind her. The little boy gave a choking sob and wiped the back of his hand across his nose. "Is he all right?" I asked. "Would you like to bring him inside? Does he like honey? I could give him some—"

Before I could get the words out, the child wrestled himself free of his mother's arms and went running past me, into the boathouse.

"Ned!" His mother's hand flew to her mouth. "I'm so sorry—he's very inquisitive."

"It doesn't matter." I smiled back. "It's awfully dark in there, though—I'd better open the shutters, or he might trip over something."

Half an hour later we were all sitting on blankets on the sand. The children were dipping slices of apple into a dish of honey, and Merle and I were sipping tea from tin mugs. She told me that she and the children had been evacuated from the Channel Islands just days before the Germans had invaded, and that they'd been living in Cornwall for nearly three years.

"It doesn't seem right," she said, glancing at the boathouse, "you having to sleep in there while we're in the house."

"I don't mind it. It's very peaceful. After London, I mean." I felt myself blushing at the lie. I hoped she wouldn't notice. "It must be hard for you," I went on, keen to steer the conversation away from myself. "You must miss your home."

"I miss some things." Merle turned her head away, toward the estuary. "It seems so long since we left. Danielle has memories of Guernsey, but the others don't—not really. Louis says he remembers being on the boat and feeling sick. I was sick, too, but I didn't mind—I was just thankful to get away before the Germans came."

"It must have been terrifying."

Merle nodded. "I'd never been off the island before. The day we left it was hot, and I had a heavy suitcase, full of clothes for the children. While we were waiting for the bus to take us down to the harbor, I fainted." She cradled the tin mug in both hands, staring into it. "I can't remember getting onto the boat. It was chaos—hundreds of children, babies crying. Women crying, too—for children who were going with-out them or for husbands they were leaving behind."

I wondered what had happened to Merle's husband. She hadn't mentioned him—and I didn't like to ask.

"It took a day and a night to get to Cornwall," she went on. "So many people had come to rescue us. The government had put out an appeal over the radio, and all these boats—big and small—came across from the mainland. We were in His Lordship's motor yacht, *Firefly*."

His Lordship? Who was she talking about? Jack had written the name of that boat in the tide tables: I had assumed it was his. Did it belong to someone else? To a lord? I couldn't ask. As Jack's cousin, I would be expected to know such things. Instead I nodded, hoping Merle would carry on with the story of their escape.

"There was a storm on the way back, and the boat hit a rock," she said. "It was taking on water. We made it here—just—but the yacht was damaged beyond repair."

"I can't imagine what it must have been like to make a journey like that with four children." I glanced at Ned, who had a blob of honey on the end of his nose. "This one must have been a baby still."

"He was—but he's not mine." Merle mouthed the last few words over Ned's head. Then she turned to the oldest girl and said, "Take them to the rock pools to wash their hands, will you, Danny? We'll have to be getting off to school soon."

When the children had gone, she turned back to me. "Ned's one of the children who left without their parents." She drained the last of the tea from her mug. "Like I said, it was chaos when we heard the Germans were coming. People had to decide whether to stay on the island and face what was coming or abandon their homes and businesses and go. Children under school age were supposed to be accompanied by their mothers." She fiddled with the empty mug. "I don't know who Ned's parents are. His Lordship came onto the boat with Ned in his arms, saying that a man had come up to him in the harbor and begged him to take his little son. Apparently the mother was ill and in hospital."

Merle tilted her head, mirroring my puzzled look. "Did he not tell you that he rescued us?" Her expression changed to a wry smile. "He's very modest, for a viscount, isn't he? Fancy not telling his own cousin something like that."

I looked away from her, toward the rocks, struggling to process what she'd said. This man who had found me, bound my wounds, fed me, and housed me was an aristocrat. A peer of the realm. It seemed impossible. Incredible. Why would a person like that go to such trouble for someone like me?

"He's always telling us to call him Jack," Merle went on. "But it seems disrespectful. The children call him Lordy, which he doesn't seem to mind."

At that moment Ned came hurtling across the sand, clutching something to his chest. To my surprise he skidded to a halt in front of me, dropping his trophy into my lap. "It's a present," he said, smiling at me from under his dark eyelashes.

"Thank you, Ned—how lovely!" I picked up the mussel shell, which was as big as his hand, and angled it so that the sun caught the mother-of-pearl inside.

"Will you come and play with us?" He sat down on the blanket beside me, tugging at my other hand.

"Come on, Ned." Merle stood up. "It's time for school."

"Oh!" His mouth turned down at the edges.

"Another time, maybe." Merle turned to me. "They go to the school round the bay. We don't usually come this way. You can only get to it from here at low tide. But they were up early, and they wanted to come to the beach."

I glanced down at Ned, who looked as if he was about to cry. What had happened to him on Guernsey was unimaginably awful. He would have been too young when he was rescued to have any memory of his parents. His story was a chilling echo of something that had happened in Africa. A piece of wickedness whose legacy haunted me still.

"Go and tell the others," Merle said to Ned. "Mrs. Graham will be cross if we're late."

"Do his parents know where he is?" I asked as he darted off across the beach.

She shook her head. "It's been impossible to get letters to and from the island since the Germans took control."

"They must be desperate."

"I know. I can't imagine not having my three with me. When the planes are flying over, and you hear about places being bombed, I think, well, if it happens to us, at least we'll be together." She brushed a wisp of blond hair from her face. "That must sound selfish—but the thought of them being somewhere else, living with strangers, hundreds of miles away . . ." She trailed off as the children came running up to us.

I was gathering up the blankets after waving them goodbye when Brock, Jack's dog, came bounding across the beach. He jumped up, wetting my chin with sandy licks.

"Brock!" Jack wasn't far behind.

The sound of his voice threw me into a panic. I was tongue-tied. Why had he kept back the fact that he was Lord Trewella? I had no idea of the proper way to address a viscount.

"Good morning!" He closed the distance between us. "Oh—you're walking. Good." However, he didn't look pleased. "There's something you need to do." He ushered me into the boathouse. "I've got you one of these." He handed me a buff-colored card, folded in two.

"What is it?"

"Your identity card—you just need to sign it."

I opened it and scanned the inside. There was my name and my date of birth. And another line headed "Marital Status," with the word *Unmarried* printed in bold black type beside it.

"How did you manage to get it so quickly?"

"It's easier, with the house being used by the military." He pushed his hair back from his forehead. "Without it, you'd be in danger of being arrested. Aliens need permits to get into Cornwall—it's a protected area."

Aliens. It sounded unpleasant. But that was what I was.

"I met someone from the house this morning," I said. "The mother of the evacuees. Sh . . . she told me you have a title. I . . ." I trailed off. What could I say? *I wish you'd told me? I'd never have had the impertinence to ask if I could stay here if I'd known?*

He grunted. "The Fourteenth Viscount Trewella—at your service." He made a mocking bow. "Would it have made a difference if I'd told you?"

"Well, I . . ."

"You would have behaved quite differently." He finished the sentence for me. "We're similar in that respect, Alice. You don't want it to be known that you're a nun because you're afraid of being judged, of being put into a box. It's the same for me: I'd rather be taken for who I am—not what people expect me to be."

His eyes were lit with an intensity I hadn't noticed before. I seemed to have hit a raw nerve. I wondered if he wished he hadn't inherited the title. If, like me, he longed to reinvent himself, to shed a skin that had become too tight.

"It's just that I . . . I don't know what to call you," I mumbled.

"You can call me what you like." There was a hard edge to his voice now. "It really doesn't matter. By the way, I've brought you these." He tipped up the knapsack he was carrying. Shoes, Wellingtons, a gas mask, and a little alarm clock tumbled onto the floor. "I hope those boots will fit—you'll need them when you come up to the farm. And you'll need to carry the gas mask with you whenever you go out."

I nodded. "We had them on the ship," I said.

He reached inside his jacket. "This is a ration book," he said, tossing it onto the bed. "We'll need your coupons up at the house for buying what we don't produce ourselves. I must get back now. Come on, Brock!"

His whole demeanor seemed different from before. I wondered what had happened since our last meeting to change his mood. The life I'd led had not equipped me to be the best judge of men, but to me, he seemed to carry his own climate with him. And today that atmosphere was dark and dangerous.

Chapter 6

My first day at the farm was Maundy Thursday. At the mission hospital that would have been a day of minimal duties and maximum prayer—the start of the holiest festival in the Christian calendar. But to the cows, it was a day like any other. They still needed milking. And when that was done, there were eggs to be collected, there was butter to be churned, and, Jack assured me, there was endless weeding and hoeing to do for the vegetables being raised on every available patch of earth.

I'd set the alarm clock to go off at six o'clock. I was ready, in my dungarees, with the emerald scarf knotted around my head, when Jack came with Brock to show me the way up through the valley. The path followed a stream that trickled out onto the beach. The trees that fringed the cove were tamarisk and pine. They gave way to copper beech, alder, and elm. But as we climbed higher, I found myself in a landscape that was more like a tropical jungle than an English woodland. Everything was giant sized. There were massive tree ferns and towering palms; great stands of bamboo rose forty feet high, some of the canes thicker than a man's arm. Monster rhododendrons and camellias made splashes of color in the sea of green: vivid pink, burnt orange, saffron yellow, and delicate creamy white.

Native British plants fought for space with the tropical ones. Edging the stream that ran down to the cove were carpets of bluebells and wild garlic. Red campions, buttercups, and daisies sprouted in open patches between the trees. Tiny violets clung to the mossy banks of the path.

I paused to examine a strange group of plants that were stunted and brown, like an army of dwarfs. The tips of green leaves were beginning to protrude from the stumpy stalks, unfurling from their winter slumber. I'd never seen anything like them in Dublin.

"Giant rhubarb," Jack called over his shoulder. "From South America. It'll be six feet tall by June."

As I hurried to catch up, I brushed against a branch, bringing a shower of petals down on my head. I caught the scent of them—something like vanilla with a hint of pepper. It reminded me of walking under the jacaranda trees in Katanga. In the Congo, spring came in September, and the lilac-blue jacaranda blossoms heralded the beginning of that season. Here it was camellias and rhododendrons—which I'd seen in Irish gardens, but never the size of these.

After a few minutes of walking I could no longer hear the gentle lap of the waves breaking in the cove. Instead I heard the splash of waterfalls and the calls of birds—wood pigeons, rooks, robins, blackbirds—nesting in the trees and bushes. I caught the bright flash of a jay as it darted through the branches. And from somewhere in the green canopy above my head came the sound of a woodpecker rapping on a tree trunk.

It gave me a giddy feeling, being able to see things without having to turn my head. Being without my nun's wimple and veil was like seeing the world through a wide-angle lens.

"Are you all right? Foot not hurting?" Jack smiled as he turned to me. His mood seemed altogether better today.

"I'm fine, thanks." I paused, breathing hard. I couldn't remember the last time I'd walked uphill. My journeys in Africa had mostly been by car or by boat, with very little walking involved. "It's so beautiful," I said between breaths. "So peaceful."

"It's gone very wild, I'm afraid. We used to have a gardener with a team of men, but they've all gone off to war."

"Where did all these plants come from?" I recognized the tree ferns and palms, but others were unknown to me.

"My family used to own a shipping agency in Falmouth. My ancestors commissioned ships' captains to bring home seeds from all over the world."

"What a wonderful idea—and how amazing that they can grow here."

He nodded. "It's unusually mild for England. The valley's quite sheltered, but my great-great-grandfather planted trees to give the place even more protection from the southwesterlies we get here." He pointed to a row of what looked like pine trees, their topmost branches piercing the sky. "They were planted the year Queen Victoria came to the throne. They're Monterey pines, from California."

As we climbed higher, I spotted a little church, half-hidden in the trees. Its walls were dotted with moss. As I glanced up at the metal cross on the roof, a swallow flew out of the porch. I didn't need to ask if this was his church. The gravestones broadcast it loud and clear. I counted seven with the name "Trewella" within sight of the path. I would have liked to linger for a while. The stories graveyards tell have always fascinated me. But that would have to wait.

Through a gap in the branches of a scarlet rhododendron, I glimpsed another building, more substantial than the church, with ancient-looking walls of honey-colored stone and mullioned windows glinting in the sunlight.

"Is that your house?" I asked. It was much bigger than I'd imagined.

"That's Penheligan." He must have seen the expression on my face and guessed what I was thinking. "Like the valley, it's seen better days," he went on. "We only use part of it. The whole of the east wing is unin-habitable—the roof leaks and the floorboards have rotted."

Now I understood why he'd said there was no room for me. The boathouse might smell of fish, but at least it had a sound roof and a solid floor.

The path leveled out, taking us through a phalanx of palm fronds, then out into the open, toward a pair of tall gates, each with a coat of arms of wrought iron. The shield bore an image I'd often seen in church buildings. It was a pelican pecking at its own breast, shedding drops of blood to feed the babies in its nest. It was a symbol of sacrifice—of a mother to her children and of Christ crucified. I shaded my eyes, trying to read the motto inscribed below.

Gever kyns dha honan. It wasn't Latin or French.

"It's Cornish," Jack said when he saw my puzzled expression. "It means 'Duty before thyself.'" He grunted. "Heck of a thing to live up to."

Yes, I thought, *insert the words* to God, *and you'd have something identical to one of the guiding principles of the order.* It was a maxim I'd failed miserably to live up to.

Jack led me through the gates into a walled garden whose crum-bling brickwork was dappled with sunlight. We passed through an avenue of trees—not as tall as the ones in the valley—some thick with blossom. I asked Jack what they were.

"These are pears, mostly. We have a few peach and cherry trees—and that one up against the wall is a fig," he replied. "Those apples I brought you came from the orchard on the other side of the house. We had a bumper crop last autumn."

I heard a low buzzing sound and spotted beehives in among the trees. Chickens and ducks were pecking about in the grass at the other end of the garden. Brock went over, sniffing at a cockerel with a ruff of iridescent feathers as green as a peacock. The bird pecked the dog's nose, and he came scurrying back with his tail between his legs.

"Almost there now." Jack opened a small wooden door in a wall that had several bricks missing at the top. The remaining ones stood out like broken teeth. "I just need to get something from the potting shed." He disappeared inside a hut with a thatched roof, Brock at his heels. Through the open door came a smell of tobacco mixed with earth, onions, and turpentine. He came out with a length of rope slung over his shoulder.

"The cowshed's just across the yard." He gave me a sideways glance. "I'd better come in with you. You'll have to make allowances, I'm afraid—they're a rum lot."

I tried not to gag at the stench of dung wafting out of the milking shed. Above the lowing of the animals I could hear a high-pitched cackle that could have come from a duck or a chicken. But as I followed Jack through the door, I saw a woman in a blue-striped turban holding her sides as she emerged from under a cow.

"Well, I told him straight," she said, still laughing as she talked over the animal's flank, not seeing us in the doorway. "Do you think I'm going to drop my knickers for a pair of nylons and a pint of shandy?"

Jack cleared his throat, cutting short the muffled giggles coming from behind the cows. "Good morning, ladies. This is my cousin Alice. She's come to help us out. Alice, this is Edith—she'll introduce you to everyone." With that, he turned and left me.

I stood on the threshold, feeling like Daniel about to walk into the lions' den. "Hello, Edith," I began, stretching out my hand. She didn't take it. She stood with her hands on her hips, looking me up and down.

"His cousin?" She pursed her lips, which were a waxy purple, like tulips. I'd never seen anyone with lips that color, other than a patient with severe heart failure I'd nursed in Africa. She looked as if she was sizing me up, trying to decide if I'd be an ally or an enemy. I hoped she didn't think Jack had sent me to spy on them.

She caught me staring at her mouth. "Cowgirl's lipstick." She gave a theatrical pout. "You want some?" She cocked her head toward the door of the cowshed. "Beeswax. From the hives. Mixed with beetroot juice." She wiggled her shoulders, making her bosom wobble under the bib of her dungarees. "You have to look your best, don't you? Never know who you might bump into."

One by one the other Land Army women emerged from under the animals they'd been milking. There were five of them. The youngest looked about the age I'd been when I entered the convent. Another looked old enough to be that girl's mother. Edith and the other two looked like they were in their midtwenties. None of them looked pleased to see me.

Edith reeled off their names so fast I couldn't take them in. Then she said: "Have you ever milked a cow before?"

"Yes—but not since I was a child." That was true. When I was very young, and my mother was still alive, my parents had taken me to stay on a farm in Kilkenny. My attempt at milking had ended in tears when the cow trod on my foot.

"We don't need another milkmaid." The older woman, whose name was Mary or Marjorie—I couldn't remember—folded her arms across her chest. "What we need is someone to clean up the muck in this place." Her eyes darted left and right, casting sly glances at the others. "But we can't ask His Lordship's cousin to do a thing like that."

I took a step toward her. "Of course you can. Where's the shovel?"

I felt their eyes on me, like X-rays, as I worked. I wondered if it was just because I was a newcomer—and a relative of Jack's—or whether they thought I was odd for offering to do the job none of them could stomach.

I was used to doing things I didn't want to do. It had been ingrained in me for so many years. I hoped that shoveling muck would make them like me. But after I'd spent an hour heaving it into piles at the end of the yard, not one of them had said a word to me. It dawned on me then that if I wasn't careful, this habit of doing what I was told without protest would mark me out with a certain strangeness. I was going to have to *unlearn* behaving like a nun.

My foot began to throb a little. It made me limp as I carried the slippery dung from the shed. I knew they'd noticed I was struggling—but it was only when we stopped for a tea break that one of them spoke to me. It was the youngest one, whose name was Janet. She had thick brown braids pinned up like a halo around her head and wire-rimmed glasses whose thin arms curled right around her ears and stuck up like tiny horns.

She came up to me as I stood alone, leaning against a wooden fence, and asked me if I was all right. When I said yes, she asked me how old I was. I saw a flicker of disappointment when I said that I was thirty. Then she asked me if I was getting paid the same amount as she and the others were: twenty-eight shillings a week.

"I'm not getting paid anything," I replied. "I'm working in return for food and a place to sleep."

Her eyes widened. "But you're his *cousin*—you shouldn't have to do that."

"I don't mind." I shrugged. "I can't sit around doing nothing. No one can."

I asked her where she was from.

"A place called Thirsk. It's up north. Took me two days on the train to get here."

"What about the others?"

"They're all from different places. No one's from round here. We live in the Scouts' hut down the road—at Constantine."

I didn't want her to think I was getting special treatment—that I'd been given a room in Jack's house while they were all sleeping on camp beds. I told her I was living in the boathouse down at the cove.

"Aren't you scared, being there on your own at night? I would be."

"Cousin Jack comes to check up on me twice a day—it's where he walks his dog." It felt odd, calling him that. But it was what he'd told me to say, and I thought I'd better stick to it.

Janet suddenly leaned closer. "They're all in love with him," she whispered. "Even Marjorie. Is it true that he's got a secret wife?"

I'd just taken a first sip of the very hot tea. I coughed and spluttered as it went down the wrong way. Edith came over and clapped me hard on the back. She couldn't have heard what Janet had said. I'm sure she would have tried to get more out of me if she had. But thankfully she had something else on her mind. She tugged at the scarf on my head, which had slipped off when she'd whacked me.

"What happened to your hair?"

I grabbed at the scarf, trying to cover myself. "Head lice," I muttered.

"Ugh!" Edith shrank back. Out of the corner of my eye, I saw Janet edge away, too.

"I don't have them now. I caught them at the hospital in London, where I was working." I undid the knot in the scarf and tied it back on—tighter. Doing something with my hands seemed to help me to lie. "We were bombed out. That's why I was limping—I got glass in my foot."

I saw something like respect in their eyes then. The older woman, Marjorie, brought me a milking stool to sit on while I finished my tea. I sensed, though, that while their initial hostility might have abated, it would only be a matter of time before, like Janet, they started quizzing me about Jack.

A secret wife. I told myself it was none of my business if he was married. Marital status wasn't something I'd thought about much when I'd encountered men in Africa. They were forbidden—and over the years I'd come to view them less as people of a different gender and more as individuals whose personalities I either warmed to or struggled with, just as I did with my fellow nuns.

So why had Janet's words made my insides shrivel like burning paper? A man of Jack's age—kind, good looking, and titled—was bound to be married. If I'd really thought about it, I suppose I should have wondered why it was him, and not his wife, who brought me what I needed each day. But I hadn't thought about it. Perhaps it was because everything was so new to me. Or perhaps it was because I hadn't wanted to.

"Have you met her?" It was a tall, slim woman who asked the question. Her hair was the same dark auburn as mine but much longer, fashioned into a loaf-sized bun that was held in place by a hairnet. Her name was Rita. She came with the teapot to top up my mug, overfilling it as she looked me in the eye.

"Met who?" I tried to sound nonchalant.

"Lady Trewella." Her eyebrows arched. "There's a rumor that His Lordship's married—but his wife has never been seen."

"Oh. Who told you that?"

"The woman who comes up from the village to do the washing. Her mother was the old viscount's housekeeper—before the war." She held my gaze, unblinking. "You're his cousin—so, go on, is it true?"

I drew the mug to my lips so that I could look away in a manner that would seem natural, not as if I was trying to hide something. I'd learned this discipline as a nun—of concealing my thoughts, my reactions. It helped me to parry the questions that followed, thick and fast.

"He's a very private man," I said, "and our families have never really been close. Until I came here this week, I hadn't seen him since I was six years old. You probably know as much about him as I do." I felt a twinge of guilt. I was getting better at it—this mixing of lies and truth.

"But you could *ask* him, couldn't you?" Rita wasn't going to be fobbed off.

"What am I supposed to say?" I shrugged. "I've already foisted myself on him at short notice, when he hardly knows me from Adam. I can hardly drop it into casual conversation, can I—'By the way, Cousin Jack, are you married? Because if you're not, there's a queue of women who'd like to audition for the part of Lady Trewella.'"

To my relief, this made them laugh. Then a cow got loose and there was pandemonium in the yard while we tried to round it up. A man in uniform came to see what the commotion was. He didn't look much older than Janet, but he had film star looks and oozed self-confidence. By the time the animal was caught, the Land Army women seemed to have forgotten about Jack.

Back inside, they taught me how to skim cream off the milk and turn it into butter. By the end of the morning my arm ached from turning the handle of the barrel-shaped churn. I watched Marjorie fashion the pale yellow lumps that emerged into pats, using wooden paddles to shape them. Tomorrow, she said, that would be my job.

At lunchtime they headed off in a truck, bound for some other farm. I wasn't sure what my duties for the afternoon would be. I walked away from the cowshed, past a row of stables with decaying wooden doors, some of which hung open at crazy angles. There were no horses inside—just antiquated hay carts and a penny-farthing bicycle whose enormous front wheel was pitted with age. Above the middle doors was a huge clock with a rust-speckled face. I stood looking at it, wondering if the time really could be twenty past two. But the hands didn't move. They'd probably been stuck like that for years.

The cobblestone path took me on, past pigsties and a tractor shed, until I spotted the house whose imposing stone walls I had glimpsed through the trees. I hoped I wouldn't run into Jack. I needed time to process what the Land Army women had said. I couldn't put a name to the feeling their gossip had triggered. But it gnawed away at me as I approached the brick wall that formed the boundary between the farm and the house.

Passing through metal gates like the ones in the walled garden, I came to a set of wide stone steps in front of an arched portico. Carved into the apex of the arch was the same coat of arms I'd seen on the garden gates. Inside was a massive wooden door with ornate curlicued hinges. The words "No Entry" were printed in large black letters on a notice nailed to the door. Beneath the words was the symbol of an anchor and the letters *RF*.

Merle appeared as I stood staring at it. She was wearing an apron over her clothes, and her face looked flushed.

"Hello," she said. "You've finished in the dairy?" She wiped her hands on a corner of the apron.

"The others have gone," I said. "I wasn't sure what else needed doing."

"Are you hungry?"

"Well . . ." It was five hours since I'd eaten the last slice of the loaf Jack had brought me. And the muck shoveling was the hardest physical work I'd done in years. But I was reluctant to admit how ravenous I was feeling, knowing how little food there was to go around.

"Come with me."

She led me round the back of the house, in through a door with peeling green paint, and down a passageway whose flagstones had been worn down in the middle from centuries of footsteps. I could smell baking—something savory, like sausage rolls or a meat pie.

"It's for tonight, really," she said over her shoulder, "but it's almost ready."

She sat me down at a long table whose surface was as timeworn as the floor of the passageway. When she brought me a glass of water, it was difficult to find a place where it would stand upright.

"This house goes back to Tudor times." Merle ran her fingers along a deep groove at the other end of the table. "Generations of servants, cutting and chopping. We could do with a few of them now."

I watched as she thrust her hands into a pair of oven mitts criss-crossed with burn marks. Bending her knees, she drew an enormous metal baking tray out of an old-fashioned range.

"Rabbit pie." She set it down on a marble slab, her cheeks pink with the heat from the oven. "We don't often have meat these days, but there's going to be a houseful tonight."

"I heard that there was military training going on here."

She took a knife and sliced into the pie. "They come and go. We're never quite sure how many will be staying on any one night."

"And you have to cook for them?"

"Not only me; there's a girl from the village who comes to help." She put a steaming slice of the pie down in front of me. "I used to run a restaurant on Guernsey—before the children came along. I like cooking. It gives me something to do while they're at school."

"It smells delicious."

"I should wait a minute before you eat it—you might burn your mouth."

I was dying to taste it, but I laid the knife and fork back down on the table.

"Do *you* like cooking?" she asked.

"I . . . haven't had much opportunity." It felt better, telling the truth. But her eyes had a searching look. "Being a nurse," I went on, "we had all our meals provided at the hospital in London."

"Which hospital was it?"

I wasn't expecting her to put me on the spot. I should have thought of that, of course. Had an answer ready. "Not one you'll have heard of," I replied. "It was an isolation hospital on the outskirts—for tuberculosis cases."

"And it was bombed?" She sounded surprised. I realized I'd tripped myself up.

"They don't always fall where they're supposed to," I said, paraphrasing what Jack had said about the bombing raid in Falmouth. "It was such a shock," I added, trying to look as if I meant it.

"Were many killed?"

"Thankfully, no." To lie about people dying was more than I could stomach. "But the building was too badly damaged to be usable."

"What happened to the patients?"

"They were all transferred—up north." I borrowed Janet's expression. My knowledge of the geography of northern England was sketchy. I hoped Merle's was, too.

"Didn't they want you to go, too?"

"I . . . I couldn't. I got glass in my foot. It's only just started to heal."

I was racking my brain to come up with a reason why I couldn't go and join the patients I'd abandoned, now that I was better. But Merle seemed satisfied. "Sorry," she said, "your pie'll be going cold. Would you like another glass of water?"

I spent the afternoon weeding rows of onions and potatoes that had been planted in front of the house, where once there must have been lawns and flower beds. Merle had given me an old cushion to kneel on, which took the pressure off my foot. She was concerned about how I was going to get back down to the boathouse.

"Why don't you come with me when I go to get the children from school?" she asked. "The path down to the village isn't as steep as the one down the valley. High tide's not till just before seven, so you'll be able to get around the rocks to the cove."

At half past three she came to find me. The route to the village took us through the apple orchard, whose trees were gnarled and spotted with lichen. They looked very old, but the branches were swathed in blossom. We passed a patch of land with potatoes and beans growing on it, enclosed by high wire netting. Merle told me that when she and the children had first arrived, this place had been a tennis court.

As we started to go downhill, I glimpsed the estuary, dappled gray green where clouds scudded over the water. Merle asked me about my life before the hospital in London. She had never been to Ireland and wanted to know what it was like. I was able to tell the truth, mostly—apart from saying that my late mother came from Jack's side of the family and had left Cornwall to marry my father.

It felt strangely liberating, chatting about the past after years of bottling it up. I got the sense that Merle wanted to befriend me. But I was acutely aware that I was acting a part, that I had already told her lies and would have to go on lying. I wondered whether, by asking Jack to conceal my old life, I had made things worse for myself. How could I exchange those confidences that build a friendship when I was holding back such a big secret?

As a novice, I had yearned for a friend. But any hint of it was nipped in the bud because of the ban on attachments. There had been a girl at the convent who was the same age as me. Her name was Clodagh. We sat together at recreation, and when I was put on a week of half rations for being late for chapel, she smuggled food to me after lights-out. But we were called out in the mea culpa. Steps were taken to keep us apart in future.

"Did you miss Ireland when you moved to London?" Merle's voice broke my train of thought.

"It was very different," I said, "but I didn't have much time to miss things—it was so busy at the hospital." Another half-truth. I hoped it would suffice. I didn't want to talk about the life I could have had if I'd stayed, the life my father had been so fiercely opposed to.

"Cornwall isn't all that different to Guernsey." Merle took my arm as the path turned from smooth shingle to uneven cobblestones. "Apart from Guernsey being an island, I mean. We had a farm there. My husband, Maurice, grew tomatoes."

I thought it strange that she talked about her husband and the farm in the past tense. I wondered if he'd been killed during the invasion.

"He decided to stay when the Germans came, because of the business."

"That must have been hard for him—with you and the children having to leave."

"Hmm." There was something in the tone of her voice—wistful with a tinge of bitterness. I glanced at her, trying to gauge whether it was an invitation to probe further or to shut up. But as I did so, something else caught her attention.

"Oh God! Get down—quick!"

I hadn't even heard the high-pitched whine of the plane's engine. We'd only just hit the ground when it screamed over our heads. I shouldn't have looked up, but curiosity got the better of me. I saw the pale gray undercarriage with its yellow-tipped wings, a black cross emblazoned on each one.

"A Focke-Wulf fighter-bomber," Merle breathed, as we both stared after it. "Probably coming to see what damage they did the other night."

I thought she must have seen these enemy planes often, to know them by name. I wondered if they'd flown over Guernsey before the invasion, the noise of their engines shattering the tranquility of the tomato farm where she'd lived with her husband and children. I had only a vague idea of the geography of the Channel Islands. All I knew was that they were much closer to France than to England.

"I think we're okay, now." She shaded her eyes, scanning the horizon. "I don't think he's coming back. Sorry if I scared you, but a couple of months ago the children and I were strafed on the way to school: we were lucky not to be hit."

"They fired on the *children*? Deliberately?"

Merle nodded. "I couldn't believe it, either. Come on—we'd better get going."

As we rounded a bend in the path, I caught sight of the village—the same huddle of cottages I could see from the beach. They were stone-built houses with slate roofs, sitting right on the edge of the estuary. To the southwest—where the boathouse was hidden by a rocky promontory—the receding tide had exposed mudflats where herons, egrets, and oystercatchers prodded about.

Yellow-flowered gorse bushes lined the final stretch of the route downhill. Washing was spread out to dry on some of them. Shirts, skirts, sheets, socks—even underwear—were draped over the prickly branches, the breeze tugging in vain to blow them away.

A wooden bridge took us from the path to the edge of the village. I could see thin green strands of eelgrass swaying in the shallow water lapping through the channel beneath. *Like a mermaid's hair,* I thought. I wondered if this was how the cove had got its name.

I followed Merle into what appeared to be the main street through the village. Despite the uniform gray of the cottage walls, it was a place of vivid colors. Pots of fuchsias and pansies lined windowsills and porches. Baskets of geraniums hung at either side of front doors. Chickens and ducks wandered around the cobblestone streets, and I could hear budgerigars and canaries chirping away inside the houses.

"It's very quaint," I said, as we passed a half-open stable door where an old, toothless man stood smoking a clay pipe.

She nodded, turning to wave as the old man raised his pipe in a greeting. "It's like the whole place is preserved in aspic. Shame about the smell, though."

Living in the boathouse, I'd become used to breathing air tainted with the odor of fish. But here the stench was overpowering. The smell was tinged with something else—a bitter, tarry scent that Merle told me was pitch boiled up to preserve the fishing nets.

We saw the nets draped out to dry in the sunshine as we neared the quayside. Wooden boats, left high and dry by the receding tide, were moored to metal rings in the wall. Their names were hand painted in bold letters. I shaded my eyes to read them. *Fleetwings, Seasquirt, Mabel, Stella.* Farther out in the estuary, moored to buoys, were bigger fishing boats.

A few yards from the quay was the fish cellar. "That's where the stink comes from," Merle said. "They store the pilchards in there after they've squeezed the oil out of them."

Two men in sailor's caps were sitting outside, mending nets strung with floats made of cork. Merle nodded to them as we passed by. "Those two are Eddie Downing and Leo Badger," she murmured. "Eddie's granddaughter is the same age as Danielle. Leo's his uncle. He's seventy-four, but he still goes out fishing every day. Last summer he caught a shark and it bit him when he tried to haul it in." She glanced back at the men, her lips pressed together, as if she was trying not to smile. "I would have introduced you—but every time I stop to chat, Leo rolls up his trouser leg to show me the teeth marks!"

We dodged across the narrow street to avoid a donkey that was coming up behind us pulling a cart laden with seaweed. "They use it for compost up at the farm," Merle said, as it trundled past. "The banks are too steep for tractors."

There was another man sitting outside a cottage, making some sort of basket out of withies. When Merle called out a greeting, he raised his head and I saw that his eyes were opaque. "That's George Retallack," she whispered. "He's amazing: He makes those crab and lobster pots even though he's been blind since he was born. He can find his way around without any help—people say he can even sense the state of the tide."

I wondered why there didn't seem to be any women in the village. When I asked, Merle told me that they were out selling fish. "They go to Falmouth by donkey," she said. "Turbot's the prize catch, along with halibut and red mullet. There are oysters in the estuary, too."

"Oysters were my favorite thing when I lived in Dublin," I said. "But it's . . ." I bit my tongue. I'd almost told her that they were the food I'd missed most when I went into the convent.

"What?" Merle said.

"It's . . . just been a while since I've had any." I smiled to cover my awkwardness.

There was a sudden commotion farther up the street: the whoop of children let loose for the Easter holiday. "Oh—they're out early." Merle opened her arms to catch Ned, who came hurtling down the street like a missile.

"Slow down!" She caught him and lifted him off his feet. "He's really too young to go to school," she said, ruffling his hair as she put him down. "He's only four and a half." She glanced past me to the woods above the village, where Penheligan's monumental walls were hidden in the trees. "It was a bit of influence from you-know-who. He persuaded the headmistress to allow Ned to come here with the others."

Watching the little boy as he darted down the street with Merle's children, I couldn't help thinking about his parents. What must it be like for them, I wondered, not knowing where he was or who was looking after him? And what would it be like for Ned when the war finally ended? How would he feel, being handed back to people who were total strangers?

"We'll walk you back to the boathouse if you like," Merle said. As we headed for the rocky spur that separated the village from the cove, she produced a paper bag from her pocket. Inside it were licorice bootlaces. She gave one to each of the children, then handed me one.

I tried to give it back—it didn't feel right, taking what she'd bought for the children—but she insisted. "Everything with sugar in it is supposed to be rationed," she said, "but there's a woman up the street with jars of these hidden in a cupboard in her front room—and she never asks for any coupons."

I put mine in the pocket of my dungarees to save for later. Merle went to catch up with Louis and the girls, who were kicking the head of a dead fish around the cobblestones. Ned fell into step beside me. He tugged at my hand, and when I looked down, he opened his mouth to show a tongue and gums stained black with licorice.

With a poker face, I retrieved my bootlace and stuck it under my nose to make a drooping mustache, curling my top lip to hold it in place.

This made Ned laugh so much he almost spat his out.

He held my hand as we made our way around the rock pools left behind by the tide. "Can we go fishing?" he asked. "There's a net in your house—I seen it."

"There is." I smiled. "But we'll have to ask your . . ." I trailed off, wondering what he called Merle.

"Auntie Merle?"

"Yes—we'll see what she says."

I almost had a fight on my hands when we got back to the boat-house. When the others heard what Ned planned to do, they all wanted to go fishing. Luckily there were two shrimping nets. I took charge of the boys and Merle the girls. By the time the incoming tide had driven us back, we'd caught half a dozen shrimps, three crabs, and a starfish.

"But I want to stay here," Ned wailed when Merle said it was time to go back for tea. She went to take his hand, but he wrapped his arms around my leg.

"You can come another time," I said. His little arms were gripping me like a vise. I bent down, slipping my fingers under his, trying to pry them off as gently as I could. I hoped that Merle hadn't caught the emotion in my voice, that she wouldn't see that my eyes were filmy with tears and ask me what was wrong.

I didn't notice that two other figures had appeared on the beach. It was only when I raised my head that I saw Jack, just feet away, with Brock at his heels. There was the strangest expression on his face. He looked as if he'd seen a ghost.

Chapter 7

Merle shooed the children up the beach toward the woods. Ned had let go of my leg as soon as he spotted Jack. I wondered if the children were afraid of him.

Once they'd gone, he behaved as if nothing was amiss. He'd brought more kindling for the fire, and he smiled at me as he tipped it into the willow basket, asking how I'd got on in the milking shed with the Land Girls.

"They were a bit wary at first," I replied. "I don't think they liked the idea of me being your cousin. I had to remember my training."

"Training?"

"The rule of the convent—that a nun must always act with grace and politeness. Smile, whatever you're feeling inside." I didn't tell him about the interrogation I'd received. Something must have happened up at the house to make him look the way he did when he'd come onto the beach. I didn't want to darken his mood by telling him how the Land Girls had been gossiping about him.

Is it true that he's got a secret wife? Janet's words rang in my head. How could it be true? Why would a man like Jack have to hide the fact that he was married? But if it *were* true . . . would that explain the dark cloud that sometimes seemed to hover over him? I used to think I was good at reading people, after so many years of nursing. But Jack was a mystery.

"Merle's been very friendly," I said, trying to steer the conversation in a different direction. "She showed me around the village this afternoon."

"Oh?" He snapped a stick of wood over his knee and threw the pieces into the glowing belly of the stove.

"She's very easy to talk to," I went on. "It's years since I've chatted like that. I didn't realize how much I've missed it."

"Didn't you have any friends in Africa?" He looked up, incredulous.

"Not among the other nuns, no. It wasn't permitted."

He shook his head. "That's barbaric. You were thousands of miles from home, working in primitive conditions—there must have been times when you needed someone to talk to."

"Oh, there were." I nodded. "But the only person I ever really confided in was a Belgian priest. His name was Father Armand. He came to the hospital twice a year to be checked for leprosy."

"Leprosy?" Jack grimaced.

"He'd set up a leper colony on an island in the river. I used to take medical supplies there while I was on my rounds of the villages in the bush." I saw my old friend in my mind's eye. A Santa Claus face, with white hair and a bushy beard. "He was the kindest person I ever met. And he had a knack of picking up on what troubled a person. I think he knew, long before I did, that I wasn't really cut out for the religious life."

"Do people really do that?" Jack was shaking his head. "*Choose* to live among lepers? Did he have a death wish? Or was he some sort of saint?"

"I used to think he was saintly," I said. "But one day I heard his story—not from him but from the local barber, who used to come to the hospital to give the patients haircuts. He said that as a young priest, Father Armand was stationed in a remote part of the Congo. He was very lonely, and one day he just disappeared into the bush. His mission gave him up for dead, but years later a touring priest discovered him living in a hut in the jungle with a native wife and three children."

Jack's eyes narrowed. "What did they do to him?"

"This other priest persuaded him to hand the children over to nuns and to leave his wife. He was sent back to Europe in disgrace. But the following year he came back to Africa. He'd asked the church for permission to devote the rest of his life to lepers as a penance for what he'd done."

Jack blew out a breath. "Had he really done anything so terribly wrong? How cruel of the church to separate a man from his family! He'd only done what's considered natural for most people."

"I know. Being a priest is a life against nature—just like being a nun. They drummed that into us from the beginning. It's what I struggled with more than anything—but in Father Armand's case, at least, something good came out of it."

"Well, yes, I can see that. But it came at a terrible price." He raked his hair with his fingers. "Did he ever tell you what became of his children and their mother?"

I shook my head. "He never knew that I knew any of it. I think he told himself that it was God's will—something that he had to accept. He had a saying, which he often came out with when I told him about my own troubles: 'The Lord allows what must happen for our own good.'"

Jack turned back to the stove, muttering something I couldn't make out. I realized, too late, that in relating the story, I'd probably turned his nagging doubts about organized religion into outright condemnation.

You call that doing good?

The voice inside my head was Sister Clare's.

So much for going it alone, she hissed.

The next day was Good Friday. When I opened the door of the boathouse, I could smell the salty tang of the sea carried on the breeze blowing in from the southwest. I stood for a while, watching the white-capped waves and listening to the fluting cries of the oystercatchers. I remembered something I'd once read about the wind affecting people's moods: how a dry wind from the mountains made people clear sighted and logical, but a damp sea wind turned human minds mystical and sensuous. I wondered if my own mind had been affected by the sea voyage that had brought me here, whether that longing to break free had come not from God but from something elemental. And whether living in this place, just yards from the water's edge, might lure a person to a different, more primitive kind of spirituality.

The thought of that unsettled me. My life was too new and too uncertain; I wasn't prepared to give up everything. I had to hold on to some of the old assurances as I had clung to the wooden table that had saved me from drowning. I said the rosary before setting off for the farm, using the mussel shell Ned had given me and some fragments of sea glass I'd collected, to work my way through the sorrowful mysteries.

Jack had left a fresh loaf of bread for me, but I couldn't decide whether to have any breakfast. At the convent, this would have been a day of fasting. I wondered if I'd be able to get through the morning ahead on an empty stomach. I needed the stamina to do my share of work. Fasting would help no one—and yet breaking the Lenten rule felt wrong. In the end I tucked a slice into the pocket of my dungarees.

I made my way up the valley on my own. The sun hadn't yet appeared over the top of the hill. In the dark green shadows of the arching tree ferns and bamboo thickets, birds were singing their hearts out. I stopped for a moment, just to listen. There was something supernatural about it: blackbirds, thrushes, wrens, robins—a dozen songs, all different, that somehow harmonized. It had the same ethereal quality as the plainsong chants that had marked dawn and dusk at the chapel in Africa. Singing in the choir was something that had made my heart soar, however difficult the day had been.

I walked on, wistful at the memory of that singing—and mortified by the realization that, apart from my nursing, this was the only thing I really missed about being a nun.

I paused again when I passed the graveyard that bordered the little woodland church. I had a sudden urge to climb over the wall and see if the door was unlocked. But I was already late for my shift at the milking shed.

As I made my way through the walled garden, I tried to prepare myself mentally for more questions from the Land Girls about Jack. But the yard outside the milking shed was strangely silent. No muffled giggles or cackled obscenities. All I could hear was the rhythmic squirting of milk into buckets.

"Good morning!"

It was Merle, peering round the tail end of a cow.

"Good morning," I called back. "Where are the Land Girls?"

"They've got Easter weekend off, to go and see their families."

"So, it's just you and me, is it?"

"No—we're helping." Merle's eldest child, Danielle, popped out from behind one of the other animals. The grinning face of Louis, her brother, appeared from under the flank of the cow in the next stall over.

"They like it much better than going to school," Merle said, ducking as a tail swished over her head.

The children were much more skilled at milking cows than I was. I thought I'd remember how to do it, but my technique produced nothing but a dribble. Danielle came to give me a quick lesson.

"How old were you when you learnt how to do this?" I asked.

"Quite little," she replied. "There were cows at the farm next door on Guernsey. Me and my dad used to go and help the old man who lived there." She was looking down at the udders, not at me, so I couldn't see her face, but I caught a small sigh at the end of what she said. I wondered how she coped with not seeing her father—not even being able to write to him or speak on the telephone.

My mother had died when I was five, a bit younger than Danielle would have been when she left Guernsey. All I could remember about that time was asking why she wasn't coming to tuck me up in bed and read me a story. I couldn't grasp the fact that she only existed as a memory. I thought about how hard it must be for Merle, trying to explain their situation to her children.

I couldn't think of anything to say about the life they'd left behind that wouldn't sound trite. Instead I asked Danielle what the other children were doing while she and Louis were milking.

"They're helping in the kitchen," she replied. "They're making pastry with Molly from the village, but they'll probably end up eating most of it before it's even been cooked." She grinned as she stood up to let me sit on the milking stool, revealing a gap in her top set of teeth.

"I used to love raw pastry when I was your age," I said, reaching for the slippery udders. "Here goes—let's hope I get it right this time."

It took a while to master what Danielle had tried to teach me. I managed to squirt milk into my eye, which had us both in fits of giggles. I finally got the hang of it—but it was past midday by the time all the milking was done.

At the end of the afternoon Merle and the children walked with me as far as the church in the woods. Danielle and the others played on a rope swing attached to one of the yew trees while Merle and I went inside.

The scent of beeswax and incense made my stomach flip over. If I'd entered the place with my eyes closed, I'd have known instantly what kind of building I was in. It was the smell of churches the world over—so familiar but, now, strangely troubling. As my eyes adjusted to the shadowy interior, an image leapt into my mind—of Judas kissing Christ in the Garden of Gethsemane. Was that what I was? A traitor?

"Shall I put the lights on?" Merle's voice was a whisper.

"If you want to," I whispered back. "I don't mind it like this, though." I caught the glimmer of stained glass in a wall of rough granite. It cast jewel colors onto a worn tombstone set in the floor. Somehow, I felt safer in the dark. Perhaps I thought that with the lights on, Merle would see the guilt written on my face.

"Would you like a candle?" She stepped away from me, to a metal stand to the right of the nave.

"Yes, please."

I shielded the flame with my hand, following Merle as she carried hers. The flickering light illuminated ancient pews with birds and animals carved into them. We passed a lectern in the shape of a pelican—an echo of the symbol on the Trewella family coat of arms. A huge Bible rested on the bird's outstretched wings. The pelican's graceful neck was curved, its beak embedded in its breast. The light was too dim to make out the drops of blood trickling down its carved feathers to the two baby birds in the nest below.

We placed our candles in a tray of sand beneath a marble bas-relief of the Last Supper. I wondered who Merle's was for. Her husband, I supposed. Mine was for me. A way of saying what I would have said to the Mother Superior, if I'd had the courage to go back to Dublin and face her: that I hadn't lost my faith—but I couldn't go on as I was.

As we turned to leave, a shaft of sunshine lit up the choir stalls in front of the altar. They looked even older than the pews. The dark wood was pitted with centuries of wear.

"I suppose you've heard the story about the mermaid," Merle said.

"What story?"

She led me over to where the sunlight pooled on the smooth stone floor. "Can you see that?" She ran her fingers over the carved end of one of the choir stalls, tracing the outline of something I couldn't quite make out. "It's a mermaid. There's the tail. And the hair."

Suddenly I saw it. A bare-breasted, fish-tailed woman with hair hanging to her waist. She held a mirror in one hand and a comb in the other. Her nose and mouth had almost disappeared, as if generations of admirers had kissed her image. But her eyes were intact, big and round, as if they flashed a warning.

"People in the village say that long ago, a beautiful woman appeared in the church. No one knew who she was. She wore silk dresses and fur capes, and her voice was sweeter than anything they'd ever heard. She took a shine to a man in the choir—the best singer in the parish—and one day he followed her home from church." Merle glanced at me, arching her eyebrows.

"Neither of them was ever seen again," she went on, "until one Sunday a ship anchored in the cove. According to the legend, a mermaid appeared and asked the sailors to raise the anchor, as one of its flukes was resting on the door of her home, and her children were trapped inside. They weighed anchor and sailed away as fast as they could, because a mermaid was a bad omen. But when they described what they'd seen, people said the mermaid was the same woman who'd lured the man away—and that the children must be his."

"So, the cove is named after the myth?"

Merle nodded.

"What a strange story." I leaned forward to touch the carving. The surface of the wood was waxy from years of polish. "I mean, you can believe the bit about a rich woman visiting the place and luring a man away, but sailors seeing a mermaid . . . where did that idea come from?"

"Goodness knows. We have mermaid stories on Guernsey. People used to say that if a man followed a mermaid into the sea, she'd take him down to the depths of the ocean and eat him up."

"That's gruesome," I said.

She nodded. "My grandfather knew a man who said he saw six mermaids playing on a beach when he was walking along the cliffs. They were probably seal pups, but he swore they were *sirènes*."

She'd used the French word for mermaid. I asked her if people on Guernsey spoke French as their first language.

"Most people speak English these days," she said. "But we have our own version of French—we call it *Guernésiais*. Do you speak French?"

I hesitated. If I told her I was fluent, she'd ask me where I learned it. Then I would have to tell her about Belgium, which would lead to more questions. "I learnt it at school," I said. "But I wasn't very good." Both statements were true. I'd simply left out part of the story. That felt better than telling an outright lie while standing in a church, right in front of the altar.

"Have you ever been in love?"

The question came like a bolt from the blue. I looked up, blinking as a beam of sunlight caught my eyes. "Yes, I was, once," I said. "It was a long time ago, in Ireland. It didn't work out." Dan's face appeared against the afterimage of the sun's rays. I'd met him at a bus stop in Grafton Street. I'd been struggling with my cello in a high wind, and he'd offered to help. His blue, sparkling eyes and big smile had made me forget all about the miserable music lesson ahead, on an instrument I was never able to master. He'd brought a sense of joy into my life—something I hadn't really felt since my mother died. The memory of him had to be locked away when I joined the order. I hadn't breathed his name for twelve years.

"And there's been no one since? You haven't left someone behind in London?" The look of gentle concern in Merle's eyes made me want to let out what I'd been holding back. But I felt trapped in the web of lies I'd spun. "No—there's been no one else," I said.

"That's a good thing, in a way," she replied. "It's hard, when there's a war on, to be in love."

There was a poignancy in her voice. "You must miss your husband terribly," I said.

Merle's eyes darted to the timeworn stones beneath her feet. "It's harder for the children," she said. "They don't understand. Jacqueline doesn't even remember him."

"I can't imagine what it must have felt like," I murmured, "to be separated in that way."

For a long moment she said nothing. I heard her draw in a long breath. "It was a blessing, actually." Her eyes met mine. "Does that make me sound awful?"

I shook my head. "No, it . . . makes you sound as if you've been very unhappy." I bit my lip. "I'm sorry—I'm not trying to pry."

"It's all right. I shouldn't have said anything. But it's so hard sometimes. Everyone thinks I must be missing him—that I must be longing for the war to end, so we can be together again. But I *don't* miss him. If I'm honest, I hope I'll never have to set eyes on him again."

I glanced at the carving of the mermaid, searching for the right thing to say.

Say nothing—let her do the talking.

The voice in my head was Sister Clare's. She'd spoken those words to me in my first week at the mission hospital, when I was struggling to deal with a distraught patient in the maternity ward—a woman whose husband had just been killed in a mining accident.

"Our marriage was in trouble long before I left the island," Merle went on. "I was pregnant with Jacqueline when I found out Maurice had been having an affair." Her eyes darted in my direction, as if she was weighing up my reaction. "It was with our housemaid, Ruby. She was eighteen years old—young enough to be his daughter." Another pause. In the silence I heard her swallow. "He'd got her pregnant at almost the same time as me. Her baby was born on my thirtieth birthday—two weeks after I'd had Jacqueline."

"What on earth did you do?" I whispered.

"What could I do?" Merle shook her head. "I had no money of my own—nowhere else to go. And I had two other children to look after." She traced the carved edge of the choir stall with her finger. "He set her up in an apartment in St. Peter Port. I used to see her, pushing the pram, when I went to do the shopping."

"How long after that did the Germans arrive?"

"Jacqueline was two and a half. I remember taking her and the others to buy ice cream one afternoon, and hearing gunfire on the mainland. That was the day they invaded France. I used to lie awake at night, panicking about what we'd do if they came to Guernsey. I had this terrible fantasy about killing Maurice and saying the Germans had done it. That's how much I hated him." She closed her eyes. "Listen to me, saying a thing like that in a place like this."

"I don't think anyone would blame you for thinking it," I said. "It must have been torture, having to go on living with him."

Merle opened her eyes. "It was. When the announcement came on the radio that we had to get the children off the island, I couldn't pack fast enough. Maurice said he had to stay behind to look after the farm—but we both knew that wasn't the real reason. I expect he moved Ruby in the minute we stepped on that boat."

"Did you know Cousin Jack?" I asked. "Before the evacuation, I mean? Is that why you came here?"

"No, I'd never met him before. It was like Dunkirk—yachts and motorboats and fishing trawlers—all kinds of people, just wanting to help. None of us knew where we'd end up—we were just glad to get away."

A sudden loud creak made us both turn our heads. Danielle came running up the nave. "Jacqueline's fallen off the swing," she panted. "She's hurt her hand."

Merle raced out to the churchyard. I hurried after her, my injured foot not yet sufficiently recovered to run. Louis and Ned were kneeling beside Jacqueline, who lay facedown on one of the graves, sobbing.

"She fell on that." Danielle pointed to a gravestone that had toppled over and split in half, its jagged edges half-hidden in the grass.

"Oh, love! Show me what you've done." Merle dropped down onto the grass. "Which hand did you hurt?"

"It's this one." Louis pointed to his sister's right thumb, which was bent away from the hand at an alarming angle.

"Can you sit up for me?" Merle slipped her arm under Jacqueline's head and tried to turn her onto her back, but the child cried out in pain.

"I think she's dislocated her thumb," I said. "Would you like me to look at it?"

Merle looked up, her face pale. She nodded. Her lips were pressed together as if she didn't trust herself to speak.

"I'll be as gentle as I can." I lifted the hand at the wrist. There was a cut in the fleshy part of the palm, but not much blood. The child cried out again as I placed my own thumb on the base of hers. "I'm just going to make this better, Jacqueline. It won't take a second, I promise." With my other hand, I grasped the top joint of the injured thumb and gave a swift, hard pull. The popping sound it made as it slipped back into place was drowned out by Jacqueline's scream.

"She'll be fine now," I said, turning to Merle as I released my grip. "It'll be tender for a while, but all she needs is a sticking plaster on that cut."

We'd just got Jacqueline sitting up when Brock came hurtling across the churchyard. Jack wasn't far behind. He came running across the grass when he saw us.

"What's happened, Mrs. Durand? Is she all right?"

He sounded strangely formal, compared to the way he always spoke to me. And yet Merle had been living under his roof for nearly three years.

"She fell off the swing and dislocated her thumb." Merle gave him a weak smile. "But your cousin fixed it."

He looked at me, his face unreadable. Then he crouched down beside Jacqueline. "It sounds as if you've been a very brave girl." He took a sixpence from the pocket of his shirt and handed it to her. Then he turned to Merle. "I came to find you because we've had a group of new arrivals out of the blue. Could Alice and Danielle look after Jacqueline?"

I glanced at Merle. She looked tense. I wondered why Jack couldn't deal with these new people without her help.

"Is that all right?" she asked me.

"Yes, of course," I said.

"I won't be long, love." She stroked Jacqueline's hair, then stood up.

As I watched her disappear into the trees with Jack, I saw him raise his hand. I thought it came to rest, momentarily, on Merle's back. But I wasn't certain. It might have been a trick of the light—the dappled shadows of leaves moving as the breeze lifted them. I glanced at Danielle. Had she noticed it, too? It seemed unlikely—she and Louis had their arms hooked around their little sister, trying to scoop her up off the ground.

I went to help the children, telling myself that if Jack *had* done what I thought he'd done, it was probably just a gesture of comfort. But my mind was charging ahead. Of course, it was entirely natural that Jack would be attracted to a warm, pretty woman like Merle. And after what she'd told me in the church, I could understand why she might be tempted.

I thought about what the Land Girls had said about the mysterious wife no one had ever seen. Surely Merle couldn't have sparked that rumor? They must have run into her often when they came to do the milking. If they thought she was involved with Jack, why hadn't they said so?

I tried not to listen to the chatter inside my head. I liked Merle. She'd been kind to me, as had Jack. They'd both gone out of their way to help me. But like that other Alice, I felt as if I'd tumbled down a rabbit hole into another world—a world where nothing was quite what it seemed.

Chapter 8

I didn't see Jack that night, or the next day. And Merle wasn't in the milking shed when I arrived for work. Danielle told me that her mother was busy, and Molly from the village was going to help with the cows until the Land Girls returned.

Molly was late arriving. Danielle said that she was the sister of George Retallack, the blind man I'd seen mending nets. She was only a few years older than Danielle—and she seemed so overawed by the fact that I was Jack's cousin that she hardly spoke to me, other than to say that a basket of food had been left in the kitchen for me to take back with me.

When I went to collect it, the house seemed strangely quiet. Where were the new arrivals Jack had talked about? Why hadn't I seen anyone going in or out of the place while I'd been weeding, just yards from the front door? In the three days I'd been working at Penheligan, the only other adult male I'd seen, apart from Jack, was the young man in khaki fatigues who'd helped to round up the escaped cow.

The next day was Easter Sunday. I took my good clothes—the silk blouse and the heather-colored skirt—to change into when I'd finished in the cowshed. I'd found a cloche hat on top of the basket of food that had been left for me. It was wrapped in layers of tissue paper and looked brand new. It was pearl gray, with a band of grosgrain ribbon of the same color fashioned into a small bow on one side. I didn't know if it had come from Jack or from Merle—but it was just what I needed. It covered my hair and was more appropriate for church than the bright green head scarf.

The path up through the valley was wetter than it had been before. Heavy rain during the night had ravaged the camellias and rhododendrons. Their sodden petals stuck to my boots as I squelched through them. The trees and bushes were eerily quiet, as if the birds had disappeared or gone into hiding. It was very different from Easter morning a year ago, when I'd walked to chapel under a burning sun, with the deafening chirp of cicadas all around.

Merle wasn't in the milking shed. Danielle said they were all going to church later, but her mother still had a lot to do in the house. I was getting faster at milking, but with only four of us it was hard work. I thought Jack might come looking for me. I was supposed to be helping him ring the church bells, but he hadn't mentioned it again since he'd asked me. By ten o'clock there was still no sign of him.

I got to the church early, just in case he was waiting for me there. The place was empty, so I wandered around the graveyard, looking at the tombstones. I found the place where Jack's parents were buried. His father's stone was shiny black. The inscription read:

JOHN AUBREY CECIL, 13TH VISCOUNT TREWELLA.

DEPARTED THIS LIFE ON FEBRUARY 5, 1942, AGED 66.

"FOR UNTO WHOMSOEVER MUCH IS GIVEN, OF HIM SHALL BE MUCH REQUIRED."

I recognized the line from Luke's Gospel—appropriate for a man of wealth and privilege.

I thought about the day I'd received the news of my father's death: of the shock of learning that the funeral had already taken place. Thousands of miles away, in a remote part of Africa, I'd been the last person to be told, even though I was his closest blood relative. Sister Clare had come to find me in the operating theater to break the news. There was no comforting touch, no hug of sympathy, because nuns were not permitted to lay hands on one another.

I'd been assisting at an emergency appendectomy—the teenage daughter of one of the mineowners, who had awoken tearful and bewildered from the anesthetic. I couldn't allow my grief to show when I came back into the room, couldn't allow myself to cry until that evening, during the hour of recreation, when I stumbled out into the garden to sob in the shadows of the mango trees.

The burial had been arranged by my uncle—my father's brother—who had also inherited his estate. As a nun, I was debarred from any inheritance. I didn't mind that, of course. What crushed me was never having had the chance to say goodbye.

I ran my hand across the smooth surface of Jack's father's stone, wondering if that relationship had been better, warmer, than the one I'd had with my dad. Things had improved for us after the bitter row we'd had over Dan. He hadn't wanted me to become a nun—but he'd come to see me take my vows. He'd told me how proud my mother would have been. That had made me cry.

I stepped away from the tombstone. The one next to it was the same size and shape, but older. Lichen had grown in the crevices, making Jack's mother's name more difficult to pick out. She was Hermione Mary Foxton, Viscountess Trewella. She had died in 1910. I stared at the inscription. I didn't know Jack's exact age. I'd guessed that he was in his early thirties. The date suggested that his mother had died giving birth to him.

I went farther into the churchyard, to smaller, more ancient stones. Some leaned at precarious angles. Others had toppled over. Some were so worn the inscriptions were impossible to decipher. But I recognized some of the names Merle had mentioned when we were walking through the village. There were several Badgers, including a father and son who had both drowned during a storm at sea. An ancestor of George Retallack had met the same fate. There was another more recent Retallack gravestone: HILDA, MOTHER OF GEORGE AND MOLLY, HOUSEKEEPER AT PENHELIGAN. She had died the year before Jack's father. As I read the inscription it dawned on me that this woman must be the person Rita had mentioned when she'd been quizzing me about Jack. Molly Retallack must have repeated gossip her mother had passed on about him having a secret wife.

"Alice!"

Jack's voice made me jump. I hadn't seen him coming across the grass. And if I had, I might not have recognized him. He was a vision of elegance, in a chocolate-brown double-breasted suit and matching fedora. A mulberry-colored silk tie with a paisley pattern was knotted precisely at the neck, with a handkerchief of the same design tucked into the jacket pocket. I felt a treacherous surge somewhere deep in my belly.

"Sorry—I didn't mean to scare you." He lifted his hat in a greeting.

"I . . . wasn't sure if you'd be coming."

"I should have left a note for you—but there wasn't time." He adjusted the fedora, pulling it down to shade his eyes. "I had to go away."

I wondered where, and why, but he was already walking back toward the church. I followed him inside. There was a low door behind the pulpit, which he had to duck to get through. It led to a tiny circular room with paint flaking off the walls and three ropes hanging down through holes in the wooden ceiling. Jack took off his hat and jacket and hung them on a hook beneath a mildewed handwritten sign.

"What's the drill?" He glanced up at the ropes. "Which one do we pull first?"

I was looking at the sign, trying to decipher the smudged letters. "The silencer's on," I replied. "We'd better have a practice before we take it off. You might want to tuck your tie into your shirt—it could get caught in the rope. You'll probably need to roll up your sleeves, too."

"Oh, yes, of course." I caught the glint of tigereye cuff links as his hands went to his collar. While he was getting ready, I looked around for something to stand on. There were a couple of apple boxes by the door. I stacked them on top of each other in front of one of the ropes.

"What's that for?"

"I need to be higher than you to show you what to do," I replied. "If you stand on the other side of the rope, I'll explain." I stepped up onto the boxes. My chin was level with his nose. "Take the tail end of the rope and hook it over your hand. Grip it tight between your thumb and your index finger, then put both hands around this." I pointed to the woolen grip, striped red, white, and blue, that encircled the rope at his eye level. "It's called a sally," I went on. "The idea is that you pull down on the sally, and when it shoots up, you keep hold of the tail end and pull the rope back down again."

"That sounds easy enough."

"It's not as easy as all that." I smiled. "It's more about technique than strength. It'll come to you with practice. But I'll start you off. Ready?"

He nodded.

"So, I'm just going to give it a gentle pull . . ." I tugged on the sally, then let it go. The rope shot up through the hole in the ceiling. The speed of it took Jack by surprise. His lost his grip on the tail end.

"Huh!" He huffed out a breath as I caught the rope and passed it back to him.

"Try again," I said.

The second time he kept hold of it.

"Now try pulling the sally yourself." I was going to step off the boxes, to give him more room, but in his eagerness, he grabbed the rope before I could move. "Don't look up!" My warning came too late. He lost control of the rope, which swung toward me. He made a grab for it and knocked me off balance. Somehow, he managed to catch me before I hit the floor.

"Alice! Are you—"

I don't know if it was the shock of my body against his, but suddenly I was laughing. It was a strange reflex that I just couldn't control. Then he started laughing, too. I could feel the vibration of it in his chest as he held me.

"I'm . . . dreadfully sorry," he gasped, raising himself up and setting me gently down on the bench. "You were quite right: it's harder than it sounds."

"We'll have another go," I said, jumping up and reaching for the rope. I could feel my cheeks burning. When he took the rope from me, I stood behind him, willing the fire inside me to die down.

He got the hang of it very quickly. After a couple of minutes, I took the silencer off the bells and stood between the other ropes.

"You're going to ring *two* bells?" He looked at me, astonished.

"I have to," I replied. "We need a three-bell sequence, starting with yours, which is the highest pitched, and ending with the one on my left, which is the lowest. Don't worry—I've done it before. Just stamp your foot when you want to stop."

It took a few strokes to get the timing right, but as we got into a rhythm, we began to produce a sound that was truly uplifting. I only caught glimpses of Jack's face. He had a look of intense concentration—but it was lit with a smile.

After what I judged to be about ten minutes, he gave me the signal to stop. We were both panting for breath, so talking was difficult.

"That . . . was . . . amazing," he gasped. "Thank you!" He grabbed his tie and knotted it round his neck. "Is it straight?" he asked, as he turned around.

"Not quite." I went to adjust it. Our faces were so close I could see the flecks of amber in his dark eyes. I could feel the heat of his body through his shirt.

"I'm afraid I have to go and join the choir," he said. "They'll be getting ready in the vestry. Will you wait for me—after the service?"

"Yes, if you want me to."

He grabbed his jacket and hat and ducked through the little door. My heart was beating very fast—and I knew that it wasn't just because of the bell ringing. My emotions seemed to have come alive the way seeds do when rain comes. Pale stalks of desire sprang up from the desert place where I had buried them.

The church was already half-full when I emerged from behind the pulpit. Merle and the children were there. She beckoned me to come and join them, her smile as open and welcoming as it had been that first morning on the beach.

"How's Jacqueline's thumb?" I whispered as I sat down.

"A bit bruised and sore—but the cut's almost healed," she replied. "I like your hat—very stylish. Did you get it in London?"

"Er . . . yes." I fingered the brim, making an unnecessary adjustment, unable to look her in the eye as I lied. It must have been Jack, then, who'd provided it. Had it belonged to the same woman who had left the clothes behind? She must have a vast wardrobe, not to miss such expensive items.

I glanced over my shoulder at the people in the other pews. It was mainly women and children, with only a few elderly men. The organ struck up and everyone stood as the choir came up the aisle. They were led by Jack, who had a red cassock and white surplice over his suit. Behind him was George Retallack. His sightless eyes darted from side to side as he walked up the aisle unaided, tapping the floor in front of him with a white stick. They were followed into the choir stalls by five men who looked to be in their late sixties or seventies, and a group of boys aged about ten to fourteen.

A lump came to my throat when they began to sing. It was the *"Regina Caeli"*—the Latin chant Jack had told me they'd been rehearsing for weeks. This kind of singing was my passion—the centuries-old music of the church. It was the thing that, more than anything, had drawn me to the religious life, and it had soothed my troubled soul as I struggled to become a nun. Hearing that pure sound as the first light of day slanted down from the chapel windows had made the daily hardships and humiliations seem bearable.

Jack's clear tenor voice soared up to the rafters. The young boys watched him intently, following his lead. His left hand was resting on the end of the choir stall, above the image of the mermaid. I thought of the story behind the carving—of the mysterious woman who had been mesmerized by a man's singing. I wondered if Merle had been thinking of Jack when she'd related it.

When the service was over, she was in a hurry to get away. "The children have been invited to a birthday party," she said, as she ushered them out of the pew. "Sorry I can't stay and chat. See you tomorrow."

I stayed in my seat while the rest of the congregation filed out. Jack appeared a few minutes later, minus the cassock and surplice. He came up to me, fanning his face with his hat. "Shall we go outside?"

On the way out, he introduced me to the vicar—a man in his eighties with pale, watery eyes and webs of purple veins on his cheeks.

"My cousin Alice," Jack said. "Bombed out of London—so she's come to help us." He came out with it so easily, so confidently.

The vicar took my hand in both of his. I burned beneath his warm smile. Lying to a man of the cloth—on Easter Sunday. Could any number of Hail Marys blot out a sin like that?

Rain began to spot as we stood there. Jack took my arm and led me down the path through the churchyard. The feel of his hand through the sleeve of my cardigan made me blush even deeper. I supposed that to the vicar, it would have looked like the most natural thing in the world—a man escorting his cousin home from church. I wondered if that was why Jack was doing it, to keep up the pretense.

"I thought you might like to have lunch with me," he said, as we walked under the arch formed by two aged yew trees. "It's not much, I'm afraid—but it'll be a change from what you've been living on for the past few days."

He led me through the trees and around the side of the walled garden to a building I hadn't seen before. It was a thatched cottage, the roof green with mildew around the eaves. There were four tiny windows in the front wall—two up and two down. One of the top panes was open, and a frayed edge of curtain flapped in the breeze.

"This was the head gardener's cottage," Jack said. "He died just before the war. We were looking for a replacement, but once conscription came in that was impossible. Anyway, it's been very handy, with the house being taken over for training."

"It's funny," I said, "I've never seen any of the military people. Apart from one man, when I was with the Land Girls."

"Oh, they come and go," he replied. "We're never sure exactly how many will be staying on any one night."

He'd used the word *we* again. It seemed to imply that he was sharing the responsibility of running the house with someone else. I wondered who that was. Could it be Merle?

He unlocked the door and shoved it with his shoulder to open it. A furry missile hurled itself at us as we stepped over the threshold. "Hello, boy!" He bent to stroke Brock's head. As he straightened up, he swept his hand at a fireplace with a smoke-blackened chimney breast, in front of which was a rough wooden table and two chairs. "Sorry—it's not very elegant. Just me and the dog living here."

He pulled out a chair for me. "Would you like some wine? That's one thing we've still got plenty of."

At the mission house, wine had been a rare treat, served only on special feast days. The glass Jack handed me was a large one.

"Happy Easter!" He clinked his glass against mine.

After a couple of sips, I felt the tension in my body melt away. Jack left me at the table, disappearing through a curtain that divided the dining room from the kitchen. I could hear the clatter of plates and cutlery. He emerged with a tray and set it down in front of me.

I caught my breath. Arranged on a silver platter were a dozen glistening oysters.

"Mrs. Durand told me they were your favorite thing to eat." He smiled. "I got them from the estuary this morning. Go on—dig in."

I closed my eyes as the first one slithered onto my tongue. An image from my old house in Ireland filled my head—of my father, who loved the Dublin Bay oysters as much as I did, puffing away on a cigar between courses. We'd been eating them the night he told me that Dan and I could never marry. The night I'd decided to become a nun.

"What did you think of our choir?" Jack's voice broke into my thoughts. "We're a raggle-taggle bunch—half the number we used to be."

"But you sang beautifully." I put down the empty oyster shell and took another. "It reminded me of the services we had at the mission. I was a choral sister—which I loved. It's one of the things I know I'm going to miss."

"I wish you could join our choir—but it's only ever been men and boys. You'd think the war would have changed that, like it's changed so many things." He took an oyster and swallowed it down in one swift, smooth movement. "Thank you for teaching me bell ringing, by the way. I wouldn't have had a hope of doing it without you."

"Well, I'm glad to have been of help." I gave him a wry look as I took another oyster. "It's funny—I still love to hear bells, even though my whole life was regulated by them. I can't get used to not being woken up by them, to not having them to tell me when to stop what I'm doing to go and pray."

Jack nodded, reaching for a napkin to wipe his mouth. "I used to travel overseas a lot before the war—while I was learning about the family shipping business. I remember once we were in port at Istanbul, and I was woken by the Muslim call to prayer. It was alarming at first, but there was something quite enchanting about it, too. I heard it four more times that day—and saw people just stop in their tracks and get down on their knees. Strange, isn't it? What they were doing was quite like what you've described."

"Not so strange," I replied. "We worship the same God."

"Really?"

"Yes." I paused, wondering if this was a further test. Perhaps the interrogation he'd given me when he found me hadn't been enough, and he'd invited me to lunch to find out how much I really knew about religion. "Muslims claim descent from Ishmael, who was a son of Abraham," I went on. "And their holy book, the Koran, has passages about Jesus. But they believe Jesus was a messenger of God, not the son of God. They don't believe he was crucified, or that faith in him grants forgiveness of a person's sins."

"Hmm. I didn't know that." He folded his arms and leaned back in his chair. "My father stopped believing in God when my mother died giving birth to me. I suppose that rubbed off on me. I'd never stop going to church—it's what my family has always done, part of who we are—but how can you believe in a God of love when there's so much misery in the world? When a monster like Hitler is rampaging across Europe?"

I realized then that this wasn't a test. What he'd revealed was too personal, too heartfelt for that. It was the kind of question I'd been asked many times by patients who were sick or dying. It wasn't easy to answer. I said to Jack what I'd said to them. "You know the story of Jesus, asleep in a boat, when a storm blew up that terrified the disciples?"

He nodded.

"When they woke him, he calmed the waves and asked them why they'd been so afraid. He thought they'd realize they couldn't come to any harm while he was with them." I took a breath, hoping that what I was about to say wouldn't sound preachy. "What I take from that story is that God doesn't create the storms in our lives—but he's there with us, in the boat."

"I wish I could believe that," he said. He got up and went into the kitchen. But I'd seen the change in his eyes. Like a pond when ice forms on its surface.

Chapter 9

*J*ack walked with me back to the boathouse. Brock, who had been
cooped up for longer than usual, darted between us, tearing off
into the undergrowth when he caught the scent of a rabbit. As we
passed the church, I couldn't help thinking about the moment when
I'd lost my balance and Jack had caught me.

The stirring I felt as I remembered it alarmed me. In the past I
would have tried to quell such unacceptable feelings in the way I'd been
taught when I took my vows. The flailing device had been given to me
along with the robes and the rosary beads. It was a ring with five chains
on it. At the end of each chain was a pointed hook. The instruction was
to whip the thing over your bare shoulders—not too hard, but enough
to drive away temptation.

*Neurotic women whipping themselves to take their minds off the natu-
ral life that God intended for them.*

My father's voice echoed down the years. He'd never said that—but
it was exactly the sort of comment he would have made if he'd known
about it. In the letters I wrote home about my life in the convent, I
never mentioned the painful ritual I carried out every Wednesday and
Friday night after lights-out, because I knew he would be violently
opposed to such a thing.

I glanced at Jack. He was bending over Brock, who had got his fur caught on a bramble bush. *No wonder you wanted to leave.* The words he'd spoken that first day came back loud and clear. Like my father, the idea of a woman punishing herself for what most people regarded as a normal human urge was repellent to him.

I watched him as he gently disentangled the thorns and set the dog free. There was no longer any compulsion for me to subdue the feelings he'd ignited. I didn't have to feel guilty for the way my body had responded to his in the bell tower. But the thought of allowing those feelings to develop scared me. I knew so little about him. What if he really did have a secret wife? Or was having an affair with Merle?

The sound of children's voices cut across my thoughts. I could hear shouts coming from the beach below. Through the trees I caught a glimpse of Merle's son, Louis, running across the sand. Ned was chasing after him, arms outstretched, as if he were pretending to be a plane.

"Hello, Louis," I said, when I caught up with them. "Where's Mummy?"

He cocked his head in the direction of the village. "At Meg Downing's party. It's all girls. Mum said we could play outside."

Ned reached for my hand and tugged it. "Can we go fishing?"

"Yes, if you want to." I smiled. "Just give me a minute to change out of these clothes."

I came back in my work dungarees, which were rolled up to the knees. I had the fishing net and a bucket. Ned and Louis didn't see me at first—they were too busy throwing sticks into the waves for Brock to run after. Jack was crouching down beside Ned, showing him how to throw overarm, so that the stick wouldn't fly up in the air. He straightened up when he spotted me.

Brock came bounding out of the sea and shook himself, which made the boys jump back, howling with laughter.

"I'd better be getting back." Jack clipped the leash to the dog's collar. "Don't let them run you ragged." He glanced at Ned, who had waded in up to his knees, his shorts soaking up the seawater. I saw that look again—the same expression that had come over Jack when he'd said he wished he could believe what I believed about God. It was a wistful look, as if he wanted to stay and play with the boys but felt he shouldn't. I wondered if he was afraid of what people might think, of the gossip that might arise from him spending time with Merle's children and the little boy she was looking after.

Ned came splashing up to me. He grabbed the pole of the fishing net and pulled me toward the rock pools. Looking back over my shoulder, I saw Jack disappear into the trees.

"Auntie Alice, can we catch a big crab?" Ned was gazing up at me, his eyes touchingly innocent. With one word he'd melted my heart. I'd never been "auntie" to anyone.

"You mustn't call her *that*, Ned!" Louis said in a stage whisper. "She's *Miss* Alice."

Ned's dark lashes fluttered as he glanced from Louis to me and back again. He was too young to grasp the social distinction that Merle must have drummed into the children—that I was Jack's cousin and must be addressed in a different way than the other women they knew. I had to fight the urge to gather him up in my arms and tell him that he could call me "auntie" if he wanted to. To contradict what Merle had said would be wrong, however much I longed to.

After half an hour of fishing in the rock pools, I told the boys I had to take them back to the village. They didn't want to go. I had to bribe them with honey sandwiches. Ned held my hand all the way along the beach.

As we neared Cliffside Cottage, where the party was being held, I could hear children singing. The sound transported me back through time and space, to my first week at the mission, when Sister Clare had taken me to see the orphanage. The children had been shy at first, but within days they'd composed a song in my honor. African voices, singing in French, to the tune of an old folk song:

Bienvenue à Soeur Antoine,
Elle est jolie, elle est jolie.
Bienvenue à Soeur Antoine,
Elle est jolie, elle est bonne!

"Welcome to Sister Anthony. She is pretty. She is good." The words had made me blush. But I couldn't help being moved. Sister Clare had warned me not to visit too often. I knew the reason behind the seemingly harsh attitude. I could see how easy it would be for a nun to form an attachment to such children. But I couldn't have foreseen what would happen—years later—to make me do the exact opposite of what she'd advised.

"They're singing 'Happy Birthday,'" Louis said, bringing me back to reality. "Do you think there'll be a cake?" The smooth skin between his eyebrows wrinkled as he looked at me. "What's the matter? Your eyes are all funny."

"Nothing," I said, twisting my mouth into a smile. "It's just the sun making them water. Come on, let's go and find Mummy."

Merle was surprised to see me—and horrified when she heard where the boys had been. "Louis! I told you not to go any farther than the fish cellar!"

"It's Ned's fault," Louis said. "He wanted to go and find Miss Alice."

"I'm sorry," Merle said. "I didn't mean for them to foist themselves on you."

"It doesn't matter—honestly. We had a lovely time, didn't we, boys?" I glanced down, but Louis was gone, heading toward a woman who was dishing out slices of birthday cake.

"Don't you want any cake, Ned?" I said.

"Will you come with me?" He fixed me with his melting, dark eyes.

I turned to Merle, embarrassed that he'd asked me instead of her.

"I think you've got an admirer," she whispered, smiling.

It started to rain as I made my way back along the cove to the boat-house. I'd planned to sit outside and read, but there was no chance of that. Instead I curled up on my makeshift bed with *Frenchman's Creek*.

I didn't want to finish the story, but I couldn't put it down. When I reached the last page, I sat with the book still open in my lap, mulling over the ending. The main character had paid a terrible price for the freedom she sought. She was brave and beautiful and had fallen in love with a kindred spirit in Cornwall. But she had a husband in London—and two young children, whom she didn't think twice about leaving with a servant while she set off on a dangerous voyage with her pirate. Did I like her? As Sister Anthony, I would have said no. But now? I wasn't sure.

There was a black-and-white photograph of the author inside the dust jacket. She was a dainty woman, not much older than me, with gentle, pensive eyes. The biography beneath the image said that she was married with three children and lived by the sea in Cornwall. I wondered if, like Merle, the war had separated her from her husband. *Frenchman's Creek* was set three centuries ago, but I couldn't help thinking that the author must have experienced the feelings she'd written about, of being trapped in a loveless marriage and longing to escape a life that was narrow and confined.

I closed the book and put out the lamp. Outside the rain was still lashing down. The noise of the wind screaming up the estuary was far louder than the enemy planes I'd heard a few nights ago. I fell into a restless sleep, full of wild and troubled dreams. The only one I remembered when I woke up was a scrambled version of the story I'd been reading. The pirate had Jack's face and the woman had Merle's. And as I watched them sail away, I was holding the hands of two children, who were crying. But the children were not English. They were African.

The storm was still raging the next day. Waves whipped up the estuary, spitting foam onto the beach, making the sand look as if it had a covering of snow. Then the rain came again, washing it all away.

Returning from the farm, the path down through the valley was so slippery I had to grab at tree trunks to stop me from falling. The bark of the giant ferns felt rough and hairy, like the hides of the cows I'd been milking. Even with the rain lashing down, the valley was a magical place. The perfume of the rhododendrons and camellias was intensified, and the volume of water in the stream amplified the trickle into a symphony of sound. I stood there for a moment, sheltering under the unfurling leaves of a giant rhubarb. It was like being in a green cathedral. I shut my eyes and breathed in the cool, scented air. I felt closer to God in this place than I had in a long time.

The next morning the weather was no better. The rain blurred the horizon, turning sky and sea into a curtain of slate gray. I wrapped myself in a tarpaulin sheet that smelled of fish and started up the muddy path. It was a good thing my foot was no longer giving me any pain; otherwise I doubt I'd have made it to the farm.

I could hear the Land Girls long before I reached the milking shed. They were back from their Easter break and were catching up with each other's escapades, raucous laughter punctuating every other sentence.

"Good morning!" I had to shout to be heard above the clamor.

A sudden hush descended. Edith had been in the middle of describing what she and a Spitfire pilot had got up to in a bus shelter outside a dance hall in Birmingham. Apparently she considered it too racy for my ears.

"We're glad to see *you*," Marjorie, the older woman, piped up. "We're one short this morning—Janet's in hospital."

"In *hospital*? Why? What's happened?"

"She was knocked down by a car." Marjorie clicked her tongue against the roof of her mouth. "She's all right—but her hip's in plaster."

Edith took up the story, filling in the details. Janet had been on her way to catch the train back to Cornwall when the accident happened. Because of the blackout, she hadn't spotted a car coming toward her when she crossed the road. "The weather made it worse," Edith said. "I think the whole country must have had this rain. We nearly didn't get here this morning—there's flooding all along the road from our village."

I walked along the row of animals waiting to be milked and sat down on the stool that would have been Janet's. I wondered if I could find out the name of the hospital she was in and write to her. I was about to ask when I heard Jack's voice.

"Is my cousin here?"

"Over there." Marjorie, who was nearest the door, pointed to where I sat.

I looked up and saw three heads turn Jack's way, following him with their eyes as he came toward me. Rita raised a hand to smooth her glossy auburn bun as he strode past her.

"Good morning, Alice." There was a terseness in his voice, and no hint of a smile. "I need you to come with me." Something in his eyes told me not to ask why. I felt the others watching me as I followed him out of the shed.

"There's been an accident," Jack said when we were out of earshot. "A fisherman from the village crushed his leg trying to land his boat. The road from Falmouth's flooded—we can't get him to hospital and no doctor can get through." He pushed his hair off his forehead. The skin beneath was glistening with perspiration. "You're the only person around here with any medical knowledge."

"Where is he?"

"They've taken him back to his house. They think his leg might be broken, but they're not sure. And he's lost a lot of blood."

"What's his name? Where does he live?"

"It's Leo Badger—Rose Cottage. I'll take you there."

"No. You go back to the house and get me bandages, iodine, a needle, and strong cotton—and something to make a splint. I can find my own way."

He searched my face, surprised, it seemed, that I'd taken command of the situation. "Yes—all right. I'll see you there."

Rose Cottage wasn't hard to find. It was near the fish cellar where I'd seen men mending their nets when I'd gone with Merle to meet the children. It was the end house in a terrace of three, sheltered from the sea wind by the school building. It had a tiny, well-kept vegetable garden. A fig tree, as well as a rosebush, grew up and around the front door.

Leo Badger was lying on a table in the small downstairs room with a pillow under his head. His weather-beaten face was taut with pain, his lips lost in the white whiskers that framed them. He looked as if he were afraid to open his mouth, ashamed, perhaps, to reveal to the men gathered around him just how agonizing his injury was.

"Who's that?" George Retallack heard me come through the door before the others noticed. He turned his face toward me, his unseeing eyes flickering from side to side. I saw that he was holding Leo's hand.

"I'm a nurse," I said. "Alice McBride—cousin to His Lordship." It felt strange referring to Jack in that way. But it had an immediate effect. George and the two elderly men standing on the opposite side of the table stepped back to let me through. A fourth man stayed where he was. I saw that he was pressing down on a bloodied rag just below Leo's left knee.

"'E's hurt bad, miss." The man looked familiar. I realized fleetingly that I'd seen him at the birthday party. "'E were tryin' to land the boat, and a big wave come and trapped 'im 'tween the gunwale and the quayside."

"You've done the right thing, putting pressure on the wound. How long have you been doing that?"

"Since we got 'im in 'ere—about 'alf an 'our or so."

"Okay. Let me look at him now."

They'd cut away the fabric of his trousers around the injury. Blood had seeped from the rag into the frayed edges. As I watched, the dark stain began to spread. "I'm going to need someone's shirt," I said. "And something short and strong—a stick or a big spoon."

George was the first to unfasten his shirt. He held it out to me. I wasn't sure if it was my voice or the smell of the blood that enabled him to locate my hands so precisely.

"There's a wooden spoon in the sink," one of the other men called. "Will that do?"

"Yes. Can someone boil a kettle? And I'll need more pillows—or anything soft to prop up his leg."

A flower-patterned cushion and a woolen jersey appeared at the end of the table. I lifted Leo's leg and tucked the shirt under his thigh. He cried out in pain and clapped his hand over his mouth.

"Hold on, Mr. Badger—I'm just going to stop the bleeding, then I can have a proper look at you." I tied the arms of the shirt in a double knot, with the wooden spoon caught in the middle of it. Then I started to turn the spoon, tightening the makeshift tourniquet.

"Could you hold it there for me?" I asked the man from the birthday party. "I need to check his pulse."

I moved down the table and put my thumbs on the leg, below the knee and above the wound. As gently as I could, I palpated the flesh at the back of the leg with my fingers. I could feel no pulse. That was good. It meant I'd stopped the flow of blood.

As I straightened up, I saw Jack coming through the door. Without a word he came to stand opposite me, passing me what I needed to clean up the wound. Then I asked him to thread a needle with cotton for me.

"Damn!" In his haste, he dropped it on the floor.

"Don't worry," I said, as he bent down to retrieve it. "It needs sterilizing anyway—just pour some water from the kettle over it."

I watched him out of the corner of my eye as he darted across the room. He didn't need to be told to put the thread through the eye of the needle before dangling it into the boiled water. Soon he was back, passing it to me. As I stitched the ragged edges of skin together, I felt the break in the fibula, at the back of the old man's leg.

I glanced up at Jack. "Did you find something we could use as a splint?"

He gestured toward the door, where two lengths of wood were propped against the wall. They were thin and flat—the sort of thing that might be used for fence panels.

"Perfect." I nodded.

He went to get them, watching me as I bound them to the shin and the calf.

"We'd better keep the tourniquet on for a while longer," I said. "Would anyone in the village have any morphine?"

"I should have thought of that." Jack shook his head. "The military people up at the house might have some—I'll go and find out."

Leo Badger let out a muffled grunt as I tied the ends of the bandage. But it wasn't a cry of pain; he was trying to say something, waving his hand at the elderly man standing over by the sink. The man went to him, bending so that his ear was close to Leo's mouth.

"He says he's got morphine," the man said. "It was for his wife, Gladys. She died last year—terrible bad, she was, at the end."

"Could you find it for me? Then we can try getting him into bed."

When the drug had taken effect Jack and I tried to work out how to get the sleeping man up the narrow, twisting staircase to the bedroom. Jack thought that, with the help of one of the men, he could carry him, but I thought it was too much of a risk. In the end we brought his mattress downstairs and made up a bed for him on the floor.

When he was settled, we stepped outside, sheltering from the rain in the doorway of the fish cellar.

"Is he going to be all right?" Jack asked.

"I hope so. The bleeding seems to have stopped now—but he needs to see a doctor. I'm worried about the risk of infection."

"I'm going to drive the tractor up to the main road," he said. "I'll see if I can get through the floodwater."

"Is that wise?" I bit the inside of my lip, imagining him lying trapped beneath the thing if it should overturn.

"I'll know when I get there." He glanced up at the sky. "It seems to be easing off a bit, anyway."

"I'll stay here," I said. "I won't leave him until the doctor comes."

"Thank you. I can't think what would have happened if you hadn't been here. You were so calm—even when I dropped that wretched needle."

"I've had far worse things happen during operations." I smiled. "At least you didn't faint on me."

He grunted. "I'd better get going."

I watched him as he walked back up the cobblestone street. When he reached the corner, he turned and waved. It was a simple gesture— nothing out of the ordinary—and yet I suddenly felt lighthearted and curiously elated.

It was just after midday when my patient opened his eyes. He looked around, blinking, not fully awake because of the morphine. He didn't see me sitting in the chair, and when I spoke, he looked bewildered.

"It's all right, Mr. Badger. I'm Alice, the nurse. You had an accident— do you remember?"

Half an hour later he was sitting up in bed, smoking a clay pipe. He looked remarkably well for someone who'd been through such an agonizing ordeal, and he remembered most of what had happened, including Jack's presence at the makeshift operating table.

"You're 'Is Lordship's cousin, aren't you?" He studied me through a curl of smoke.

"That's right. I was working in a hospital in London, but it was bombed."

"You don't sound like a Londoner," he said.

"I'm from Dublin—the Irish branch of the family."

"Oh." He tilted his head, like someone examining a portrait. "You know, you remind me of someone. A girl 'Is Lordship used to knock about with."

"Really?" My hand went to the scarf tied round my head. I doubted that any girl Jack had been involved with in the past could have had hair like mine.

"You've got the same color eyes—and that fairy look about you." He sucked on his pipe. "'Er name was Morwenna Martin. Does 'e ever speak of 'er?"

Morwenna. It was an unusual name—but I knew it from somewhere. It came back to me in a heartbeat: Jack had written that name in the back of the tide tables, along with a date in 1938. "No," I said, "he's never mentioned her to me."

"No, I don't suppose 'e would," the old man went on. "She were from Sithney: worked as a maid at the rectory. Not the sort of girl the old viscount would have approved of . . ." He trailed off, rubbing his beard. "Not that I blame 'Is Lordship, mind. Nothing wrong with sowin' your wild oats." He chuckled, spluttering as the smoke caught his throat. "'E'd squirm like a bag of eels if 'e knew that folks round here knew. Never brought 'er 'ere, of course. Used to take 'is boat round the coast to Porthleven to pick her up. But I spotted 'em more than once when I was out fishin': saw 'em jumpin' into the sea and frolickin' about in the waves."

"What happened to her?" I was thinking of what the Land Girls had said. Had Jack secretly married the girl, against his father's wishes? Was he keeping her somewhere, at a discreet distance?

"She went away." He shrugged. "I 'eard someone say she'd gone over the border to Devon, to work in a big 'ouse there." He went to knock his pipe out on a saucer next to the mattress he was lying on. But he stretched too far, toppling over onto his side. He let out a cry of pain.

"Mr. Badger!" I jumped up to help him. "You mustn't strain yourself. Those stitches in your leg won't hold unless you keep still."

He grunted. "I'll have a matchin' set, now, won't I, Nurse? A scar on this leg, in the very same place that shark bit the other!"

For a moment I thought he was going to try to roll up the remaining leg of his trousers to show me what the shark had done. I managed to persuade him to take a second dose of morphine, and soon he was sleeping again.

I went to the door and looked out. The rain had stopped, but the cobblestones were still wet, with a miniature stream trickling down the street toward the quayside. I wondered if Jack had managed to get through the floodwater to the doctor.

I went back inside and sat down beside the mattress. I couldn't shake the image Leo Badger had conjured, of Jack and the girl, Morwenna, together in the sea. I pictured them clinging to each other, kissing, her hair, long and sleek, snaking over her wet, naked shoulders. Was it true, what the old man had said—that my face was just like hers? Was *that* the reason why Jack had taken me in?

Chapter 10

The doctor arrived as I was boiling eggs to go with the freshly baked bread George Retallack's sister, Molly, had sent round. Leo Badger was propped up on pillows, directing me to where the plates and cutlery were kept. His face fell when he saw the doctor following Jack through the door.

"You're not goin' to cart me off to 'ospital, I 'ope," he said, as the bandages were peeled back.

"I don't think that'll be necessary, Mr. Badger." The doctor pushed his wire-rimmed spectacles up his nose as he straightened up. "Miss McBride seems to have done an excellent job."

I stepped outside with him while Jack helped Leo to relieve himself in a chamber pot.

"I must congratulate you, Miss McBride," he said. "Not only did you save the leg, but probably his life as well. He'd lost a lot of blood by the time you arrived. Lord Trewella tells me you were working in a London hospital until recently?"

I nodded, praying he wouldn't ask me which one. A doctor wouldn't be fobbed off with the vague answer I'd given Merle when she'd asked that question.

"But you're not nursing here in Cornwall? I hear you're helping at the farm."

"That's right."

His searching look was disquieting. "Hmm. If you don't mind me saying so, that's a terrible waste. You should be working at the hospital in Falmouth, not milking cows."

The sun had gone down when I got back to the boathouse. Its dying rays tinged the surface of the estuary copper and crimson. The water was flat calm—so different from earlier in the day, when the wind had whipped the water into foaming fury. I stood outside for a while, watching the colors change in the fading light and listening to the haunting cries of the birds gathered along the shoreline.

I thought about what the doctor had said. He'd made me feel guilty about being here, in this beautiful place. And what he'd said was, undeniably, right. Milking cows and weeding vegetables could be learned quickly by any able-bodied person. Even a child could do farmwork, as Danielle and Louis had demonstrated. But it took years of training to be a nurse. How could I justify remaining here if there was a need for nurses in Falmouth?

I wondered what it would be like to live in that city, with the constant threat of bombs dropping. Even as I imagined it, I knew that it wasn't the fear of a German attack that made me want to stay in Mermaid's Cove. It was the newfound joy of living in a place that made my soul soar every time I stepped outside, of having my own space after years of communal living, and—what I hesitated to admit, even to myself—the way I felt every time I set eyes on Jack.

My conscience told me that these were very selfish reasons not to follow the doctor's advice. I would have to talk it over with Jack. Perhaps the doctor was already discussing it with him, on the journey back to Falmouth. My heart sank as I imagined Jack nodding at the words that had made me feel so uncomfortable. I tried to push the image away, telling myself that at least my being here had done some good. I murmured a prayer for Leo Badger's speedy recovery, picturing him smiling as he sat up in bed. Jack had organized some of the neighbors to take turns sitting with him. I planned to go back and see him in the morning when I'd finished in the cowshed.

"Alice!"

I spun round at the sound of Jack's voice. I hadn't expected to see him down at the cove.

"I thought you were taking Dr. Williams home," I said, when he came jogging across the beach, the dog at his heels.

"I did," he said, catching his breath. "But the flooding's not so bad now—we didn't need the tractor—so I got back in time for a walk. Poor old Brock's been cooped up all day, haven't you, boy?" He smiled as the dog gave an answering bark. "Oh—and I brought these, to say thank you."

From his knapsack he produced a bouquet of scarlet camellias. "They were Leo's idea," he said. He glanced down as he handed them to me, as if he were embarrassed to be giving flowers to a woman. "This is from me." He pulled out a bottle of claret. Château Latour 1934—a vintage my father would have driven the length and breadth of Ireland to get hold of.

Jack had brought something else as well: an enormous mullet—another gift from Leo—for supper. "He was bringing it in when the accident happened," he explained. "In the old days I'd have cooked it over a driftwood fire on the beach," he said. "But that's another thing the war's deprived us of. We'd better go inside."

I glanced up at the sky. The rain clouds had disappeared. A single star, or more likely a planet, was just visible on the eastern horizon. "We could eat outside even if we can't have a fire," I said. "Looks like it's going to be a fine night."

As twilight descended on the cove, we sat on a blanket on the sand with a glass of the claret to wash down the fish. The only sounds were the lap of the ebbing tide and the rustle of birds roosting in the trees behind us. Jack's face was silhouetted against the darkening sky. I couldn't make out his features, but he seemed to be looking far out into the distance, across the black, shimmering water. I wondered if he was thinking about those other nighttime picnics he'd alluded to. Perhaps he'd sat like this with the girl Leo had told me about.

I followed Jack's gaze, out to the vanishing horizon, thinking about what Leo had told me: how he'd spotted the boat, *Firefly*, anchored farther along the coast, and seen Jack and the girl jumping off it, into the sea. *Frolicking about*—that was the phrase he'd used. It conjured faded memories of my own—of the summer before I joined the order, when Dan and I would cycle to the dunes at Portmarnock beach. We'd throw down our bikes and flop onto the cool sand, shielded from prying eyes by clumps of waist-high marram grass. It was a ten-mile ride from Dublin, but we were hungrier for each other than for the food and drink in our saddlebags. It was on one of those days at the beach that he'd asked me to marry him. I remembered teasing him, saying he'd only proposed to make me go further—to do what I longed to do but didn't dare. I'd ridden back home elated, carried away by the idea of a wedding. It hadn't crossed my mind that Dad would be so vehemently opposed to our plans.

I wondered if Jack had wanted to marry Morwenna, whether he and his father had fallen out about it. A match between a viscount's son and a maid would almost certainly be frowned upon. Perhaps we had something in common, then, Jack and I: both of us denied the choices we might have made.

Leo had said that Morwenna had gone away. Perhaps, if Jack had told her there was no future for them, she'd decided she couldn't bear to go on living in Cornwall. Or had she slipped over the border into

Devon so that they could carry on the relationship without the risk of being seen together? But if he hadn't married her, where had the rumor of the secret wife come from?

I suppose I could have tried to raise the subject. I could have said I'd been looking at the tide tables and come across a name scribbled in the back. But I suspected he would see right through me, realize that people in the village had been gossiping about his private life, the same way the Land Girls did. Curious as I was, I couldn't bear the thought of embarrassing him. He'd done so much for me. Gone out of his way to help me. I told myself that if he had secrets, they were no business of mine.

"It's so peaceful." Jack's voice came out of the darkness. "It's hard to imagine the horrors going on out there."

"How far is it to the French coast?" I asked.

"About a hundred miles, as the crow flies."

"Is that where the German planes came from? The ones that bombed Falmouth?"

"Yes—but they won't come tonight."

"How do you know?"

"It's a waning moon," he replied. "It won't rise until the early hours of the morning—too late to give a clear view of any target."

"Dr. Williams told me I should go and work at the hospital in Falmouth." I had to say it, however much it pained me. "He thinks I'd be of more use there than on the farm."

"That's probably true." He paused, still looking out across the estuary, not at me. "Yes," he went on. "That's what you should tell the others in the milking shed: that you'll be doing shifts at the hospital every so often." Something in the tone of his voice had changed, as if he was thinking aloud, working out the solution to something that had been puzzling him.

"You want me to go? To Falmouth?"

"No, I don't." He turned his face toward me. I caught the glint in his eyes. "I have something else in mind for you, Alice—something that requires a different kind of bravery from nursing but could save many more lives in the long run."

I'd been about to take a sip of wine, but I stopped, the glass suspended in front of my mouth. "What?"

"I want you to work for us."

"*Us?*"

"Churchill's secret army—otherwise known as the Special Operations Executive." He reached for his glass and drained it. "Do you know about the French Resistance?"

I stared at him, uncomprehending. "Only what I read in newspapers on the ship."

"We run undercover missions between Cornwall and France. Ferrying secret agents to help the Resistance and picking up downed Allied airmen to bring them back to England."

Suddenly I grasped why nothing seemed to make sense up at the house, why I'd only ever seen one of the many people who came and went each week. No wonder Jack had seemed to have an air of mystery about him.

"It's dangerous work," he went on. "We need people like you, Alice."

"But . . . what could *I* do?"

"You speak fluent French, which gives you the ability to blend in. Last month we lost four men. They were rowing out to the pick-up boat from a beach on the coast of Brittany. A German patrol vessel came by, wanting to know what they were doing. None of them had more than a few words of French. They were shot dead on the spot."

Somewhere in the trees behind us I could hear an owl hooting. Now I saw why Jack had gone to such trouble for me, why he had fed me, clothed me, and let me hide away from the world I'd left behind. From the moment he'd found me, when I'd muttered words in French while hovering between life and death, he must have realized that I could be of value. What the sea had washed up was bounty, to be taken and used.

"Why didn't you tell me this before?" My voice sounded very loud in the stillness. "Why did you pretend to be a farmer?"

"I didn't pretend." There was a note of indignation in his voice. "Farming takes up as much of my time as the other work. Don't you see? We had to check you out. Gauge what sort of person you are, whether you're cut out for the sort of thing we have in mind."

"*We?*"

"Merle Durand is part of the operation. She'd go to France herself if it wasn't for the children. I asked her to keep an eye on you—get a sense of how good you'd be at sticking to the story I'd invented for you."

A hollow sensation seeped from my stomach to my chest. How convincingly Merle had acted her part—even down to the tone of awe in her voice at that first meeting on the beach. And those whispered confidences about her marriage in the church. Was any of it true? Or was it something she'd concocted to make me believe that she liked me, trusted me, wanted me for a friend?

"She told you she did the cooking for the people in the house," Jack went on. "That's partly true—but her main role is translating radio messages from the Resistance."

He paused. No doubt he was expecting me to say something, to express surprise at what he and she had so cleverly concealed from me. But I couldn't speak. My throat was swollen inside, as if I'd swallowed a wasp.

"I suppose all this is something of a shock," he said. "I hope you won't take it to heart. Merle really likes you. She thinks you'd be perfect for the work we're trying to do."

I tried to shift the lump in my throat. "I . . . don't think I could do it," I mumbled. "The kind of thing you have in mind. I . . . I'm not brave enough. Just the thought of getting onto a boat . . . any sort of boat . . . terrifies me."

"I can understand that, after what you've been through. But it's like falling off a horse: the only way to conquer that fear is to get back on as soon as you can." He fell silent again. I heard him take a deep breath. "You said you wanted to do some good, Alice. This is your chance."

I knew that he was right—about overcoming my fear of traveling on water. But could a person like me really make a difference in the kind of clandestine mission he'd described? "What exactly would I have to do?" I asked.

"You'd be part of a fake French fishing crew," he replied. "With luck, you wouldn't have to do anything. You'd go ashore with the agents we send out and come straight back with the escaping airmen. If I could split myself in two, I'd do it myself—but I have to skipper the bigger boat."

"So, I'd have to pretend to be fishing?"

"That's right. If there was a challenge from an enemy craft, you'd have to convince them the only thing you're landing is mackerel."

"I'd have to dress as a man?"

"Yes." There was a smile in his voice. "With that haircut, you'd be quite convincing."

I was glad that it was dark. Glad he couldn't see my cheeks burning with humiliation. Wasn't it enough that he'd robbed me of the illusion that I'd made a friend? Did he have to add insult to injury by telling me I looked like a man?

"You'd be properly armed, of course," he went on. "We'd teach you how to use a pistol. Do you think you could handle a violent situation? I don't suppose there was much of that in a convent, was there?"

The burn of humiliation gave way to a flash of indignation. If he thought I'd been living in a bubble of serenity, he was very much mistaken. "If you want to know, I've twice seen violent death." I kept my voice neutral, matter-of-fact. "First in Belgium, in a mental asylum where I was nursing: when I went to relieve the nun on night duty, I found her slumped in a chair with a knife in her back."

I heard him blow out a breath.

"Secondly in the Congo, where the sister on ward duty with me was clubbed over the head by a native man whose witch doctor had told him that if he killed a white woman, it would drive away the spirit of the dead wife that haunted him."

"Good God," he whispered. "You *saw* that happen?"

"Yes."

"Did he try to attack you, too?"

"He didn't see me. I was in a side room, filling up the medicine trolley for the evening round. I heard a scream—not from the sister, but from one of the patients. It was a maternity ward for the wives of the men who ran the mines. Any one of them could have been killed."

"What did you do?"

"I went to the woman who had screamed. I didn't grasp what had happened at first, because Sister Beatrice—the one who'd been attacked—was still on her feet, walking toward the man, making him back off, away from the patients. I don't know how she did that. It was almost supernatural, as if a spiritual energy was coming from a body that must have already been dead. When her body was examined, it was found that only the skullcap under her veil had kept the brains in place."

It was a long time since I'd thought about that dreadful day, but the memory was as vivid and shocking as a sequence from a horror film. We weren't allowed to talk about it at the mission house—but I remembered one of the nuns whispering that Sister Beatrice had been lucky, because she had died for Christ. I hadn't cried until then, but I'd shed bitter tears in bed that night. How could such a caring, skillful, dedicated person be better off dead? I couldn't, wouldn't accept that.

"What happened to the man?" Jack's voice brought me back to where I was.

"He disappeared into the bush," I replied.

"Weren't you afraid after that?"

I considered for a moment before answering. "I was more shocked than afraid," I said. "The native men who worked as orderlies found the attacker the next day and dragged him into the hospital, trussed up like a chicken. They wanted to kill him in front of us, to do to him what he'd done to the sister they'd admired and respected. We had to stop them, of course."

"Was that an order? Did *you* want to stop them?"

"If it had happened when I first arrived in Africa, I probably wouldn't have wanted to, no. But I didn't have to be given an order to know what was right in that situation. We were trying to win souls, you see. We had to set an example. Forgiveness. I told them that Sister Beatrice wouldn't have wanted him to die and neither did the rest of us."

"And did it work?"

"Well, they didn't kill him. The police took over then, of course. He went to prison."

"I didn't mean that. Did you win any souls?"

"Some of them had already become Christians. But after that most of the others handed in the necklaces of birds' claws, bones, and feathers they wore around their necks—the things that welded them to the power of the witch doctors."

For a long moment he said nothing. "I underestimated you, Alice. I thought your life was all prayer and care." He stood up, his feet crunching shells as he moved. "You don't have to get involved in this work if you don't want to. Sleep on it." He called Brock, who was rooting about in the seaweed at the water's edge. "One more thing, you mustn't mention anything we've discussed to the Land Girls or anyone in the village. Do you understand?"

"Yes."

When he and the dog had vanished into the darkness of the woods, I stood for a moment, staring up at the stars. *You don't have to get involved in this work if you don't want to.* His voice echoed inside my head. *You said you wanted to do some good, Alice.*

Yes, I thought, *but this is way beyond what I imagined when I said it.*

Chapter 11

J couldn't sleep that night. I lay awake, trying to imagine the life that Jack had in mind for me. He'd said I could save more lives by working for Churchill's secret army than by going to Falmouth to nurse at the hospital. I wondered how many men were stranded in France, and how it would feel to be shot out of a plane and come down, probably injured, in a place that was swarming with enemy soldiers.

How can I know God would want this from me?

It was a question that had often been the focus of my prayers when I was a nun. Jack had made it clear that the work could be dangerous. I wasn't afraid of that. What was I afraid of? Being killed? Having to kill someone?

In the morning I dragged myself out of bed, having had hardly any sleep. When the milking was done, and I'd called at Rose Cottage to check Leo Badger's progress, I made my way back up to the house and took the path that led down to the church. I peered round the door to make sure no one was there. I tiptoed in and sat in one of the pews. My eyes were drawn to the crucifix above the altar. The figure of Christ was as pale as the candlesticks on the table below. He looked emaciated, defeated—a stark contrast to the buxom, fiery-eyed mermaid carved into the choir stall a few feet away.

Please, tell me what I should do.

I knew God wasn't going to speak to me. I'd sat like this too many times to hope for a clear voice inside my head. But I prayed that he would answer through my conscience. I closed my eyes. Jack was there, waiting in the darkness. I saw myself sitting beside him at the helm of a boat, dressed in oilskins and a sailor's cap like the old fishermen in the village. I almost smiled. It was such an absurd image, a risible imitation of the novel I'd been reading, where the heroine disguised herself as a cabin boy to go plundering ships with her pirate. But even as I mocked myself, the thought of going off on a secret mission with Jack was intoxicating.

Why was my imagination so much more powerful than my conscience? How could I know if the answer God seemed to be giving was nothing but my own cloaked desire?

"Hello."

The voice made me jump. I'd been so wrapped up in my thoughts I hadn't heard the door open, or the sound of footsteps.

"I thought I might find you in here." Merle was standing at the end of the pew. "I wanted to apologize."

I didn't know what to say. It stung me that the friendship she'd seemed to offer had an ulterior motive. But how could I criticize her when I'd lied about myself?

"I'm sorry." She sat down beside me. "He said we had to test you out. But as soon as I met you, I felt guilty, because you were so warm and so kind to the children. I wanted us to be friends."

"How much did he tell you about me?"

"That you were a nun, but couldn't go back to that life," she replied. "And that you spoke fluent French. He wanted to know if you were capable of concealing who you really are, that you'd be convincing. That's important, in the sort of work our people do."

Our people. I couldn't help wondering what else Merle and Jack might be concealing from me. Knowing that they were working together so closely only stoked the suspicion that had taken root that afternoon in the churchyard, when I thought I'd seen him place a hand on her back.

"I hope you'll forgive me," Merle went on. "There'll be no more pretending. You know everything now."

"Everything?" The expression on my face must have betrayed what was going through my mind.

"You think there's something between us?" Merle gasped. "Goodness, no!"

"I . . . I'm sorry, I—"

"You thought that because of what I told you about Maurice, I'd be looking elsewhere." She pursed her lips. "That's understandable, I suppose. And it's true. I have fallen in love with someone else." She opened her handbag and pulled out a leather wallet. Inside was a black-and-white image of a dark-haired man in workman's overalls standing in the doorway of a greenhouse. "His name's Fred Bechélet. He worked on our farm on Guernsey." She handed the photograph to me. "He was there for me when I was at my lowest ebb, when I found out about Maurice's affair and the baby Ruby was expecting. After a while it developed into something more than a friendship." She glanced at me, her eyes wary, probably wondering if I'd disapprove.

"I don't think anyone would blame you," I said.

She grunted. "Maurice did. He was furious when he found out. Fred lost his job."

"Where is Fred now?"

"Somewhere in North Africa." Her face clouded. "He's not allowed to say exactly where. He joined the Hampshire Regiment a few days after the war broke out." She took something else from her bag. "This is his last letter." She stared at the smudged postmark on the envelope. "Everything he writes is censored. He always tries to make me laugh. He draws funny little caricatures of the officers in his camp. But the newspapers are full of what's been happening out there. The Germans are trying to cut off the Suez Canal and the Persian oil fields. There's so much at stake he must be in terrible danger."

"How long is it since you've seen him?"

"Almost two years. He came to Cornwall on leave, just before heading out to the Mediterranean." She ran her finger around the edge of the photograph. "Sometimes I dream that he's been captured. We've had men staying here who've escaped from prison camps. I've heard such awful things about what happens in those places."

I thought about the men Jack had told me about—shot dead because they didn't have enough French to throw the Germans off the scent. Somehow the photo in Merle's hand made it all seem much more real. That face, smiling into the camera with no notion of the horrors that lay ahead, had a powerful eloquence. My doubts fell away at that moment. I knew what I had to do.

"You won't say anything about Fred, will you?" Merle went on. "People can be so judgmental. I have to think of the children—I wouldn't want them hearing hateful things in the school playground."

"Of course not. And I'm sorry . . . I shouldn't have jumped to conclusions about you and Jack."

She smiled. "It's human nature, isn't it? And he's the kind of man that sets hearts fluttering. I've heard the way the Land Girls go on about him."

"They told me he had a secret wife." I made myself sound amused, contemptuous, as if it mattered not one iota whether such a thing was true or not.

"Oh dear—and you thought that was me!" Merle laughed as she tucked the snapshot of her lover back inside her bag. "Well, I don't know where that rumor came from. He's never mentioned a wife to me. But he keeps things very close. You've probably realized that by now."

<hr>

My induction to Churchill's secret army began the following afternoon. Merle took me through the kitchen to the main part of the house, through a locked door that bore the same "No Entry" sign I'd seen at the front entrance.

"What does that symbol mean—the anchor with the initials beside it?" I asked.

"It's the insignia of the River Forces," Merle replied. "It's the branch of the military that deals with operations launched from inland waterways, like the Helford estuary. The sign's meant to fool anyone nosing around into thinking the house is being used for conventional military activities." She led me into a lofty room with carved wood paneling on the walls. Jack's ancestors stared down at me, painted in oils. The largest picture was of a man in Elizabethan costume, whose rather sinister-looking face was encircled by an extravagant lace ruff. It hung beneath an ancient-looking minstrel gallery.

"This is the great hall," Merle said. "It was used for banquets in the old days. But it's been turned into an extra bedroom." She pointed to a pile of mattresses stacked in a corner of the room. "We're quiet now, but we're expecting a full house tomorrow. There could be as many as twenty. Most of them will be parachuted into France, but some will be going with you. It's a new moon next week. That's when we do the airdrops and the pickups—it's the only safe time. You'll be leaving on Sunday morning, before it gets light."

I hadn't realized it would be so soon. The thought of boarding a boat and heading out across the sea that had almost taken my life made my stomach flip over.

"The agents you take will be carrying equipment that's too fragile to parachute in. Once you've dropped them in Brittany, you'll be bringing other people back. We don't know how many at this stage. Some might be injured. There'll be first aid equipment on the boat if you need it."

She opened the door to a room off the great hall. The smell of this room was different to the rest of the house. Musty and slightly stale, as if no one had used it for many years. "This is the library." Bookshelves covered two walls, and on the others hung oil paintings of hunting scenes. Long windows looked out over what once would have been lawns. Now the vista was the rows of onions, beans, and potatoes I'd been spending my afternoons hoeing.

I followed Merle across the room to a large desk with a briefcase on it. She flipped open the lid of the briefcase and pulled out a headset. "This is how we communicate with the Resistance groups," she said.

Moving closer, I saw that the headset was connected to an apparatus inside the briefcase.

"It's a Morse code transmitter," Merle explained. "Most of what we plan is done via sets like this. The trouble is, the Germans attack any group they get wind of. Equipment is either destroyed or confiscated. So, for backup, we use this as well." She went over to the window, where a conventional wireless radio, identical to the one we'd had at home in Dublin, sat on an ornate bureau inlaid with ivory. She turned one of the knobs and music came out of the speaker. "It's tuned to the BBC's French service," she said. "Twice a day the announcer in London drops coded messages for the Resistance into the broadcasts. It allows us to let people in Brittany know that a boat is on the way."

The music faded out and a man, speaking in French, began reading out what sounded like messages of greeting sent in by listeners: birthdays, wedding anniversaries—that sort of thing. "That's how we do it." Merle inclined her head toward the set. She took a piece of paper from the pocket of her skirt and handed it to me.

I read the handwritten message aloud: "*Bonjour à Tante Marie et Oncle Pierre de la part de tout le monde à La Maison de La Sirène.*" I looked up, mystified. "Good day to Aunt Marie and Uncle Pierre from everyone at the House of the Mermaid?"

She nodded. "That's the code name for this place. Aunt Marie and Uncle Pierre are the aliases of the Resistance people organizing the pickup." She turned off the radio. "All being well, your fishing trawler will drop anchor offshore in the early hours of Monday morning. The men you're going to collect will be waiting in the dark, on the beach. You and the agents will go ashore in a dinghy, along with weapons, ammunition, and medical supplies. Once everything's been unloaded, the others will climb in and row back with you."

She made it sound so simple. "How long has this been going on?" I asked.

"Only for a couple of months," she replied. "This'll be our third operation. I suppose you heard what happened last time?"

I nodded.

"The men who were shot were all pilots—three British and one American. If the Germans had turned up just five minutes earlier, it wouldn't have happened, because the agents would have been in the dinghy, and they all spoke fluent French. But they'd just been dropped, and the dinghy was on its way back." She paused, her eyes on mine. "That's why we need you there."

She went back over to the table where the Morse code machine sat. She slid her hand under the machine and pulled out an envelope. "For the purpose of the mission you'll have a code name. We use names from Shakespeare. *The Tempest*. Yours is Ariel."

"Ariel." It was the second time in as many weeks that I'd taken another name.

"That's what you'll be called while you're away from here. Everyone else on board will be going under an alias, too."

"What do I call Jack?"

"He's Prospero," she said.

I wondered if Jack had chosen his name and mine. Ariel had been imprisoned in a tree by a witch, and Prospero had set him free. In other circumstances that would have made me smile.

Later that afternoon Jack took photographs of me for the fake documents I would need. Then he took me down to the woods to show me how to use a pistol. I didn't want to carry a weapon and I told him so.

"I do understand," he said, as we walked through the walled garden, past the chickens scratching around the roots of the fruit trees. "The idea of killing another human being goes against everything you believe in. But try to imagine how you might feel if a German pointed a gun at someone you cared about." He turned his face to me as we wound our way past the beehives. "Remember the other day, when you were on the beach with the children and I appeared with Brock?"

I nodded.

"Ned was clinging to your legs, wasn't he? I think he wanted to stay and play with you instead of going back with the others."

"Yes, he did." I looked at him, puzzled.

"Imagine if I'd been a Nazi—just landed on the beach and wielding a gun. How would you have felt if I'd pointed it at Ned?"

The question took me by surprise. "I . . . I'd have thrown myself on top of him—Ned, I mean."

"But once I'd shot you, I could have killed all the others." Jack paused to open the gate that led to the path through the palms and tree ferns. "What if *you'd* had a gun?"

I didn't reply at first. I knew that he'd argued me into a corner. "You can't use Ned as an example. If someone was going to kill a child, I would have to shoot them. Any right-thinking person would do the same—but that's not the same as using a gun in the kind of mission you want me to go on."

"Why not? Weren't those men who got shot last month just as worthy of protection? If they'd lived, they would have gone back to fighting the Nazis, gone on trying to bring this war to an end." He kicked a fallen palm frond out of the way. "I'm not saying you'll ever have to use a gun; the reason we want you out there is to diffuse any confrontation before it escalates to that level. But—please forgive me for saying this—if you're going to help us, you need to stop thinking like a nun."

What could I say? Ever since I'd been washed ashore, I'd been trying to do exactly that. But it was one thing to set aside the rituals that had governed my life—and quite another to contemplate breaking one of the Ten Commandments.

Thou shalt not kill. There was no qualifying sentence following those words: nothing to say that it was all right to take someone's life in certain circumstances, that taking one life was justifiable if it saved many others. And yet thousands of Christians were out there fighting the Germans. They had taken the same moral position as Jack—that defending against evil was justified, even if it meant killing people.

I followed him in silence as he led me away from the path, through overgrown camellia bushes whose branches caught my scarf as I ducked underneath them. Through the flowers and foliage, I glimpsed a wooden structure standing in a clearing. It was a dilapidated summerhouse with a thatched roof, parts of which had slid down the eaves, giving the place the look of an old man in need of a haircut. There was no glass in the windows, and the door was hanging open at a crazy angle, as if it could fall off in the slightest breeze.

"That's what we'll use for practice." Jack pointed to a stack of hay bales a few yards in front of the summerhouse. "Come and stand on the steps and I'll show you."

The weapon he gave me looked like a tiny telescope. It was slightly longer than my hand and about two inches wide. "It's called a sleeve gun," he said. "You see this ring at the end?"

I nodded.

"You thread a rubber band through it, which goes around your arm, above the elbow. It's designed to be worn up the sleeve, out of sight. You're left-handed, aren't you?"

"Yes." I was surprised that he'd noticed.

"So, you'd wear it on your left arm. If someone threatens you, you slide it into your hand, point the muzzle, and operate the trigger with your thumb."

I rolled up the sleeve of my blouse, and he showed me how to affix the rubber band to hold the pistol in place.

"It's already loaded," he said. "It has a silencer, so it won't make a noise. The idea is that you pull it out quickly and when you've used it, it will just slide back into your sleeve, out of sight."

He showed me how to operate the trigger. "There's not much of a kickback on it, so you don't have to worry about your arm being forced back when you fire it. You can only fire a single shot. Ready?"

I stared at the bales of hay. My legs were shaking. My arm felt like lead when I tried to raise it. There was a small popping sound as I pulled the trigger, and a puff of dust as the bullet hit the target. As it cleared, a memory of my father flashed before my eyes. He was standing at the kitchen sink with his shirtsleeves rolled up, washing blood off his hands. I was seven years old—too young to understand that he'd been dealing with the aftermath of a grenade attack by the IRA on British soldiers a few streets away from our house. When he'd seen me watching him, he'd turned to me and said: "It takes such a long while to make a man, Alice—and so little time to destroy one."

Chapter 12

$\mathcal{A}$t half past three on Sunday morning, I let myself out of the boathouse. I hadn't been able to get much sleep. I'd been ready an hour earlier, dressed in the latest set of clothes I'd been given: a man's long-sleeved undershirt, a thick woolen jersey, and a pair of corduroy trousers with oilskins worn over the top of them. A cap like the one Leo Badger wore completed the outfit. The whole ensemble was even more cumbersome than a nun's habit. I wondered how on earth real fishermen managed.

I made my way around the rocks to the village. It was tricky in the dark. The tide was coming in, and I couldn't use a flashlight because of the danger of drawing attention to what I was about to do. Gradually my eyes became accustomed to the dark. The sky was clear and studded with stars. I could see the white foam of the encroaching waves as the tide crept closer.

Above the lapping of the waves I caught a throaty growling sound. The motor launch. Jack had told me they kept it hidden in one of the creeks along the river. "It's very fast," he'd said, tracing our route with his finger on a map. "Forty knots. It'll get us over to New Grimsby in a couple of hours."

I'd never heard of New Grimsby until then. It appeared as a red dot on the tiny island of Tresco—one of a group called the Isles of Scilly, off the southwest coast of Cornwall. It was where the fishing boat we were to take to Brittany was moored—a real French sardine boat that came over during the Dunkirk evacuation of 1940 and had been commandeered for secret missions.

The sound of the motor launch faded as it passed me by, heading for the quayside. When I reached the village there wasn't a light to be seen. Roofs wet with dew glistened in the starlight. Five figures were standing at the water's edge. The boat was already moored, bobbing gently in the water. As I drew nearer, I saw Jack's profile silhouetted against the night sky.

The boat's long streamlined shape reminded me of the motor yachts I'd seen racing across Dublin Bay as a child. Jack was up on deck, ready to help anyone who lost their balance as they stepped off the quayside. Everyone was wearing the same bulky clothing as I was. I'd been told that one of the agents was a woman—but from where I was standing it was impossible to distinguish which one she was.

As I watched, I saw someone trip and almost fall into the water. But there was no cry of alarm—not even a muttered expletive. Everything was done in total silence. When my turn came, Jack stood with his hands outstretched, waiting to catch me if I stumbled. When he saw that I was all right, he cupped his fingers around his mouth and made a soft hooting sound, like an owl. I heard footsteps on the quayside, then the sound of ropes slithering into the water. Jack was already starting up the engine. As the boat pulled away, I spotted a solitary figure standing on the shore. I caught a glimpse of his upturned face, pale and round in the starlight. It was George Retallack—the blind man.

We began to pick up speed and the front of the boat lifted slightly, planing across the water. I clung to the rail, gasping as spray drenched my face. When I licked my lips, they tasted of salt.

After a while Jack called to me over his shoulder. "You should go below—get some sleep!"

"I will, in a minute," I called back.

I had no intention of going down there. I could imagine how crowded it was likely to be in the cabin—and I thought the agents were more in need of a few hours' rest than I was. They were the ones who were about to risk their lives, going ashore in enemy territory. Besides, I was too nervous to sleep.

With some difficulty, I managed to sit down on the slippery deck. I was afraid to look over the edge of the rail at the water surging around the side of the boat. Closing my eyes didn't help. Bodies in the water were all I could see. Flailing arms glinting in the moonlight. What if it happened again? What if a German submarine was lurking out there in the Channel?

Please, God, if this is what you want me to do, keep us all safe.

I looked up at the stars, trying to quell my fear by remembering evenings in Africa, and how I used to sit outside during the nuns' hour of recreation. The sharp salt smell of the sea faded as the scent of the Congo night came back to me: the mingled fragrance of mimosa and jacaranda, underlaid with the smell of dust. I began to hear the high-pitched thrum of crickets and the distant beat of drums. I remembered how, when I first arrived in the Congo, Sister Clare had interpreted the drum language for me. She said that the jungle was reverberating with the news that the new nun was of childbearing age and had big, beautiful eyes.

"Aren't you cold?" Jack's voice startled me out of the trancelike state I'd fallen into.

"No," I called back. "It's nice up here. Bracing."

"It'll be light soon. Can you see—over there—the sky's just turning pink?"

He was pointing away from the direction in which we were heading. I looked over my shoulder and saw the faint glow on the eastern horizon. It reminded me of that other morning, in this same sea, when I'd clung to life as waves washed me toward Cornwall. Was it only two weeks ago? It felt like a lifetime.

"Come up here, if you like," Jack called. "I'll show you where we are."

I didn't trust myself to stand up, so I scrambled across the deck on all fours.

"Not got your sea legs yet?" Jack said, as I grabbed the rail at the helm of the boat. In the pale dawn light, I could see his wry smile. "You'll have to put on a more convincing act when we get to France if you're going to fool the Germans."

"I know," I murmured. "I'm not as bad as I was when we first set off."

"You'll be fine. I'm sure the biggest hurdle was stepping off dry land."

I nodded.

Jack beckoned me to come closer, then pointed at something off to the right. "Can you see that?"

I craned my neck to see what he'd spotted. He was looking over to the west, where the sky was still dark gray.

"Here—have these." He took off the binoculars looped round his neck.

Lifting them to my eyes, I made out a tall, thin shape in the distance, apparently rising out of the waves. As we drew closer, I saw that it was a lighthouse, perched on a rocky ledge that protruded from the sea.

"That's the Wolf Rock," Jack said. "Normally you'd be able to see the light from the Cornish coast—but they switched it off when the war started." He turned the wheel slightly, steering the boat away from the lighthouse. "Sometimes you can hear it, though."

"Hear it? How?"

"There are big cracks in the rock and when the weather's rough, the wind makes a howling sound like a wolf."

I gave silent thanks for a calm sea. "What's that?" I pointed to a collection of gray bumps up ahead. They looked just like a school of whales I'd spotted on the voyage back from Africa.

"Those are the Eastern Isles," Jack replied. "They're the smallest of the Scillies—no one lives there, apart from seabirds and a few goats. In a minute you'll see a bigger island: St. Martin's. The one we're going to—Tresco—is a few miles west of that."

I soon realized what a competent sailor Jack was. As we approached the Scillies, he had to navigate through shoals of rocks to get us safely through the wild, deserted archipelago that guarded the main island group. The sky was just light enough for him to see the hazards and avoid them. Clearly his timing of the voyage had been critical—leaving Mermaid's Cove while it was still dark, but at the last possible moment, to catch the dawn before we reached dangerous waters.

"Just that one off the port bow, now, and we'll be through." Jack nodded toward a group of rocks piercing the waves on the left side of the boat. "That's New Grimsby Sound, up ahead."

The rising sun had turned the sea a coral pink. I could see two humps of land, shrouded in a milky mist, with a narrow channel in between. I glanced at the wicked-looking rocks Jack had pointed out as we glided past them. I spotted a rusty mast sticking out of the water— the remains of a boat that had come to grief there. I wondered how long it had taken Jack to acquire such expert knowledge of the sea between England and France. I had a sudden image of him racing across the waves in his yacht, *Firefly*, the wind in his hair and the girl, Morwenna, at his side. I felt a gnawing ache below my ribs—a feeling I didn't want to admit to, whose name hovered in the shadowy margins of my mind.

"Can you see the castle?" He passed the binoculars back to me.

Rising out of the mist was the top of a round tower. The pale walls were pockmarked and crumbling.

"It looks very old," I said.

"It dates from the seventeenth century. They call it Cromwell's Castle." He pulled the throttle back, slowing the boat as we entered the narrow channel between Tresco and the neighboring island of Bryher. The mist was beginning to clear. I could see stretches of white sand on either side of us, deserted apart from seabirds scattered along the water's edge. The deep blue of the ocean turned to a translucent turquoise where the waves lapped the shore. As we glided past a granite outcrop, I caught sight of the harbor nestled below the castle.

"That's our boat—the one at the end."

Half a dozen fishing trawlers were moored in the harbor. The one Jack was looking at was painted blue, with a narrow red stripe. As we got closer, I could read the name on the side: *La Coquille. The Shell.*

"The others will be up and about in a minute," Jack said. "Remember—it's code names only when you talk to them. But keep conversation to a minimum: the less you know about them, the better." He rubbed the dark stubble on his chin. "Once we get the other boat onto open water, you and I are fishermen. If anyone stops us and asks you to identify yourself, you're Jean-Luc Piquemal. You've got your papers?"

I patted the pocket of my oilskin trousers.

"You'll need to get some sleep before we get to Brittany; otherwise you'll be of no use at all. There are hammocks belowdecks on *La Coquille*—they're quite comfortable when you get used to them." He turned away from me in answer to a shout from the quayside. A white-haired man in a striped jersey was waiting to tie our boat to a docking post.

"Good morning." A woman's voice behind me made me jump.

"Good morning," Jack replied, as he tossed a rope over the side of the boat. "Did you sleep well?"

"Not very—one of the others was snoring like a steam train."

I could only see her eyes, nose, and mouth. Like me, her hair was hidden under a fisherman's hat, and the upturned collar of her jacket hid her throat and chin.

"Miranda." She smiled, holding out her hand to me. "And you must be Ariel."

I'd never even sat in a hammock before, let alone tried to sleep in one. Miranda was a couple of feet away. Without her hat, her hair spilled over the side of her gently swaying bed. She looked very young: about the same age as Janet, the Land Girl. She'd told me that she was half-French and came from a small town not far from London. I lay watching her, wondering what had made her decide to put herself forward for such dangerous work. I thought she'd fallen asleep, but after a while she wriggled around to face me.

"Not very comfortable, are they?" She swept her hair off her face.

"No." I tried to prop myself up on my elbow. The hammock swayed violently and we both laughed.

"We used to have one in the garden at home," Miranda said. "But my dad set fire to it when he fell asleep with his pipe in his hand."

"Oh—I hope he wasn't hurt."

She shook her head. "Mum turned the garden hose on him. She hates him smoking. He's a doctor and she's always telling him he shouldn't inflict his bad habits on his patients. His consulting room stinks of tobacco."

I told her that my father had been just the same, that I could always tell which room in the house he was in because of the telltale odor wafting out under the door. Like me, she had sometimes accompanied her dad on his rounds as a child. We swapped stories of the grisly things we had seen, heard, and smelled: people with severed arms and legs, women screaming out in childbirth, elderly patients whose ulcerous legs tainted the air and made us gag.

"It put me off any sort of career in the medical profession." She huffed out a laugh.

I didn't know if I was supposed to let on that I was a nurse, so I didn't reply. She said she thought she'd better try to get some rest, and she turned over. I must have drifted off to sleep, too. When I woke up, Miranda had gone. I scrambled up the wooden ladder and heaved myself onto the deck. I blinked as the sunlight hit my eyes. I saw Jack emerge from under a blanket. His hair was sticking up, and the shadow of stubble on his jaw was darker than when I'd last seen him. The five agents were sitting in a circle, eating something.

"Would you like some?" Miranda was holding out a plate of thickly sliced brown bread spread with butter and jam. The sight of it made me ravenously hungry.

"You'd better eat some now," Jack said, reaching across to take a piece. "You might not feel like it once we get underway."

It wasn't an idle warning. We left the shelter of New Grimsby Sound as the sun dipped below the craggy outline of Bryher island, and within an hour of reaching the open sea, the boat began to pitch alarmingly. I think I was the only one, apart from Jack, who wasn't sick. It must have been sheer terror, freezing my insides.

I went to stand beside him at the wheel. In the orange glow of the sunset, I could see the white of his knuckles. "How long until we get there?" I had to raise my voice to be heard.

"Depends on whether this wind dies down," he replied. "If it was calm, we'd do it by one or two in the morning. But at this rate, it'll be touch and go whether we make it before daybreak."

"What happens if we don't?"

"We have to mingle with the French fishing boats and sit it out until tomorrow night."

"What about the people we're picking up? How would they know?"

"They won't be there unless they get the tip-off on the BBC broadcast. Merle will only give the go-ahead for that when I message her. If she doesn't hear from us by nine o'clock tonight, it won't happen." He twisted the wheel as a big wave surged against the port side of the boat. "How are you feeling?"

"Not too bad," I replied.

"Good. In that case, you can help me. The binoculars are in that cupboard." He pointed to the place with his foot. "Keep watch for me, will you? I need both hands on the wheel."

"What am I looking for?" With some difficulty, I opened the cupboard.

"Any boat or ship. Particularly anything that looks as if it's coming fast. There's not much chance of encountering an enemy vessel yet, but the closer we get to France, the more likely we are to run into one. It'll be dark in an hour or so—you just need to keep watch until then."

I scanned the horizon, trying not to lose my balance. The ocean was alive, moving all the time. How on earth was I going to pick out any craft in such a swell? My mind started conjuring up phantom images. At one point I convinced myself that a submarine was emerging from the waves, away on the horizon. But it was just a trick of the light—the dying rays of the sun catching a lone column of rain.

By the time darkness fell I was exhausted. But the sea was much calmer than when we'd set out from New Grimsby. Miranda and the others, who'd been clinging to the sides of the boat, looking like death, had gone below to the hammocks.

"You should go down, too," Jack said.

"I don't think I'd be able to sleep again," I replied.

He nodded. "We're making good time now. In a minute I'll send that message. You can hold the wheel for me, if you like."

"But . . . I . . ." I stared stupidly at the weather-beaten circle of wood.

"It's quite simple," he said. "There's the compass—we're heading southeast. Just keep us going steady in that direction. You probably won't need to turn the wheel at all, but if the needle shifts, you'll only need to tweak it slightly to get us back on course."

He stood behind me, placing both his hands over mine until I got the hang of it. The fear bubbling up inside me dissolved into a surge of guilty longing. I wanted to pretend I couldn't do it, make him stay like that, holding me, his body braced against mine. But even as I thought it, he moved away. I heard his footsteps receding as he crossed the deck. I was afraid to look over my shoulder, terrified of taking my eyes off the needle of the compass. I wondered fleetingly what my other self would have said, had I had the ability to glimpse the future. If I'd been shown this vision of myself a year ago, a month ago, I would have dismissed it as pure fantasy. Yet here I was, a woman disguised as a man, at the helm of a French sardine boat, taking a band of secret agents into enemy territory. Would I have agreed to it if anyone other than Jack had asked me? I couldn't answer that question. And it was far too late now to think of turning back the clock.

Chapter 13

*T*he wooden dinghy was bobbing about in the water, tethered to the starboard stern of *La Coquille*. Miranda climbed down the rope ladder first, followed by the four men, and then me. We took up our positions: me sitting in the stern with a mackerel line at the ready; one of the men, whose code name was Ferdinand, at the oars; the others lying in the belly of the little boat, alongside the ammunition and the medical supplies they were taking. As Ferdinand began to row, I pulled a tarpaulin over the four people lying at my feet.

La Coquille was anchored less than half a mile from the coast of Brittany. The plan was that Jack would weigh anchor as soon as the dinghy was on the move. He would meander along the coast, dragging a net, to avoid drawing suspicion to the boat. Then, when enough time had elapsed, he would return to collect me and the men I was to rescue.

With no lights, it was difficult to navigate. We could see the land silhouetted black against an indigo sky, but we were going in blind, unable to detect any potential hazard. Jack had described the place we were heading for: a long stretch of sandy beach with no hidden rocks to threaten us. The people waiting for us were unable to signal their presence for fear of alerting any enemy craft that might be patrolling the coast. But they would be watching from their hiding place in the dunes, Jack assured us. They would see us, even if we couldn't see them.

We were told not to speak to one another unless absolutely necessary. The only sound was the lap of the oars. I sat, rigid, in the stern, listening intently, dreading the throb of an approaching engine. But this part of the ordeal was soon over. Ferdinand was powerfully built. Half an hour after setting off, he pulled in the oars and let the waves take us onto the beach. He jumped out and held the boat steady while the rest of us scrambled out.

As we stood on the beach, peering into the darkness, I heard a soft hooting sound—the same sound Jack had made when we left the quayside at Mermaid's Cove. Ferdinand cupped his hands to his mouth and hooted back. We heard the crunch of feet on sand. A figure loomed out of the dunes, coming toward us.

"Bonsoir à tous de La Maison de La Sirène." The man's whispered greeting was a version of the coded message Merle had passed to the BBC.

"Bonsoir, Oncle Pierre." Ferdinand stepped forward, his hand outstretched. *"Appelez les autres. Je tiendrai le bateau pendant qu'ils montent."*

The man hesitated, glancing over his shoulder. Ferdinand had asked him to signal to the men he'd brought to the beach so they could board the dinghy. I couldn't see the Frenchman's face, but his body language conveyed that something was wrong.

"Ils ont été fusillés. Ils ont rencontré une patrouille allemande sur le chemin." They were shot. They encountered a German patrol on the way here.

"Fusillés?" I could hear the tension in Ferdinand's voice.

We learned that all four had survived the attack, but they needed urgent medical attention.

"Je m'en occuperai." I'll take care of them. It felt strange, speaking the language again. *"Je suis infirmière."* I'm a nurse.

Six heads turned my way.

"Not here," the man said in terse French. "There are Germans everywhere."

I replied that I could treat them on the fishing boat if they were able to walk.

He said that they could, with help.

The others followed him up the beach while I crouched beside the dinghy. I said a silent prayer for them, my eyes fixed on Miranda until she melted into the darkness. After what seemed like an eternity, Ferdinand and the other men reappeared, each supporting one of the wounded escapees. I held the rope as they helped them aboard.

"None of them is in a fit state to row," Ferdinand whispered to me. "Can you do it?"

"Yes—of course." I sounded more confident than I felt. The last time I'd handled a pair of oars had been on the River Liffey in Dublin, when I was sixteen years old.

"Good luck—stay safe." And with that, he pushed the boat into the water. One of the men groaned as a wave lifted the bow. I pulled hard on the oars, afraid that if I didn't get out of the surf quickly, the boat would flip. Somehow, I got us beyond the breakers. I tried to keep a straight course, heading out, I hoped, to open sea. I had no idea how Jack was going to find us.

I was panting for breath, the muscles in my arms burning from the effort of rowing. I hoisted the oars out of the water, desperate for a rest but terrified of stopping for more than a few moments.

"I wish I could help you." The voice was American. It came from the man nearest to me. He was half sitting, half lying in the bottom of the boat. There was a crude bandage bound around the top of his right arm. It was too dark to see how bloody it was.

"It's okay," I replied. "I'll be fine—just resting for a moment."

"Jeez! No disrespect—I didn't realize you were a woman."

"Well, that's good," I grunted, as I took up the oars again. "I'm supposed to fool the Germans into thinking I'm a fisherman." I glanced over my shoulder, searching for the silhouette of *La Coquille*. I strained my ears for any sound other than the lap of the waves. What would I do if I heard the distant thrum of an engine? How would I know if it was Jack coming, or the enemy? Every time I pulled the oars, I felt the pistol Jack had given me pressing into the flesh of my arm. I prayed I wouldn't have to use it.

"You're doing great. Want me to watch for the boat?" He made a muffled groaning sound as he shifted his weight, pulling himself up so that his head was above the oarlocks.

"Be careful—don't put any strain on that arm."

"I'm okay." He huffed out a laugh. "Leastways, my eyes still work."

I wanted to ask his name, but I didn't know whether I was supposed to. We went on in silence until he reached out with his good arm, tugging urgently at the fabric of my trousers. I stopped the oars and twisted my head round. The shape of a boat loomed out of the water. There was no sound. Whoever it was had dropped anchor.

"Is it ours?" the American whispered.

"I'm not sure," I murmured back. It was too dark to make out the name on the side of the vessel. I tried to suppress the feeling of panic rising from my stomach. We were so vulnerable—four wounded men and a woman who had no idea what to do.

Please, God, help us. I fired the words like a silent arrow into the vast, inky sky. A heartbeat later, I heard the splash of a rope hitting the water.

It took nearly an hour to get the men on board *La Coquille*. Three had upper-body wounds and the fourth had been shot in the leg. None were up to climbing the rope ladder. We had to make a harness and haul them up, one at a time. Jack tried to do it unaided, but it soon became clear that he was going to need help. By scrambling up the ladder once I'd secured the harness, I was able to add my weight to his. It was a struggle, even then—especially when it came to the American, who was the tallest man I'd ever seen.

"We need to get away." Jack glanced at the sky as he pulled up the rope ladder. "Will you be able to cope on your own? The medical kit's down below, inside one of the benches."

"Is there a hospital on Tresco?" There hadn't been time—or enough light—to assess the men's injuries. I'd never had to remove bullets. But I knew enough to realize that it would be dangerous even to try on my own, in these conditions.

"No," he said, "but there's one on the main island—St. Mary's."

"We need to get them there, then."

"You don't think they can make it back to Cornwall?"

"I wouldn't like to risk it. They'll be safe, won't they, once we reach the Scillies?"

He hesitated a moment. Then he nodded. "You'd better go to them."

It was getting light by the time I went back up on deck. The men were all sleeping, helped into oblivion by a few sips of the brandy I'd found when I located the medical kit. I'd had to tourniquet three of them, including the American, who'd been shot just above the elbow. The fourth man—a Scot with an accent so strong I struggled to understand him—had gashed his head.

From what I could gather, the men had been attacked when they'd passed through a checkpoint on their way to the beach. Their Resistance courier—the man who had come to meet our dinghy—had shot the German sentry dead when he began firing. The Scot had dived for cover at the sound of gunfire, and had fallen down a railway embankment, his scalp splitting open on a chunk of concrete.

Attempting stitches on a boat that was pitching in the open sea would have been too risky, so I cleaned up the wound and bandaged his head as tightly as I could. When I was satisfied that I'd done all I could for him and the others, I went to get some fresh air.

Jack was scanning the horizon with the binoculars. There was rain in the air, the sea a charcoal smudge against the pale gray of the sky.

"How are the patients?" he asked, as I stepped into the wheelhouse.

"All fast asleep," I replied. "I'm hoping they won't wake up until we get them back onto dry land."

"Well, thank goodness you came. God knows what would have happened otherwise." He lowered the binoculars and turned to me. "You realize you probably saved their lives?"

I shook my head. "All I've done is patch them up. The people at the hospital are the ones who'll save them."

"But if you hadn't been in that boat, they'd never have made it. Not one of them was capable of rowing. They'd have been sitting ducks for the Germans." He reached into a compartment under the wheel and pulled something out—a bulky shape swathed in white cloth. "Are you hungry?" He unwrapped a loaf of bread and tore off a piece, handing it to me. I bit into it, edging farther into the wheelhouse as the wind spattered raindrops against the back of my neck.

"It's a shame there's nothing to go with it," Jack said between mouthfuls. "We could do with something hot to dip it into. Soup would be good, wouldn't it?"

I nodded. I hadn't tasted soup for years. Not since leaving Ireland.

"What's so funny?"

I hadn't realized I was smiling. It must have been a wry sort of look on my face, because what I'd been remembering wasn't very nice. "I was thinking about the convent," I said. "If you'd done something wrong, they put you on short measures of soup for a week. But there was a worse penance than that."

"What?"

"Well, if you were really disobedient, there was something else you had to do before you got your soup: you had to kiss the feet of the ten oldest nuns in the convent."

"Ugh!" He glanced at the bread in his hand as if he'd suddenly discovered it was crawling with weevils. "Why on earth did you become a nun? You could have been a nurse without all of that nonsense."

"I wanted to work in Africa," I replied. "It wouldn't have been easy to do that on my own, at the age I was then." I glanced through the rain-speckled glass at the gray-green sea, avoiding his eyes.

"That's quite a sacrifice."

There was something about the way he said it. I suspected that he'd guessed this wasn't the whole story. I hadn't intended to tell him about the boy I'd left behind in Ireland—but in this topsy-turvy world, where so much was supposed to be secret, I suddenly felt compelled to tell the truth.

"There was another reason," I said. "I had a boyfriend. His name was Dan. We were only seventeen, but we'd talked about marriage." I watched a raindrop slide down the window, gathering speed as it joined with another. "My father wouldn't hear of it. He was the local doctor, and he knew that Dan's mother had been admitted to a psychiatric institution." I took a breath. The memory of Dad's words still had the power to make my insides curl. "He said he didn't want our family tainted by madness."

Jack didn't respond for a moment or two, as if he were sizing me up. "So, you became a nun to spite your father?" He sounded less surprised than I thought he'd be.

"I think I would have done it anyway." I turned to face him. "I thought I was capable of another kind of love—the kind that doesn't involve marriage or children."

He shook his head. "But you were so young. How could you bear to make a decision like that?"

I hesitated. I didn't want to admit that I'd gone to the convent the day after the row with Dad, that I'd been fired up with a white-hot anger that drove all rational thoughts from my mind. And that if my love for Dan had been stronger, I might have chosen a different course. "I knew that it would hurt sometimes," I said at last, "but at the convent they taught us that it was like pruning a plant: cutting off one possibility of love would encourage you to grow and flourish in different ways."

"That might work for some women." He gave me a searching look. "But I've seen how you are with Merle's children. And with young Ned. It didn't work, did it? Not for you."

I felt as if a hand had squeezed my heart. How was it that in the space of a fortnight, he was able to understand me better than I understood myself?

"No," I heard myself saying. "It didn't work." It was as if I were hovering above the boat, watching the person who had once been Sister Anthony letting out what she had locked away the day the train had pulled out of the station at Elisabethville. "There were two children in Africa—a boy and a girl. I found them in the jungle when I was on my way to carry out vaccinations at a school. They were babies—newborn twins. They were about to be buried alive with their mother, who had died giving birth to them."

"Buried alive?" Jack's voice sounded as otherworldly as my own, like an echo from the depths of the ocean.

"It was a tribal custom to dispose of babies that way if the mother had died. I'd heard of it, but this was the first time I'd seen it with my own eyes."

"What did you do?"

"I had two native men with me—they were paddling the raft I was in—and through them I persuaded the villagers to let me take the babies to the mission hospital. There was an orphanage there, which I knew would take them."

"So, they survived? They were all right?"

"Yes. But I wasn't." I took a breath, willing away the sting of threatened tears. "I chose Swahili names for them. Kamaria—which means bright, like the moon, for the girl—and Kenyada, which means gem, for the boy. I used to visit them every day. I wasn't supposed to—I'd been warned about not going there too often when I first arrived in Africa. But I couldn't help myself. I developed what the sister superior viewed as an attachment to them, something that was frowned upon by the order. That was why the decision was made to send me back to Ireland."

"They *made* you leave?"

I nodded. My throat felt tight. "They let me go and say goodbye. The children were far too young, of course, to understand what was going on. I knew they wouldn't miss me, wouldn't even remember me. That helped a little. But as I walked away, I knew, with every fiber of my being, that I would never be the kind of nun the order expected me to be—the kind who displays unquestioning obedience and has the ability to give up all worldly attachments." I turned my face to the sea, but my filmy eyes and the raindrops on the glass turned the waves into a blur of gray. "I suppose, deep down, I'd always known it. But what happened with those children brought it home to me, very powerfully: that being a nun meant having no choice, meant living a life against your natural inclinations, even when those inclinations were good and loving."

For a moment the only sound was the hum of the boat's engine. Then Jack said, "Did you ever blame your father? For making you do something you ended up regretting?"

I sensed that there was something behind the question—something that concerned him, not just me. I glanced at his face, wondering what was in his mind. He had that same brooding look I'd noticed before. "I understand why my father did what he did," I replied. "I think he honestly believed he was protecting me by forbidding me to marry Dan."

"Hmm." He rubbed his knuckles against the dark stubble on his jawbone. "I can imagine my father taking a similar view. He was a traditionalist. Always quoting the family motto, 'Duty before thyself.' I never thought about it when I was growing up—the responsibilities that came with inheriting a title. I imagined myself sailing the world, running the family's shipping company."

"You did that—for a while—didn't you?"

"Yes. But it all fell apart after the Wall Street crash. Within a few years the business was unsustainable. We had to liquidate all the assets. And by the time my father died, the house had become a terrible financial burden. I couldn't . . ." He stopped short. I noticed the subtle change in his eyes, the indefinable something that lingered there momentarily. I wondered if he'd been about to reveal something about the girl he'd fallen in love with.

"I shouldn't go on about it," he said. "You must be tired. You should try to get some sleep."

The way he said it was like an order. But as I turned to go, he caught my hand. "I'm sorry for what happened to you in Africa." His voice was different now: soft, almost a whisper. "But I'm not sorry that you've given up being a nun."

I gazed back at him, tongue-tied. I couldn't tell if he was offering me sympathy, or something more. I felt myself blushing and I broke away, muttering something stupid about my convent haircut coming in useful for fooling the enemy.

Down in the cabin, the men were all still asleep. I sank into one of the hammocks and closed my eyes. But I couldn't settle. For the rest of the journey I lay awake, tortured by what Jack had stirred up.

I'm not sorry that you've given up being a nun.

What had he meant by that? Was he simply glad that I'd washed up at Mermaid's Cove, desperate for a new life and with the abilities required for the secret work he was involved in? Or was he like the men on the *Brabantia*? The ones who used to cast sly glances as I walked past their deck chairs?

Men always want what they can't have. Sister Clare's voice floated into my head, all the way from Africa. Was that true for Jack? If Leo Badger was to be believed, Jack had flouted convention to run after a girl from a very different background to his own. Was that something he was drawn to? Pursuing women who were out-of-bounds?

All I knew of romantic love was the summer I'd had with Dan. At the convent, I'd tried to forget what it felt like to have a man's hands on my body. I'd often drawn blood with the twice-weekly flailing of my shoulders, battling to suppress the rush of desire those memories unleashed. Twelve years as a nun should have squeezed all that out of me, along with all the other human yearnings. But it hadn't.

Thinking about Jack in that way was like standing in front of Pandora's box. Did I want to lift the lid? Could I take the consequences if I did?

Chapter 14

When we got back to Cornwall, I slept for nearly twenty-four hours. I had no idea what time it was when I woke up—I must have knocked the little alarm clock onto the floor when I fell, exhausted, into bed. I jumped up, my heart pounding, unable to work out where I was. The boathouse was pitch dark. The only clue that I was on dry land, not in the belly of *La Coquille* or the motor launch, was the lack of movement. Not fully conscious, I stumbled out of bed and felt my way along the wall. I knocked over a row of fishing rods, which clattered like dominoes to the floor. "Mary, Mother of God," I muttered. "Just tell me where I am!"

My hand found the doorknob, and below it the large metal key. When I opened the door, I saw that the sky was gray with clouds and the tide was a long way out. I couldn't work out what time of day it was. I gazed at the shoreline, where the crisscrossed poles of the sea defense lay exposed like the skeleton of a monstrous fish. It added to the air of unreality, to the dreamlike memories that swam into my head as I stood, motionless, in the doorway. Had I really been to France? Had I imagined those men and that desperate escape in the dinghy? I ran my fingers up and down my arms. The ache in my shoulders from pulling on the oars told me that I hadn't dreamed it.

A glimmer of orange sunlight touched the western edge of the estuary, dying away as the clouds scudded across the sky. Afternoon, then, not morning. As I watched the seabirds digging their bills into the wet sand on the tide line, my stomach grumbled for food. The tame robin that always appeared when I opened the door came hopping along the sand, eyeing me expectantly. I couldn't remember what, if anything, there was to eat. I opened the shutters, then went back inside to see what I could find.

Minutes later I heard someone knocking. I expected it to be Jack, out for his customary walk with Brock. But it was Merle.

"He's gone to London," she said, as I put the kettle on to boil. "He would have been taking the men you picked up, but that'll have to wait until they're well enough to travel." She sat down on one of the apple boxes. "He'll have to report back on what happened, though. It'll help the SOE to plan your next mission."

I nodded. In the euphoria of getting back to my little sanctuary alive, I'd forgotten that I'd be going to France again when the moon had waxed and waned.

She asked me what it had been like, rowing a boatload of wounded men out to sea.

"If I'd known about it in advance, I don't think I could have done it," I said. "But there wasn't time to think. That was a blessing, really."

"Well, you were incredibly plucky." She took an envelope from her jacket pocket. "This is for you."

I stared at the name—*Ariel*—in bold black type. "What is it?"

"Your wages," she replied. "They don't expect you to do this kind of work for nothing." She smiled as I tore open the flap. "I thought we might go shopping in Falmouth together when the children are back at school. There's not much to spend your money on—but we might be able to buy some dress fabric. There's a sewing machine up at the house."

I emptied the contents of the envelope into my hand. It felt so strange to have money. I turned the coins over. They had the image of King George on one side and pictures of a ship, a bird, and a flower on the other. The notes were the same color as my skirt: mauve with a thread of silver running through them. The idea of going into a shop, of choosing cloth to make into a dress, was intoxicating. But the thought of it set off a tidal wave of guilt.

"What's the matter?" Merle asked. "You don't look very pleased."

How could I explain the feeling? It would be difficult for anyone outside the religious life to comprehend—that adjusting to life in the material world was something like shaking off an addiction. "I'm just trying to get used to the idea of having money of my own," I said. "I'm a bit afraid of it, to be honest."

"Well, you don't have to worry—I'll be there to make sure you don't blow it all in one go! Shall we go on Friday?"

Before I could answer, Ned and Louis burst through the door. Merle had sent them to play on the beach while she came in to see me. Ned was covered in sand. Even his hair had sand in it.

"Oh, Ned!" Merle stood up. "What on earth have you been doing?"

"I be dead." He rubbed the back of his hand across his eyes, blinking as more sand fell from his eyebrows. "Louis says."

"Louis! Did you bury him? Is that why he's in such a mess?"

Louis hung his head. "He was being naughty, Mum. He said he didn't want to live with us anymore—he wants to live here with Miss Alice."

Merle's eyes went to the ceiling. "He does, does he? And I suppose he came out with that all on his own—nothing to do with you teasing him?"

"It was his fault," Louis muttered. "He threw a dead crab at me. I threw it back, and he started to cry, the big baby. Look—he's crying again: because he knows it's true!"

Merle cast an exasperated look at me. "What a pair! What would you do with them?"

"Let me clean Ned up," I said. "He can stay here for his tea, too, if that'll help. I can bring him back later, when they've both had a chance to cool down."

"Would you like that, Ned?" Merle asked.

He gave a loud sniff and a violent nod.

When the others had gone, I heated up some water and gave Ned a bath in the metal tub that hung behind the door in the bathroom. I'd often washed patients at the mission hospital, but I'd never given anyone a proper bath. I was worried about the soap going in his eyes and making him cry again, but he was very good. He didn't make a whimper—even when I poured water over his head to get the last of the sand out of his hair. His brown curls stuck to his skin like the slick fur of a seal, parting over his ears. When I went to rub him dry, I noticed a small hole at the top of his left ear, as if someone had stuck a needle through the skin.

"Louis hasn't been hurting you, has he?" I asked.

His hand went to the place my fingers were examining. His face told me that he was unaware of anything being amiss there. "He did kick me," he said. "Not on my head—on my leg."

"Has he done anything else?"

He shook his head.

"Well, if he hurts you again you must tell Auntie Merle—or me."

When he was dry, I sat him on my lap, swathed in the towel, and fed him fish-paste sandwiches. While he was eating, I told him a story that my mother used to read to me, about a giant whose legs were so long he could step across the Irish Sea without getting his feet wet. I would have kept him all evening if I could. But I'd promised to get him back to the house by seven o'clock.

Ned held my hand as we walked up the valley, through carpets of bluebells, with swifts and swallows darting through the air after insects.

He wanted to know the names of all the birds that we heard, and the flowers that we saw. I picked a foxglove and showed him how to put the petals on the ends of his fingers. When we passed the church, I caught a glimpse of an owl perched in a branch of a yew tree. I pointed it out to him, and we stood watching as it flew across the churchyard, swooping low to perch on a Celtic cross that stuck out of the ground at a crazy angle.

"Will you be my mummy?" Ned whispered.

His words took my breath away. He was looking up at me, his big, dark eyes so vulnerable, so trusting.

"Oh, Ned," I murmured. "I'd love to be your mummy. But you have a mummy already."

He shook his head. "That's what Auntie Merle says. I asked her to be my mummy, but she says she can't because she's my auntie."

His eyes were glassy with tears. I crouched down beside him, my feet squashing last year's dead leaves, the damp smell of them rising from the muddy ground. "Your mummy would be with you if she could," I said. "She lives across the sea, and she has to stay there for a while, but one day you'll see her. She'll come and take you home."

"When?" The look he gave me was heartbreaking.

"I don't know," I whispered. "Soon, I hope."

"But I want a mummy now."

I didn't trust myself to speak. I wrapped my arms around him and hugged him to me. I felt his tears on my skin. "I could be a pretend mummy," I murmured into his ear. "What about that?"

"A pretend mummy?" He moved his head away from the crook of my neck, his eyes searching my face.

"Like in a game," I said. "Like when you put your gas mask on and pretend to be a monster."

He nodded.

"We'll pretend we're birds, living in the woods." I cocked my head toward the owl, who was still perched on the tombstone, preening its feathers. "I'll be the mummy owl and you be the boy owl. We need to go hunting for mice for our supper. Where shall we look?"

"Over there!" He ran to a fallen tree whose trunk was covered in moss and got down on all fours, peering underneath it.

I watched him as he scrambled about catching imaginary mice. I knew that I was going to have to be very careful. It was so easy to love him. But I didn't think I could bear that pain again—the agony of having, one day, to say goodbye to him.

The next day, when my work at the farm was over, I went to see Leo Badger. He was sitting in a chair, pipe in hand, chatting away to George Retallack. George got up when I came into the cottage and said he'd wait outside while I looked Leo over.

There was no real need for me to examine Leo, as he was getting regular visits from the district nurse, but he seemed keen to show me how his injuries were healing. He asked me to recount exactly what I'd done to his leg on the day of the accident. His eyes gleamed as I described fashioning a tourniquet out of George's shirt to stop the bleeding.

"That's twice I've nearly bled to death, then." He looked as pleased as if he'd just netted the biggest catch of pilchards in history. "Did I show you where the shark bit me?"

He looked disappointed when I said that he had—but he cheered up when I produced the apple pie that Merle had made for him.

When I went outside George was sitting on the doorstep. I offered him a slice of the pie, which he politely refused, saying that Leo needed it all to build his strength up. We chatted for a while about the practicalities of getting Leo in and out of bed, and about how long it would be before he could go fishing again. As George talked, his eyes darted this way and that, as if he were constantly monitoring his environment even though he couldn't see it. I wondered if he would be at the quay-side again the next time we went to France, ready to untether the rope when Jack gave the signal. It dawned on me that there was great wisdom in picking a blind man for that job: if anyone tried to get information out of him, he wouldn't be able to say who had been on the boat.

"Forgive me for askin'," George said, "but you're not the cousin who ran off to South Africa, are you? With the tin miner?"

The question was such a surprise that I laughed. "No—that's not me." I gave him a wry smile, hoping he wouldn't probe further, wouldn't expose my ignorance of Jack's family. But, of course, he couldn't see me.

"She had all her goin'-away clothes delivered to the 'ouse—a wedding dress an' all," he went on. "The parcel was addressed to 'Is Lordship—not the old viscount, mind, but Mister Jack. My old ma was 'ousekeeper in them days, and she opened it. Teased 'Is Lordship somethin' rotten, she did: thought it was 'im getting wed on the quiet until 'e told 'er it were for 'is cousin."

The story filled me with a mixture of exultation and relief: it had been a joke, then, that talk about a secret wife.

Jack was still away on the day of my shopping trip to Falmouth with Merle. I'd become used to seeing him morning and evening when he brought the dog down to the cove for a walk. I tried not to listen out for Brock's joyful barking when I was getting ready to go up to the farmyard. I missed Jack's visits. I didn't like to admit it, even to myself, but it wasn't just the company I missed—it was him.

The Land Girls were rowdier than usual that morning. They'd just heard that there was to be a dance hosted by a platoon of American soldiers newly arrived in Cornwall. The talk was all about the gifts they expected to get if they managed to get their claws into a Yank, as they called them. Silk stockings, chocolate, and cigarettes were the most sought-after items.

Edith gave me a sly smile as she emerged from under a cow. "I suppose you met lots of Americans in London."

I didn't answer. I couldn't tell her that the only American I'd ever encountered was the one I'd rescued from a beach in France.

"I bet you went dancing every night when you lived there," she persisted.

"Are you joking?" I grunted. "Most nights I was so worn out all I wanted was my bed. I haven't been dancing in years." This blend of truth and fiction seemed to satisfy her—although the look she gave me as she ducked down spoke volumes. In her eyes I was a pitiable creature with terrible hair who didn't know how to make the most of herself, nor how to have a good time.

I applied myself to the teats of the next cow waiting to be milked, unable to shake the image she'd conjured of people in London living fast and free despite the bombs raining down. I couldn't help wondering whether Jack was making the most of being there on government business, going out at night to escape the twin pressures of running an estate and a secret military operation. I imagined him in a crowded, smoke-filled room with a whiskey in his hand, attracting admiring glances from women like Edith. Women who would be all over him, like ants on honey, once they got him onto the dance floor.

"You're missing the bucket!" It was Marjorie, to my left, who alerted me to what I was doing. I'd been so wrapped up in thoughts of Jack that I'd squirted milk all over my boots.

After the milking was done, I went to find Merle. She was in the kitchen, up to her elbows in flour, making bread dough.

"I won't be long." She slapped a ball of dough onto the marble slab beside her and started kneading it. "Could you do me a favor? I need to post a letter in Falmouth. There are stamps in the bureau in the library. Could you fetch them for me? I'll be ready to go by the time you come back."

I wondered if the letter was for Fred. Merle hadn't mentioned him since the day she'd told me about their love affair. I thought I'd better not ask. If she hadn't heard from him, she was bound to be worried, and raising the subject would make things even worse.

I went down the passage that led to the great hall. The portraits of Jack's ancestors seemed to stare down accusingly as I crossed the room, as if they knew how I felt about him. When I reached the door of the library, I opened it noiselessly—another legacy of my years as a nun. It had been a rule of the convent, no rasp of hinge or lock. If a nun allowed a door to slam, she was supposed to kiss the floor and say three Glorias.

The musty smell of old books hung in the air. The Morse code machine looked incongruous in such a room—modern and alien against the hunting scenes hanging on the walls. The briefcase that contained it lay open on the desk in the center of the room, with the codebook Merle used to decipher messages from France beside it.

The bureau was over by the window. Like all the furniture in the house, it looked as if it had seen better days. Slivers of the mother-of-pearl inlay had fallen out, and when I pulled down the flap, one of the legs wobbled precariously. There were rows of pigeonholes down both sides. I suddenly remembered, as I searched for the stamps, that I'd intended to write to Janet, the Land Girl who was in hospital. In all the drama of the past few days, it had gone out of my head. I made a mental note to write to her as soon as I got back from Falmouth.

My fingers went in and out of the pigeonholes but found no stamps. I tried a drawer at the back of the bureau, but the brass knob came off in my hand when I went to open it. Frustrated, I grasped the sharp end of the screw protruding from the wood. It took a few seconds of determined pulling to open it. But the only things inside were a few paper clips and a dog-eared envelope.

Curiosity got the better of me when I spotted the name on the envelope. It was addressed to J. Trewella, 14 Cadogan Square, Belgravia, London. The stamp bore a Guernsey postmark, dated April 14, 1940. I shouldn't have taken it out of the drawer. And I certainly shouldn't have opened it. But I felt an inexplicable compulsion to see what the envelope contained.

What my fingers found was not a letter but a photograph. It was a black-and-white snapshot of a sad-eyed girl holding a baby wrapped in a fringed shawl. I turned it over. On the back was written "Edward John" and the date January 15, 1939.

I flipped it over again and stared at the girl's face. I couldn't help but see the likeness. The elfin face, the sprinkling of freckles on the cheekbones. It could have been a picture of me from when I lived in Dublin.

You know, you remind me of someone. A girl 'Is Lordship used to knock about with. The words of the old fisherman Leo Badger came back to me as I gazed into the wistful eyes. I pried open the envelope, searching for any clue to the identity of the person in the photograph. But it was empty. Then I spotted something, written very small, on the flap. It was the return address. I angled it to the light, struggling to decipher the tiny writing. It said: "M. Martin, 18 St. Julian's Avenue, St. Peter Port." My heart shifted in my chest. Morwenna Martin was the name Leo had revealed. But if this girl was Morwenna, why had she sent Jack a photograph of a baby? Was he the father?

I felt a sick surge in my stomach as I turned the photo over again. "Edward John." If the date written under the name was the baby's date of birth, he would be nearly four and a half years old by now. About the same age as Ned. And Ned was short for Edward.

I snatched up the envelope, staring at the postmark, then the address written on the flap. Why would Morwenna have been living on Guernsey just months before the Nazi invasion? And if Ned was the baby in the photograph—*their* baby—why had Jack taken him off the island without her?

My hands were shaking as I stuffed the image back inside the envelope. I dropped it back into the drawer as if it were on fire. I hurried out of the room, back to Merle, telling myself that it couldn't be true, that I was putting two and two together and making five. But I couldn't quell the storm of emotion inside me.

It took every ounce of my nun's training to conceal my feelings from Merle. I told her I'd been unable to find the stamps, and she said it didn't matter—someone else had probably needed them, and she could buy more in Falmouth.

We sat on the top deck of the bus. From up there I could see the landscape stretching out beyond leafy hedges sprinkled white with cow parsley and hawthorn blossom. Fields of ripening crops were interspersed with meadows where cattle and sheep grazed. The only clue that a war was going on was an airfield where a trio of Spitfires came in to land as the bus trundled past.

We drove through the village of Constantine, where the Land Girls lived, picking up more passengers outside the post office. The bus wound past rows of cottages, then plunged into a green tunnel formed by the branches of oaks and sycamores on either side of the narrow lane.

More villages followed, with quaint Cornish names: Treverva, Mabe Burnthouse, Budock Water. Merle chatted about the children during the journey. She told me that they needed costumes for a performance the village school was putting on. She was making dresses for the girls from an old tablecloth, but she wanted to look for some lace to trim them with. I was listening to what she was saying and taking in the changing landscape—but another part of my brain was miles away, playing a movie reel of the story of Jack and Morwenna, trying to make sense of what I'd uncovered.

The more I thought about it, the more plausible it seemed that Morwenna *was* the girl in the photograph. According to Leo Badger, she had left Cornwall, but no one knew where she'd gone. If she was pregnant and Jack wouldn't marry her, that sudden disappearance made perfect sense. He'd had a boat. Taking her to Guernsey would have been easy—and far enough from Cornwall to avoid a scandal. But if Ned was their child, why had Jack taken him from his mother? Could the story he'd told Merle have been half-true? Had Morwenna been in the hospital when the Germans invaded the island? And if so, what had happened to her?

"You can see the docks from here." The subtle change in the volume of Merle's voice brought me back to the here and now. She was looking away from me, across the bus, out of the window on the other side. Following her gaze, I saw a wide sweep of bay and a forest of masts. A huge ship, painted gray, was making its way toward the docks up a wide channel of water. Houses covered the hill that rose up from the waterfront. Falmouth was bigger than I'd imagined.

"Can you see that gap in the houses—over there?" Merle pointed to a place where there were no roofs, just the jagged remains of walls. "That used to be Lister Street. Thirty people died when it was bombed."

The bus wound its way through narrow streets with shops and houses painted in pastel colors. A man in a Royal Navy uniform with a pint glass in his hand glanced up at us from the doorway of the Star and Garter pub. More men, in uniforms I didn't recognize, were gathered outside the Dolphin.

"Americans," Merle whispered. "They've only just arrived in Cornwall."

I nodded. "The Land Girls told me."

We passed a building with sandbags piled around the walls. "What's that place?" I asked.

"The hospital," Merle replied.

I remembered what Dr. Williams had said about it being a waste that I was doing farmwork. Jack had told me I could save more lives working for Churchill's secret army than being a nurse. Was that true? I wondered. I'd patched up four men on that mission to France. It didn't seem much, compared to what I might have done in a hospital ward. But I knew that wasn't what Jack had meant. It was impossible to gauge the impact of those four men going back into active service.

"Do you wish you were working there, instead of for us?" Merle had read my thoughts. She'd dropped her voice to a whisper, mindful of the other people on the bus.

I hesitated before replying. "I'd like to work in a hospital again one day," I said. "But if you and Jack think the other work is more important, I'm glad to be doing it."

"It's not just important—it's vital," Merle murmured. The bus came to a stop and she stood up. "This is where we get off."

We stepped out into a wide avenue of pale brown buildings that reminded me of Grafton Street in Dublin. As Merle led me across the road, away from the alighting passengers, she said: "I couldn't tell you on the bus, but those people you dropped off—and the ones you'll take next month—they're preparing the way." She glanced over her shoulder. "The Americans are getting ready to launch a major offensive. The success of that operation will largely depend on the people we have in France gearing up the Resistance. That's why we're so desperate to get them over there."

I nodded as I took in what she was saying. That explained why American soldiers had set up a base in this area. They were gathering as near as possible to the coast for an attack by sea. "When will that happen?" I whispered.

"No one knows. It'll be determined by what happens on the eastern front, as well as the strength of the Resistance in France."

I thought about the agents we'd taken to Brittany. Miranda, Ferdinand, and the others. I asked Merle where they would have been taken when I'd left them.

"To a safe house inland," she replied. "Although *safe* isn't a very good word. The places they stay in are constantly being raided. They have a fifty-fifty chance of coming back alive."

"Do they know that?"

"Yes. We couldn't expect them to do what they're doing unless they knew the risks." She paused as a man walking a dog came to a halt a few feet in front of us. She pulled me into a shop doorway and started talking about the balls of wool arranged in a pyramid in the window. When the man moved on, she said, "All of this is top secret—you mustn't breathe a word to anyone."

A moment later, Merle was back in the persona of a mother whose only concern was trawling the shops for what she needed for her children. It was as if the conversation we'd had about the war had never happened. She took me to a store that sold blankets and suggested that I buy one to have made into a coat. Then she found a place that had rolls of printed cotton that the assistant said had just arrived from India. She explained how many coupons I was permitted to use from my ration book, and we bought enough fabric to make me a dress.

I should have savored the experience of buying things on what was my first shopping trip in years. But my heart wasn't in it. I couldn't stop thinking about the photograph in the bureau at Penheligan. It was as if I'd found a little piece of Jack's soul hidden away in that envelope.

Chapter 15

Jack came back a week after my trip to Falmouth. He emerged from the trees, Brock at his heels, as I was going to fetch water from the stream.

"Alice!" His voice had a treacherous effect on my body. It unleashed a powerful surge of pure joy, instantly tainted with dark swirls of jealousy.

"Hello," I called back. "How was London?" I tried to sound casual, carefree, but the way it came out wouldn't even have deceived a child.

"Depressing," he replied. "It's good to be back. Have you had breakfast yet?"

I shook my head.

"Good." He shrugged off his knapsack. "I have bacon and sausages. We might have to share them with Brock, though. He hardly touched his food in London. It's as if he could smell the fear."

I bent down to stroke the dog's fur. It felt warm and silky soft, not yet matted with salt water and sand, as it would be after a few minutes of frolicking on the beach. I didn't ask why or how we were having bacon *and* sausages for breakfast. It seemed terribly extravagant. But I didn't want to cast a cloud over his good humor. He'd sought me out and he'd brought me something special. For that I was happy, despite the warning voices in my head.

"I thought you might like to know how those men are," he said when we were sitting on the beach, eating with our fingers. "They arrived in London a few days after me—all in good shape. They'll be back in action by the time we do our next run." He broke off a chunk of sausage and tossed it to Brock, who caught it between his teeth before it could fall onto the sand. "They asked me to pass on their thanks. You did a terrific job in difficult circumstances."

"I'm glad they've all recovered," I replied, "but I don't like to think of them having to go back to what they were doing."

He glanced up from his plate, a forkful of food suspended on its way to his mouth. "You wouldn't say that if you'd seen what I saw in London. The Germans dropped a bomb on a school. According to the news reports, it was deliberate—not accidental. It cut the building in half. The children were having their lunch when it fell. Thirty-eight of them were killed, and six teachers."

The piece of bacon in my mouth suddenly felt like cardboard. A *school*. What kind of wickedness made men drop bombs on children?

"Those men we rescued are pilots," he went on. "So many have been lost. We need every single one of them if we're going to win this war."

I picked up what remained on my plate and offered it to Brock. "What if they get shot down again?"

"Then we'll do our best to rescue them. If anything, coming so close to being captured makes them even keener to get back out there—they've seen firsthand what it's like to live under German occupation."

Something flickered in his eyes as he said it. I wondered if he was thinking of what the injured airmen had been through in France, or whether his mind had leapfrogged to another place. Was he thinking about the girl in the photograph? No doubt people on Guernsey were experiencing the same kind of treatment the Germans were meting out to the French. If Morwenna was trapped on the island, Jack would have no way of knowing what had become of her.

I'd heard enough horror stories about the Great War when I was at the Institute of Tropical Medicine in Belgium to know that it was not only men who were victimized when soldiers invaded. Some of the older nuns at the convent where I lived in Brussels had harrowing memories of being made to strip naked by German troops who accused them of being spies. Baseless charges, they said: the only purpose was humiliation—but they counted themselves lucky not to have been raped.

No wonder Jack sometimes looked as if he were carrying the weight of the world on his shoulders. If what I suspected was true—if he'd spirited Morwenna off to Guernsey to avoid a scandal—he must be racked with guilt at having to leave her to the mercy of the Nazis.

Listen to me, Sister Anthony: the tighter you pull those strings, the better you will restrain the imagination.

The voice of Sister Margarita rang through my head, transporting me back to the novices' robing room in Dublin, where I had first put on the hated skullcap. It was as if, because I no longer wore it, my mind had lost the discipline of rational thinking. I told myself that I had no concrete evidence to support my wild theory of Jack fathering an illegitimate child with the girl Leo Badger had seen him with one summer, years ago. The baby in the photograph could be anyone's child. I didn't know for certain that the girl was Morwenna—or that the snapshot had been sent from Guernsey. For all I knew, Jack could simply have used an old envelope to store the photo. And as for Ned being the child, surely that was venturing into the realm of fantasy.

"I suppose you're thinking about the agents we dropped?" Jack's question was so far from what had been in my mind that it took me by surprise.

"I . . . yes . . . I was." I avoided his eyes as the lie came stumbling out. "Have you heard from them?"

"They all got through." He nodded. "And everything they took out with them has been safely delivered. But that creates a problem for us."

"Why?"

"They took radio parts as well as ammunition and medical supplies. That means the Brittany Resistance teams now have fourteen working radio sets instead of the half dozen they had before." He looked at me. There was nothing haunted in his eyes now. What I saw was a determined gleam. "Merle needs help translating the messages. She doesn't have enough time, with the children to look after. We're drafting in another woman from the village to relieve her of the cooking. But I'd like your help with the radio work."

I held his gaze, beyond being surprised by anything he asked me to do. "Well, yes, of course," I said. "If someone teaches me what to do."

"It'll take time to pick it up," he said. "I've brought you a set of the codebooks we use." He reached into his knapsack. "You'll need to learn Morse code first. That's this one." He passed me the thinner of the two books. "The ciphers are in here." He held the other one out to me. "There are two ways of interpreting messages: most of the time you'll be translating straightforward coded phrases—but sometimes you'll receive sentences that sound like nonsense. You'll get something like 'I love Siamese cats,' or 'Granny has eaten all the chocolates.' They convey something quite specific, for the sake of speed, such as a warning about enemy troops in a drop area, or an imminent raid on a safe house."

I opened the Morse code book. That seemed straightforward enough, patterns of dots and dashes alongside each letter of the alphabet. The cipher book looked more intimidating—it was thicker than the family Bible at the house in Dublin.

"Merle will show you how to use the transmitter." He stood up. "You're most likely to be needed in the early evenings, when she's busy with the children. I hope you won't mind—I know you're already putting in long days."

"It's not as if I have anything else to do." I hadn't meant for it to come out sounding like a complaint. I enjoyed the solitude of the boathouse. I loved walking back there, enveloped in the lush tranquility of the valley, knowing that I could spend the evening ahead reading one of the books I'd borrowed from the house, or just lie outside on a blanket, looking at the stars. It was a freedom that most people took for granted, but for me it was still new and very precious.

"I'm sorry," he said. "It can't be much fun for you, down here all alone."

"Oh, no, I'm fine, honestly," I said. "I like it—really I do."

"Hmm." He rubbed his knuckles against his chin. I noticed how smooth his skin was, not bristling with stubble as it had been when I'd last seen him. After a moment he said, "I suppose you've heard about the dance the Americans are putting on?"

I nodded. "The Land Girls can't stop talking about it."

"Would you like to go?"

"Me?"

"Why not? They've sent an invitation—to 'His Highness, Viscount Trewella.' Nice of the US Army to elevate me to royal status." He smiled. "And it would be natural to take my cousin along. 'The Honorable Alice McBride'—how does that sound?"

"It's very kind of you, but—"

"Oh, Alice," he cut in. "You always think people act from the best motives. Kindness has nothing to do with it. The truth is I'd rather not go, but if I don't, it'll look as if I'm snubbing our allies, which I certainly don't want to do." He shrugged. "It might be just about bearable with you on my arm."

I wasn't sure what to make of that. Was he afraid of being mobbed by the likes of Edith and Rita? Did he think that going with me would help him keep them at bay? I fingered a wisp of hair that protruded from my scarf, wondering how on earth I could make myself look presentable. What I wanted to say was that I couldn't possibly go to a dance. Not looking like this. But that would sound terribly vain.

That night I stayed up late, trying to memorize the alphabet in Morse code. But I found it hard to concentrate. Staring at the rows of dots and dashes, my mind kept drifting to the dance. It was two weeks away. My hair would grow a little longer in that time. I thought about asking Merle for advice about how to style it.

The thought of going to what the Land Girls clearly regarded as the social event of the year filled me with a mixture of excitement and terror. It had been so long since I'd been dancing. I wasn't sure if I'd remember how to do it. And the dances were bound to have changed since my brief foray into the ballrooms of Dublin. I was seriously worried about making a fool of myself.

I wondered if Jack knew what he was letting himself in for, asking someone like me as his guest. But I was coming to realize that he never did anything without first weighing the consequences. For him, there always seemed to be an ulterior motive. It wasn't as if he pretended otherwise. He'd warned me more than once not to mistake his apparent generosity for kindness. And he'd made it clear that I'd only been invited to the dance to make things less socially awkward for him.

But those words he'd used—about it being just about bearable with me on his arm—suggested that he did at least enjoy my company. And on the boat, coming back from France, he'd said that he was glad I was no longer a nun. What was I supposed to make of comments like that? Did he feel more for me than he wanted to admit?

Trust in the Lord with all your heart and lean not on your own understanding. A line from the book of Proverbs elbowed its way through the muddle of thoughts in my head. Chapter 3, verse 5 had been drummed into me as a novice, along with the next verse: *In all your ways submit to him, and he will make your paths straight.* That was the trouble. I'd stopped submitting to God in all my ways when I'd made the decision not to go back to the convent. Was this bewildering longing for Jack beckoning me down the right path or the wrong one?

I recalled the moment in the boathouse when I'd suddenly realized that I could cast off my old identity if I chose to. I hadn't given up the religious life to get something for myself. I'd done it to break free from the burden my vocation had become, in the hope of leading a more honest life.

Sister Clare's face appeared in my head—her eyes clouded with suspicion. I could imagine her questions, if I'd had to justify it to her: Would I have made the same decision if someone other than Jack had rescued me? Had I, even then, been subconsciously drawn to him? And if the answer was yes, how could I possibly claim that leaving the order was what God wanted?

Lean not on your own understanding. I'd never doubted the wisdom of those words. But I wasn't sure that they could help me now.

Chapter 16

I spent the next two evenings up at the house, shadowing Merle as she sent and received messages. She explained that Penheligan was the radio base for communicating with two of the many Resistance cells now operating in France. One was in northern Brittany and the other in the south area of the region—code-named Team Felix and Team Frederick. The radio operators within both teams each had their own unique "key"—a prefix to any message that came in that immediately identified the sender and made it clear that what followed was genuine and not something the Germans had put out.

On the first evening she went through these identifying codes with me. "If ever you get a message with *these* letters at the start, you must come and find me." She pointed to a place at the top of the second page of the cipher book. "It means that the sender has been captured, and anything that follows could be false information."

After that she gave me old messages, in Morse code, to transcribe for practice. I had to write out the letters, decode them using one of the ciphers, then translate the message from French to English. On the second evening, while I was scribbling away, I heard a noise overhead—what sounded like the scrape of a chair on a wooden floor. Merle saw me glance up.

"They're having a meeting in the maids' sitting room," she said. "I hope they won't make too much noise—it's right underneath the boys' bedroom."

I thought of how odd it sounded, this juxtaposition of the old way of things with what went on at Penheligan nowadays. The activity overhead was a reminder of the secret life of the house, of people I rarely encountered, who came and went, slept in the beds for a few nights, and were spirited away before anyone working outside caught a glimpse of them. Some, I knew, were agents in training, destined to be parachuted into France, or to go in by boat with Jack and me.

I wondered if Jack was the only instructor, or whether there were others. Surely, he couldn't do all that single-handed, as well as running the farm? I stared at the jumble of letters in front of me. There was so much about him that I didn't know.

A sudden bleeping from the transmitter cut across my thoughts. Merle frowned as she scribbled down the characters.

"What is it?"

"That prefix I was telling you about." She was still writing as she spoke. "It's from Team Felix. There must have been a raid."

I thought of Miranda and the men I'd last seen disappearing into the sand dunes. I didn't know which of the Resistance groups they'd joined. Would any of them have been caught up in the attack? I wondered if Merle would have any way of finding out.

"What will you do?" I asked.

"Send a message back—something completely neutral that won't alert the Germans to the fact we know what's happened." She bit the end of the pencil in her hand. "I hope to God they haven't got their hands on the codebooks. If they have, we won't be able to communicate with anyone until we can get a new set out to France."

"You'd have to start from scratch? With new codes?"

"Yes."

The machine began to bleep again. Merle's pencil flew to the pad of paper. She was standing on the other side of the desk from me. I could read what she was writing down, even though it was upside down. The message said: *"C'est la saison des vendanges."*

"It's time to harvest the grapes?" I glanced up at her, uncomprehending.

She blew out a breath. "That means the books are safe. The Germans will only get the radio."

"And the operator?"

"Yes." She looked away. Clearly this was something she'd had to learn to deal with—the trauma of knowing that the message she'd just written down was probably the last thing the person sending it would do before they were executed.

On the third evening I was on my own. Merle's mood had been gloomy as she'd prepared me for my shift. Details had come through of two more raids on Resistance houses in Brittany. That meant that three of the precious transmitters we'd delivered to France had been taken in the space of a fortnight. Far worse was the news that six people had been killed during the attacks and two were missing, probably being held prisoner.

Five of those killed were local people, Bretons who had put their lives on the line by joining the Resistance. One of them was a woman—a teacher, Merle told me, who was only twenty-three years old. One of our own agents had died. Miranda was one of the two who were missing.

"Do you think she's been arrested?" I knew I shouldn't ask, that the answer was likely to haunt my dreams, but I couldn't help myself.

"That's the most likely explanation. They've probably sent her to one of the prison camps." Merle was fiddling with the handset, not looking at me.

"But she could have escaped, couldn't she? The Germans might not have realized she's one of ours."

"That's possible." Merle nodded. "There have been agents who have escaped."

"But you don't think it's likely?"

"I think it'll be a miracle if she's still alive. The agents know what's in store for them if they're captured. They probably didn't tell you—they're given suicide pills, concealed in their clothes."

I thought of Miranda, laughing as she'd told me about the childhood visits to her father's patients putting her off a career in medicine. She'd looked so young.

Please, God, don't let her be dead, or in any kind of pain.

In the light of what Merle had said, it seemed a forlorn prayer.

"I have to go now." Merle put down the handset. "You'll be all right, won't you?"

During my first week I didn't move more than a few inches from the transmitter. I was terrified of missing something, or of not getting a message down fast enough. But as the days went on, I became more confident. The situation in Brittany seemed to have calmed down somewhat. There was no more news of raids—most of the messages I received were about ammunition supplies or possible sites for airdrops. Each time the machine bleeped into life, I hoped for word of the missing agent Miranda. But no one I communicated with had any idea what had become of her.

The next Monday, Merle wanted me to do a double shift. "I wouldn't ask," she said, "but it's the Cuckoo Feast."

I looked up from the machine, mystified. "What's that?"

"A festival they have in the village every year," she replied. "It goes back to the Middle Ages."

"They don't *eat* cuckoos, surely?"

She laughed. "No. The children know the story behind it—they learnt about it in school: Some ancient farmer was making a fire and he put a tree stump onto it. When the flames started to take hold, a cuckoo flew out of the stump. So now, every May, people round here commemorate it. The children put on a play and there's a picnic afterward. I'd love you to see it, but someone needs to be here."

She showed me the costumes she'd made for the girls. Danielle was the May queen and Jacqueline one of her attendants. The boys were going to be woodland animals—Louis a fox and Ned a hedgehog.

"I'll bring them in to see you when we come home," she said.

"Yes—I'd like that." I picked up the hedgehog costume, imagining Ned's excitement as he put it on. Merle had used sacking with bunches of bristles from old brooms she'd found in one of the farm buildings. She'd made the outfits while listening out for messages—on the same sewing machine I was using to make a dress from the fabric I'd bought in Falmouth, the dress I planned to wear for the dance.

I'd fretted over telling Merle about Jack's invitation. I didn't want to hurt her feelings. I thought that she would probably have liked to go, too, if she'd been invited. But, to my surprise, she hadn't seemed to mind.

"I wouldn't feel like dancing," she said. "It probably sounds mean-spirited, but I couldn't take a whole evening of watching other people having fun."

"You're worried about Fred?"

She nodded. "It's five weeks since his last letter. I think he was in Tunisia. But I don't know if he's all right."

Jack had told me the news of the spectacular defeat of German and Italian forces in North Africa. He hadn't said how many Allied troops had been killed.

"Anyway," Merle said, with a too-bright smile. "How's that dress coming along?"

Jack put his head around the door of the library after Merle had gone. I had the headset on, so I didn't hear him at first.

"I'm off to the village in a minute," he said, when he'd managed to get my attention. "They want me to give out the prizes." He was smiling, but it was a tight smile, as if what he was going to do was a duty, not a pleasure. "Merle's already gone, has she?"

"Yes."

He came and sat down beside me.

"Is anything wrong?" His eyes searched mine.

"No—everything's fine."

"There's something on your mind, though."

This ability of his to pick up on my thoughts was uncanny. I'd been mulling over what Merle had said about Fred, wondering if Jack could pull strings to find out what had happened to him. I'd held back because I wasn't sure whether she'd told him about the man she'd fallen for.

"It's just something Merle said," I replied. I told Jack that she was worried about a former employee from the farm on Guernsey.

"Fred Bechélet?" He rubbed the back of his neck. "I wish I could make some inquiries. But if everyone did that, they'd be swamped."

I nodded. I felt foolish. I should have realized that.

"It's hard for her," he went on. "But I think that having you here has made things much more bearable."

That word again. It made me sound like something you might put on a burn or an insect bite, a salve that would sting at first but was worth putting up with. Was that how he saw me?

"There's something I need to talk to you about before I go." He rubbed his chin with his knuckles. He was looking at the Morse code machine, not at me. "I've had a call from the people in London. They have you in mind for something different next time we go to France—something that would involve going ashore."

"What do they want me to do?" I felt a tremor in my stomach, the same panicky feeling I'd had when I'd been rowing the men back to *La Coquille*.

"They want you to act as a courier—take equipment to the Resistance: the kind of thing we can't parachute in. There's a shortage of women, you see, and it has to be a woman."

"Why?"

"The Germans are getting wise to what we're doing. They're routinely searching any man who passes through the checkpoints—however convincing a French accent they have. Women attract less attention than men, and with your background, you'd be particularly convincing." He paused, his middle finger tracing a mark on the table, a ring made by a carelessly placed wineglass. "They want you to go into France as a nun."

I stared at his hand as it circled. For a moment, I was too stunned to speak. It was like some cruel joke. Asking me to become the person I'd ceased to be to fool the enemy. But the logical side of my brain saw that the idea was quite brilliant: Who better than an ex-nun to carry off such an audacious stunt?

"I was dreading telling you." Jack's mind was running in the same channel as mine. "I can only imagine how it would feel, getting into those clothes again."

"It would be very . . . strange."

"You can say no, of course. It's much riskier than what you did last time."

"What exactly would I have to do?"

"Well, you'd do the pickup from the beach, then row back alone, to the harbor upriver at Lannion, with the equipment. There's a convent in the town. They'd fix you up with the nun's habit, and a bicycle. The stuff would be hidden under your robe. In the morning you'd cycle to a rendezvous point in the countryside. We'd be waiting offshore to pick you up, once it got dark."

"How would I know where to go?"

"You'd have a map. They print them on silk: you conceal it in the lining of your clothes." He looked up from the table. A ray of sunshine caught his eyes, lighting up the flecks of amber and gold in the brown irises. There was something in the look he gave me—a fleeting impression of pent-up emotion, of feelings he couldn't express. "You'll be taking radio parts: new transmitters for the sets that have been smashed up. And something else."

"What?"

"Explosives. The Resistance is planning to blow up roads and bridges to disrupt the German supply lines." He paused, watching me intently. "As I said, you don't have to do it."

"But someone has to." I held his gaze. "And if there are no other women, it would have to be a man. And that man would almost certainly be caught and probably shot on the spot." I could see my face reflected in his eyes. It felt as if I were glimpsing the future, my life as it would be in a fortnight's time. My life. And, quite possibly, my death.

It was a quiet afternoon for messages. Most of the Resistance people led apparently ordinary lives during the day—working on farms, in offices, or in schools—and it was in the evenings that they became active as freedom fighters. In the first couple of hours I translated only two requests, one for fresh supplies of ammunition and another for wound dressings.

When the machine fell silent, I went to sit by the window. I threaded cotton into a needle and set about sewing a tricky pleat into the front panel of the dress I was making. It seemed a ridiculous thing to be doing in light of the conversation I'd just had with Jack. But it stopped me from thinking about what I'd agreed to take on, focused my mind in a way that shut out the terrifying images his words had conjured.

I'd only sewn a couple of stitches when I heard a tremendous thud. I jumped out of my chair as a row of books came tumbling off a shelf near where I'd been sitting. My first instinct was to run out of the room, into the great hall. I stood there for a moment, wondering if anyone else in the house had heard anything. No one appeared.

I made my way down the passage to the kitchen, thinking that perhaps the gas range had blown up. When I opened the door, the room was empty and undisturbed. Molly and the other woman who helped with the cooking had gone back to the village for the Cuckoo Feast.

I ran outside, wondering if the noise had come from one of the farm buildings. I went into the milking shed—deserted at this time of the day—and then into the one where the tractors were kept. I was about to go back into the house when I caught sight of Merle running up the path from the village. She was holding Jacqueline's hand, tugging the child along. Jacqueline's white dress was torn and stained. Jacqueline had her free hand up to her eyes, as if she was crying. Behind them I glimpsed Danielle, who was dragging Louis up the hill. Both looked as if they'd been rolling about in mud.

I ran over to them. "What on earth's happened?"

"A bomb fell on the field behind the school," Merle gasped. "No one's hurt, thank God."

"We saw the plane coming," Louis piped up. He looked more excited than frightened. His fox head had fallen forward, hanging under his chin like a red beard. "There was a Spitfire chasing it."

"Where's Ned?"

Merle put her hand to her chest, too out of breath to speak.

"He ran off." Danielle spoke for her. "Lordy's gone looking for him."

"We all dived for cover," Merle panted. "It was total chaos. We didn't realize he was missing until Mrs. Graham did a head count of the children."

"Where would he go?"

"I'm not sure—we thought he might have gone back into the school, but he wasn't there, was he?" She looked at Danielle, who shook her head.

"The tide's out," Louis said. "He might have gone to the boathouse, Miss Alice, looking for you."

"I'll go and look for him."

"No," Merle said, catching my arm. "He'll be somewhere safe, I'm sure. Probably in one of the houses in the village. If you go, we might miss something." She glanced toward the house.

I didn't know what to do. What if he wasn't in the village? What if he'd wandered off in the confusion and got himself lost? I couldn't bear the thought of him being alone and afraid.

"Just look after things for a few minutes, while I get the children settled." Merle guided me up the steps to the house. "If he's not back here by then, I'll take over in the library."

An hour later I was on the path down through the valley, straining my ears for any sound that might betray the whereabouts of a small, lost child. When I reached the church, I went up and down the graveyard, looking behind tombstones and up into the trees, in case Ned was hiding there. Then I went into the church itself. It was a rather forbidding place for a child to enter alone. I thought it very unlikely that he'd choose it for a refuge, but I searched the place anyway—even the little room behind the pulpit where the bell ropes hung.

When I came out into the sunshine, I stood for a moment, listening. A magpie was rattling away in one of the ancient yew trees. When it stopped, all I could hear was the whispering rush of the stream that trickled through the trees on its way to the cove. Then I thought I heard something else. Something human. Not words, something more like a cough or a burst of laughter. It sounded like an adult—not a small child. It was coming from beyond the church, somewhere in the tangle of shrubs and trees, away from the path. I ran across the graveyard, almost tripping over a toppled tombstone half-hidden in the grass. I scrambled over the wall, and as I landed in the pile of leaf mold on the other side, I heard a familiar voice, singing.

"Row, row, row your boat. Gently down the stream . . ."

Through the foliage I spotted Jack's face in profile. On his back was what looked like a giant pine cone. My brain leapfrogged the message my eyes were sending. With a surge of joy, I realized that it was Ned, dressed as a hedgehog. Jack had one hand around two little ankles that stuck out from under the sacking hem of the costume. Ned was holding on to Jack's head. I could see his fingers moving, rubbing Jack's hair as if it were a biddable pony, not a person, carrying him. As I got closer, I saw Ned's body quiver, as if he was sobbing silently. I could just see his nose and chin protruding from the hood of the costume. In the moment before he saw me coming, Jack reached up and felt for Ned's face.

"Soon be home, little chap." He cupped the child's swaying head in his hand. "There's nothing to be frightened of. I've got you now."

The expression in Jack's eyes was intense—gentle but ferocious— words that shouldn't go together, but somehow did. I'd encountered something similar when I was in Africa, in the maternity ward at the mission hospital. I'd seen it in the faces of the women when they held their babies for the first time.

"Alice!" He'd seen me. In a flash he heaved the drowsy child off his shoulders and set him down on the ground. Ned blinked up at me from beneath a small forest of bristles. His eyes were red and swollen. Green caterpillars of snot oozed from his nostrils.

"Thank goodness you're safe!" I bobbed down and wiped Ned's nose. "Where did you find him?" I glanced up at Jack, who looked as if he were chewing on a wasp.

"In the summerhouse." He jerked his head back over his left shoulder. Through the trees I could just see the moss-covered thatch of the little hut where he'd taken me for target practice before we went to Brittany.

"Oh, Ned! Why did you run away?"

"I s . . . seed a plane." He drew the back of his hand across his eyes. "Louis says if it goes bang, I got to run."

"I'd better get you back to the house." The way Jack spoke to Ned was quite different from when he'd been carrying him on his shoulders. He sounded brisk and businesslike, as if the child were a stray animal that he'd rounded up. He gave the boy a little prod. I wondered why he didn't pick him up. Ned could hardly put one foot in front of the other.

"I'll carry him, if you're tired," I said.

"If he's not too heavy for you." He nodded. "I'll go on ahead—let them know he's been found."

I got the distinct impression that Jack was the one running away now.

Much later, when the sun was going down, Jack came by with Brock. He told me that the German plane that had dropped the bomb on the field had been shot down by the Spitfire Louis had seen chasing it out to sea. He didn't mention Ned until I asked him about the search.

"How did you know he'd go to the summerhouse?"

"It was my den when I was a boy." He shrugged. "Somewhere *I* used to go and hide."

"He's such a sensitive little soul," I said. "It must be so hard for him, hearing the others call Merle 'Mummy.' He must wonder what's happened to his own parents." I was aware that I was venturing into dangerous territory. But I couldn't forget the look I'd seen in Jack's eyes when he was carrying Ned through the woods.

"Merle told you how he came to be here?" He bent down to ruffle Brock's fur, avoiding my eyes.

"She told me that a man approached you on the quayside on Guernsey. She said he begged you to take Ned because his wife was in hospital."

Jack nodded. "But you don't believe that."

The silence hung in the air like dust motes. It was as if he'd peeled back my eyes and looked inside my head. I felt as if I were back in the convent, caught unawares, not certain which rule I had broken.

"You *know*, don't you?" His voice was almost a whisper. "I saw it in your face when you came through the trees." He looked up, straight at me. "I don't know *how* you know. But you do."

My body reacted before my brain had fully grasped what he was saying. Gravity went into reverse, my stomach lurching toward my chest. He was telling me that what I'd tried *not* to believe was true. Morwenna wasn't just a girlfriend he'd loved and lost. She was the mother of his child. Ned was his son.

"I . . . I found a photograph," I mumbled.

He searched my face, his dark eyes glinting silver in the fading light. It was like watching a thunderstorm, waiting for the explosion. "Where?"

"In the bureau in the library." I tried to swallow but my mouth was so dry I couldn't. "I wasn't prying, I promise. It was before I started the radio work. Merle had sent me to fetch stamps." My voice was croaky. I coughed and tried again. "When I couldn't find them in the pigeon-holes, I spotted a drawer. It wouldn't shift at first. Then it shot open. There was an envelope inside."

I thought he'd be furious that I'd opened what had clearly been a private letter, addressed to him. But he said nothing. Just went on watching me.

"I guessed who the girl was," I continued. "Leo Badger had told me about her—her name, and what she looked like."

A flicker of something creased the skin between his eyebrows. A mixture of surprise and indignation. I realized that I'd fanned the flames, letting out that people had been gossiping about him.

"When I saw the baby's name, and the date, I . . ." I faltered. "I'm sorry. It was none of my business. I shouldn't have looked inside the envelope."

He closed his eyes and drew in a breath. "I shouldn't have left it there. It was careless. And it was naïve of me to think that people in the village wouldn't know about her." His eyes snapped open. "What exactly did Leo Badger say?"

"Well, he . . ." I hesitated. I felt bad about revealing the source of the gossip. I hoped it wouldn't have repercussions for Leo. "He only mentioned her because he saw a resemblance with me," I replied. "I almost laughed when he said it—even with my scarf on, I look as if I've had an argument with a sheepshearer—but according to him, I have the same eyes and the same 'fairy look,' as he put it."

"Hmm. Did he say where he'd seen her?"

"On your boat. He'd spotted you together when he was out fishing." I didn't want to humiliate him by repeating Leo's actual words. "He told me she worked as a maid in a village along the coast—and that a maid wasn't the sort of girl someone like you would be expected to marry. I asked what had happened to her, and he said she'd gone away, to work in Devon, he thought."

He shook his head. "I wish to God she had," he murmured.

"Because Guernsey was invaded?"

He looked at me strangely, as if I'd said something nonsensical. "No," he said, "she wasn't there when the Germans came."

"She wasn't in hospital?"

He brought his hands up to his face, pressing his fingertips against his forehead. "Morwenna died, Alice."

"Oh, Jack . . . I . . ." The words caught in my throat.

"She disappeared when she found out she was pregnant. I didn't know she was expecting a baby—I just assumed she'd had enough of me. We hadn't known each other very long. I met her one day when I was out fishing. She came swimming out from the beach at Porthleven." He heaved out a sigh. "I'd gone out in the boat to escape what was going on at home. The family finances were at their lowest ebb, and my father had just been diagnosed with cancer. Morwenna drove the dark thoughts away. She dived under the boat and tugged the fishing line so hard I thought I'd hooked a whopper. Then she came up, laughing, and climbed aboard. We met as often as we could after that. But after a couple of months she vanished. I made inquiries at the place where she worked. They had no idea where she'd gone.

"Then a letter came, out of the blue. It was nearly two years later. And out fell that photograph." He went silent, as still as a statue, his fingers glued to his forehead, as if the memory had paralyzed him. Then he said: "She wrote that Ned was mine, and that she hadn't told me because she knew I couldn't marry her. She said she'd gone to Guernsey because a friend of hers worked in one of the hotels on the island. Morwenna got a job there, too. But with the war, the work had dried up. She said she needed money."

"What did you do?"

"I said I'd give her what she wanted if I could see our baby. I sailed over to the island on *Firefly*. She was waiting for me at the harbor, with Phyllis, her friend. When I'd seen Ned, Morwenna said she needed to talk. Phyllis said she'd take him for a walk while we went out to the boat." He shook his head slowly. "It was low tide, so I'd anchored *Firefly* to a buoy out beyond the harbor. When we got into the tender, the wind was picking up. By the time we reached the boat, there was a swell running. I climbed out first, so I could help her up. But she slipped on the ladder."

My hand went to my mouth. "That was how she died?"

His head dipped. It was an almost imperceptible nod—as if, even now, he found it hard to acknowledge what had happened. "I dived in after her, but I couldn't see her. The water was murky—and it was so cold. I couldn't swim against the swell. I had to give up."

His fingers parted. I saw that his eyes were glassy with tears. What he'd told me was too shocking for words. It brought back all the horror of the attack on the *Brabantia*—the panic and the fear as the water pulled me under. I could imagine Jack's desperation as he plunged beneath the waves, the blind terror of flailing about, unable to save her.

"The lifeboat went out looking for her. They searched for days. But her body was never found. After a week they told me to go home."

"What about Ned? What happened to him?"

"I should have taken him with me, but I panicked. I couldn't stomach trying to explain it all to my father. I paid Phyllis the money I was going to give to Morwenna—asked her to look after him until I'd worked out what to do. Then, a month later, the call came to evacuate all the children from the island." He raked his fingers through his hair. "It was the perfect cover. I could bring him back to Penheligan. There was no need for anyone to know the truth."

I remembered what Merle had said about the chaos in St. Peter Port on the day she left. It suddenly occurred to me that she might have been aware of what Jack was doing but had told me the version he had invented. "What about Merle?" I asked. "Does she know?"

He shook his head. "I sometimes wonder if she suspects. But she's terribly loyal—she's never said anything. She gets an allowance for looking after Ned. I told her it had to come via me, from the government fund for evacuees, and she's never questioned that."

"But what about Ned? Doesn't he *need* to know?"

"Yes—one day. But he's too young to be troubled by it now."

I wasn't sure about that. I thought of the time in the woods when Ned had asked me if I'd be his mummy. The child was desperate for parents of his own.

"It's hard to think of the future," Jack went on. "With this war, nobody can. When I went back to Guernsey that June of 1940, the only thing on my mind was to bring him somewhere safe."

"Wouldn't it have been easier for everyone if you'd admitted he was your son? It must be so hard, having to keep up the pretense." I stopped short of saying what I felt in my heart: that Jack was denying himself and Ned the love that had flickered into life in that moment in the valley.

"Easier?" His face changed. His eyes had a distant look, like a sleep-walker. "You know, Alice, when I found you on the beach, and you told me you wanted to leave your old life behind, I envied you. Three years ago, I could have done something similar. When Morwenna died I thought of sailing away with Ned and never coming back. But I didn't have the guts. I couldn't do it to my father. It meant everything to him—the house, the estate, our standing in the community."

"But when your father died, couldn't you have come clean about Ned?"

"I made a promise to him on his deathbed—that I'd never do anything that would bring shame on the family name." There was such sadness in his voice. I saw now why he wore his title so lightly, why he preferred to be called "Jack" and not "sir" or "my lord." He hadn't wanted it. It had shackled him. And now it was blighting Ned's life, too.

"You must think me the worst kind of hypocrite," he said. "Going to church on Sundays, putting on a show of respectability."

"I know how that feels," I replied. "I was a hypocrite for years. I clung on to the order, even when I knew I could never be what they wanted me to be. If it hadn't been for the shipwreck, I don't think I'd have had the courage to leave."

"You're very honest, Alice. That's why I had to talk to you. You don't like lies. Pretense doesn't come easily to you. But I've come to beg you to keep my secret."

I felt as a priest must feel on the other side of the confessional. But what he'd revealed wasn't going to be remedied by three Hail Marys and a few Our Fathers. I wanted to reason with him, to impress on him how much more important his son was than any amount of wealth or privilege. But I sensed that he already knew that, and that anything I said would simply aggravate his sense of guilt and make him turn away from me. For Ned's sake, I must bite my tongue. Until I had the chance to do . . . what?

I want to do some good in the world.

The words I'd come out with the day after I'd met Jack sounded hopelessly naïve to me now. What did "doing good" mean in a situation like this? Was there anything in the Bible about it? Any words of wisdom from Jesus or the disciples? Something floated into my head:

Above all, hold unfailing your love for one another, since love covers a multitude of sins.

I couldn't remember where that came from. Somewhere in the New Testament. One of the Epistles—James, maybe, or Peter.

Love. That word had so many shades of meaning. One thing that had been made very clear to me as a nun was that loving someone didn't mean turning a blind eye when they did something wrong. And what Jack was doing, what he was asking me to keep hidden, was, undeniably, wrong. The thought of Ned longing for the love of a parent—with Jack living alongside him, refusing to reach out to him—was heartbreaking.

The feelings Jack had stirred in me should have withered just thinking of that. But they were still there. I knew very well that no matter what I told myself, the next time he came to the boathouse, the very sound of his footsteps would set my pulse racing. Was it possible to subdue that longing?

With God's help, you could.

That was what Sister Clare would say. But in my heart, I knew I wasn't going to ask for that kind of help. Like a starfish that loses one of its arms, part of myself had been amputated when I left the order. What had grown in its place might look the same—but it was entirely new. And the new part of me didn't want the longing to stop.

Chapter 17

I felt more alone in the days that followed than at any time since my arrival in Cornwall. I didn't feel able to talk to Merle about the plan to send me into France as a courier. I knew that she would have been told, but discussing it with her would only have intensified my trepidation. And I couldn't confide any of what Jack had told me about Ned. It was so hard, seeing the little lad trailing after the other children—sometimes happy in his make-believe world of gas-mask monsters and mice-chasing owls, but often close to tears because of some spiteful taunt from Louis. Merle simply didn't have the time to give him the attention he craved.

I took him off to play a couple of times after school and made us picnics to eat on our own on the beach, or in his den, the old summerhouse. But I was careful not to do it too often. I didn't want Jack to know that I was giving Ned special treatment, that I was trying to compensate for what he wasn't doing.

I spent most evenings up at the house. Usually I was in the library, listening for messages, but sometimes I went up to the attic to put the children to bed while Merle stayed downstairs. Often, when I was up there, I would hear voices drifting up from the rooms below. The house was filling up again. I wondered what kind of people were preparing to put their lives on the line in Brittany, whether they had wives, husbands, sweethearts, children. Knowing that I was going to be responsible for getting some of them safely onto French soil weighed just as heavily on me as the thought of going ashore myself.

The children were a welcome diversion. Danielle was old enough to look after herself, but the others liked to be tucked in and have a story read to them before they went to sleep. They had only one book—a hardback compendium of fairy tales with a dog-eared cover. It had come from the library downstairs and had Jack's name written on the front page. Some of the stories were quite gruesome. I wasn't sure they were suitable—especially for Ned—but Louis assured me they'd heard every one of them many times before.

I loved the expressions on their faces as the story unfolded. And when it was over, I'd stand in the doorway, watching them as they drifted off to sleep. But those evenings were bittersweet. They brought home the stark reality that, in a few days' time, I would be far away from this comforting domesticity, in the middle of a war zone. And it brought something else to the surface—the deep-rooted ache of poignant memories, of keeping vigil beside the cot shared by the twins I'd left behind in Africa.

Kamaria and Kenyada had been too young for stories. In the days after they were rescued, we didn't know whether they would live or die. I'd watched them grow into sturdy toddlers, been there when they took their first steps. In a few weeks' time they would be two years old. But I wouldn't be there to see them blow out their birthday candles. Perhaps, when they were older, some other sister would tell them the story of how they were rescued by a nun traveling upriver. I hoped she would leave out the grim facts, that they would grow up blissfully ignorant of the harrowing start they'd had in life. But thinking of that was like picking at a scab. Sister Clare had told me to try to forget them. But I couldn't. It was almost unbearably painful, knowing that I wouldn't be there to see them grow up.

Two days before I was due to leave for France, Merle and I were in the library together. She was trimming my hair—trying to style the uneven growth into something acceptable for the dance, which was to take place that night.

"You mustn't worry about it," she said, as she snipped at a tuft that stuck out above my right ear. "Short styles are very much in vogue now. You're going to look just like—"

The Morse code machine beeped into life before she could finish the sentence. The scissors clattered onto the desk as she went to pick up the headset.

"There's been another raid." In a heartbeat her voice had changed completely. She bit her lip as she wrote the message down. "The Germans attacked a farmhouse near Lannion. A grenade smashed the radio. And another set was confiscated." When she'd finished writing she looked up, her face taut. "Three dead."

She pushed the message across the desk. It was so stark. A few scribbled words, the epitaph of three lives snuffed out. I looked up, reading in her eyes what she couldn't say, that she was thinking of me, soon to head off to the very town where this latest atrocity had happened.

I didn't see Merle again until the evening. She'd gone off to find Jack, to brief him about the latest developments in Brittany. No more messages came through that afternoon. I spent the time putting the finishing touches on my dress and ironing it, so that it would be ready to change into later. It seemed awful, shockingly frivolous, to be going to a dance when people on the other side of the Channel were risking their lives to bring the war to an end. But here in England, life had to go on. People couldn't be blamed for trying to retain some degree of normality—otherwise, things would become unendurable. I told myself that I was only going for Jack's sake, and that he was only going out of a sense of duty. But that didn't dispel the guilt I felt: no matter how I tried to justify it—or how nervous I was—I knew I *wanted* to go.

Putting the children to bed distracted me for a while. They'd been out on Eddie Downing's fishing boat, catching mackerel. Even Ned had managed to bring home two of the silvery creatures in his little tin bucket. He was too tired for a story—he fell asleep with his clothes on. And Louis and Jacqueline dropped off before I'd reached the second page of "Three Billy Goats Gruff."

After checking on Danielle, I tiptoed downstairs and changed into my dress. The cotton fabric still had a faint scent of the spices from the merchant ship that had brought it from India. It was hazelnut brown with white polka dots. The pattern I'd followed had short sleeves and what Merle called a sweetheart neckline. There was a single pleat below the bust to allow the dress to swing out when you danced.

I was standing by one of the windows, watching the sun dip below the apple trees in the orchard, when Merle came back to the library.

"Look at you!" She sighed. "I had a waist like that once!" She opened her handbag and took out a velvet pouch. "I thought you might like to borrow these." She pulled open the drawstring and tipped a pearl necklace and matching bracelet onto the desk. "I was wearing them when I left Guernsey," she said. "I had quite a bit of jewelry in those days—Maurice was a generous man, for all his other faults—but I left most of it behind in the evacuation." She picked up the necklace, running the pearls through her fingers. "I used to like getting dressed up, but . . ." She trailed off as she handed it to me.

There was a mirror above the bureau. As I stood in front of it, fiddling with the clasp of the necklace, I caught Merle's reflection. The wistful look in her eyes made me wonder if she was thinking about Fred. I wished there was something I could do to lift her spirits. Seeing me heading off for an evening out wasn't likely to make her feel better.

When I turned around, she smiled, but her eyes were filmy. I wondered if it was the sight of me in her jewelry, triggering memories she was struggling to suppress—or whether it was the thought of what might happen to me in France.

"You enjoy yourself tonight, do you hear?" She gave me a hug. "Shall I go and tell him that you're ready?"

I shivered as Merle went out into the hall. I wasn't sure if it was the draft or the thought of the evening ahead. When she came back, she said that Jack had gone to bring the Alvis round to the front door, and that I should go and wait on the porch.

It wasn't cold outside. The sky was still light. The sun had beaten down all afternoon, heating the stone walls on either side of the front door. I could feel their warmth through the fabric of my dress as I listened for the crunch of tires on the gravel drive. I'd never heard of an Alvis. The only car I'd traveled in during the past decade was the battered Model T Ford the nuns had used to get to and from the railway station at Elisabethville.

When Jack's car glided into view, I caught my breath. It was a vision of elegance—a two-door convertible with sky-blue bodywork and a dark blue roof. Chrome spoked wheels matched the winged eagle crest on the engine grille, which glinted as Jack pulled up. He jumped out, smiling. He was wearing the same well-cut suit he'd worn to church on Easter Sunday, but with a different tie, sea green this time, with a heraldic design beneath the knot. I recognized it at once; it was the same device I'd seen on the gate to the walled garden and engraved in the stone arch over the front door—the pelican piercing its breast with its beak, shedding drops of blood: symbol of parental devotion and self-sacrifice. It seemed bitterly ironic in the light of what Jack had told me about Ned.

"Is that a new dress?" He took my arm as I came down the steps.

I felt the blood surge up to my face. "Yes. I . . . it is," I stuttered. I wanted to tell him that I'd made it, not bought it. I didn't want him to think that I'd been extravagant, that I'd spent a lot of money for an event that he was only attending because he felt he had to. But suddenly I was tongue-tied.

He opened the door to the passenger seat, holding it as I climbed in. The warm, earthy scent of the leather upholstery enveloped me as I sank into it.

"It shouldn't take us long to get there," he said, as the engine purred into life. "You haven't been to Constantine, have you?"

"I passed through it on the bus, on the way to Falmouth."

"It's a sleepy little place—I think the Americans decided to hold this dance to inject a bit of life into it."

He told me about visiting the camp they'd set up outside the village, the huge consignment of supplies that had arrived at the Falmouth docks to feed the men who had effectively tripled the size of the local population overnight. He described things I'd never heard of: cans of something called Spam, which was cooked pork that would last for years if necessary; a fizzy drink called Coca-Cola, which had a kick like coffee; and Hershey Bars, which I could imagine the Land Girls fighting to get their hands on, because people in Britain hadn't tasted chocolate for years.

When we arrived at the village hall, the patch of ground beside it was rammed with vehicles—mostly US Army jeeps and motorbikes. But a space had been reserved for the Alvis. Two soldiers were standing guard so that no one else could take it. Their uniforms were very different from those of the British troops I'd seen in Falmouth. A pale olive color, with a symbol like a wave in blue and gray stitched onto the shoulder. A black necktie was tucked between the middle buttons of the shirt. The cap—shaped like an upturned boat—was worn so far over the side of the head that it looked as if it might blow off in the slightest breeze. They opened our doors for us and stood at attention as we climbed out.

Stepping over the threshold of the village hall was a surreal experience. We walked out of the golden light of a summer evening into a cavernous room whose windows had been covered over with blackout boards. Towering spotlights had been erected in the corners of the room. They changed color every few seconds, casting rainbow beams onto a mirrored ball suspended from the ceiling, which dappled the faces of the people sitting at the tables and lit up the strings of red, white, and blue bunting that festooned the walls. On a dais at the far end an orchestra was playing—all men in uniform—and behind them hung the Stars and Stripes and the Union Jack.

We were greeted by a man who introduced himself as Major General Leonard Gerow. He was a great bear of a man, quite terrifying until he smiled. He seated us on either side of him at the top table.

There were no other women sitting with us. I glanced around the room, spotting Edith, Rita, and Marjorie at the other end. They were in a huddle, their heads almost touching. Whether they'd expected Jack to be there, I didn't know. They looked as if they were weighing up the talent. There were dozens of other women doing the same, but the men outnumbered them. There would be no shortage of partners to choose from.

"Would you care to dance, ma'am?"

The invitation took me by surprise. It came from the general himself.

"Oh . . . I . . ." I glanced at Jack, who smiled at my reticence.

"Go on, Alice," he said. "Enjoy yourself!"

There were a few other couples taking to the floor. General Gerow took my arm, guiding me to the center of the room. I tried not to flinch as he slid one hand around my back. I wondered if he could tell how nervous I was. The thought of getting the steps wrong—of treading on his foot or bumping against him—made my mouth go dry.

Luckily the dance turned out to be a waltz, something I'd learned as a girl. As we glided past the tables, he asked me where I came from, and told me his ancestors on his mother's side had come from County Mayo.

"I love your accent," he said. "I hope to visit Ireland one day, when all this is over."

He was very polite—and his hands never moved an inch in the wrong direction, the way I remembered boys in Dublin doing. When the waltz ended, he took me back to our table. I caught one or two of the American soldiers glancing at me, possibly contemplating asking me to dance. I guessed that on the arm of their commanding officer, I was out-of-bounds.

There were two new people at our table when we took our seats. General Gerow introduced them as the bishop of Truro and his niece, Clarissa. When the bishop greeted me, I went hot with embarrassment. I could only imagine what he would say if he knew he was shaking hands with an ex-nun who had flouted church rules and was now masquerading as a relative of Viscount Trewella. To my shame, he beamed at me and said what a pleasure it was to have a cousin of Jack's visiting the county.

His niece looked a few years younger than me and was very beautiful. She had long chestnut hair, which she wore loose, with two jeweled pins holding it back just above her temples. She'd been seated next to Jack, and as soon as the introductions were over, they were chatting away to each other. It looked like an intense conversation. Her eyes glittered as the light from the mirror ball caught them. And then she said something that made him laugh. Sitting between the general and the bishop, I couldn't hear what it was that he found so amusing. I was trying to carry on a conversation with the men on either side of me while straining to eavesdrop. And all the while I was aware of a dull ache below my ribs, which turned into a stab of jealousy when Jack and Clarissa got up and left the table together.

The tempo of the music had changed to a much livelier rhythm. People were pairing off, almost tripping over the chairs in their hurry to get onto the dance floor. I lost sight of Jack. When he reemerged, I saw that he was holding Clarissa so close that their heads were almost touching. Her dress had a low, scooped back. His hand was touching bare flesh. Her hips swayed from side to side as they moved in time to the beat of the music.

As I watched them it dawned on me that Jack must have known that this girl would be coming, that he had brought me along as an act of charity, knowing that there would be other men for me to dance with while he homed in on the bishop's glamorous niece.

Suddenly the room felt suffocating. I mumbled an excuse about needing some air and wormed my way out, squeezing past the scrum of bodies on the dance floor. But before I reached the door the music came to an abrupt stop. A man's voice boomed from the stage:

"Ladies and gentlemen, the next dance is a number that comes all the way from the United States of America. In honor of the Second Battalion of the Fifth Maryland Regiment of the Twenty-Ninth Infantry Division, please take your partners for . . . the jitterbug!"

"Say, ma'am, would you like to dance?"

My way out of the room was blocked by a tall, slim American serviceman who looked like an overgrown child. His blond hair was shaved above his ears, and what remained stood up like a brush on top of his head. The pale wisps of the beginnings of a mustache clung to his upper lip. Before I could make any sort of reply, he grabbed me and pulled me into the crowd on the dance floor. His hand was clammy, like a damp washcloth wrapped around mine.

Out of the corner of my eye, I saw Edith spinning across the floor as another soldier flung her away from him in a move unlike any I had ever seen. The next thing I knew, my partner put both hands around my waist and hoisted me off the ground before thrusting me down between his legs. I emerged, breathless and indignant. But before I could draw breath, he began stepping out a fast, swaying rhythm that ended with me being thrown and spun like a yo-yo. The skirt of my dress flew so high I was afraid people would see my underwear. But as I patted it down, I saw that everyone around me was beaming—not at me, but out of sheer pleasure.

I began to relax a little, not fighting what my partner did, but trying to mimic his steps and follow whatever energetic moves he wanted to deliver. Just as I'd started to grasp the dance, the music came to an end. My American gave me a little bow and asked if he could get me something to drink.

"That's very kind of you, but she's with me." Jack was suddenly there, beside me. At the sight of him my young partner smiled nervously and backed off.

"I thought you looked as if you needed rescuing," he said, taking my arm. "I shouldn't have left you on your own—but I needed to circulate a bit. I thought you'd be safe with the bishop." There was a wry smile on his face.

"Actually, I was enjoying myself." I held his gaze, returning the look.

"Really?"

"Well, it was a bit of a shock at first—but I think I could get to like it."

"In that case, perhaps you'll have the next dance with me."

The band had started up again. The rhythm was lively, but not the wild beat of the jitterbug.

"Do you know this one?" He put his hand on my back. His touch was light, but it sent a ripple down my spine.

"It's a quickstep, isn't it?"

I placed my left hand on his right arm as he took my other hand in his. Then we were gliding across the floor, picking up speed. It reminded me of being on board *La Coquille*, with the wind tugging at my clothes.

"I can't believe you haven't done this for so long," he murmured. "You dance as if you've been doing it all your life."

I glowed inside. I didn't want it to end. I wanted to stay like this and dance every dance with him. But I knew that wouldn't be possible.

Even if he wanted to, it wouldn't be right. What would people think of a man who spent the entire evening in the arms of his cousin?

I realized that this might be the only dance I would have with him. Trapped by the deception that I had instigated, I would have to watch him take to the floor with a procession of other women: women with curvy, gyrating bodies, like Clarissa, or pouting, lipsticked mouths, like Edith and Rita.

His jaw brushed my forehead as we swerved around a couple in our path. The scent of his skin was earthy and piney, a wistful, poignant smell, like long-ago Christmases. The temptation to nestle my cheek in the crook of his neck was overwhelming. And then, just as the music reached a crescendo, the room was plunged into darkness.

Chapter 18

*J*ack grabbed my hand. People around us were laughing, whooping. No one seemed frightened. I wondered if the lights had been put out on purpose: a prank by one of the soldiers to allow the men to get more intimate with their dance partners.

"I'm not sure what's going on." Jack's lips brushed my ear—by accident, I thought, because he didn't sound pleased.

Then an American voice shouted from the other end of the room: "The power's gone down!"

The announcement was greeted with wild cheers from the crowd around us.

"Hold on to me." Jack pulled me closer. "Let's try to get outside."

We fought our way through the press of bodies. I could hear fragments of whispered conversations, men telling women things they wouldn't have had the nerve to say under normal circumstances. And, judging by the moans and giggles, some of the women were doing things they couldn't possibly have gotten away with under the spotlights.

I had no idea which way we'd been heading when the power failed. But Jack seemed to know where he was going. By the time we got near the door, someone had opened it, creating a small patch of dark gray in the blackness. We stumbled outside. The air was fragrant with the scent of newly mowed grass. Others came spilling out after us. It was impossible to make out faces, but I thought I heard Edith's voice close by. When I glanced in the direction it had come from, I saw a procession of couples, arm in arm, heading away from the hall, toward the fields.

"What's the problem?" Jack was talking to someone whose silhouette showed a military cap.

"Looks like the lights have blown an electrical circuit, sir." The accent was a deep, slow drawl.

"Any chance of fixing it?"

"I doubt it—not before daylight, anyways."

"In that case, could you pass on a message to General Gerow? I'd like to thank him in person, but I wouldn't want to bother him with all this going on. Please let him know that Lord Trewella and his cousin had a marvelous time."

"Sure, I will, sir. Lord . . ." The man faltered.

"Just say Lord Jack. He'll understand."

Jack took my arm, steering me past the looming shapes of US Army jeeps. Even in the dark the elegant lines of the Alvis made it easy to spot.

"I can wait here if you like," I said, as he held the door open for me. "If you want to say good night to . . . anyone."

I couldn't see his face, but I heard what sounded like a grunt mixed with a chuckle. "You mean Clarissa? I had a lucky escape, I think, with the lights going out. She's a lovely girl—but a bit overpowering."

I was glad that it was too dark for him to see my expression. He waited for me to climb in, then pushed the door shut. I breathed in the warm smell of leather, watching his dark shape as he moved across the front of the car to the driver's side. Luckily, he'd reversed into the parking space. Trying to back out with so many people around would have been next to impossible. The headlights were narrow slits—all that was permitted in the blackout. They cast bright arrows on the legs of the men and women still stumbling out of the village hall.

"I'm sorry it ended like that," he said, as the car glided down the narrow lane beyond the village. "It had only just got going. Not much of an evening out for you."

"I don't mind—really I don't. When you haven't been used to that kind of thing, it can be a bit overwhelming."

"Oh dear, was my quickstep a bit too quick?"

"No—I . . . it wasn't *you*. There were just so many people. I'm not used to it." I wanted to tell him how wonderful it had felt, sashaying across the dance floor, feeling the warmth of his hand through the thin cotton of my dress. But to voice that feeling would take me over the invisible line that lay between us. I was afraid of trespassing into unknown territory, afraid of embarrassing him and ruining everything.

"I suppose it must be very strange," he said. "It's hard for anyone outside that world of yours to grasp what it would be like to be deprived of the things most people take for granted."

That world of yours. It sounded as if he still saw me as a nun, however much I'd tried to shake off that persona. Perhaps it was because I was only days away from going ashore in disguise on our mission to France. The thought of it made my stomach churn.

"You'll slip into it again quite easily, I imagine," he went on. "It's all arranged, by the way: the nuns in Lannion have everything ready." He glanced at me fleetingly before turning back to the road ahead. "All the same, it's not too late to change your mind."

Once again, he'd tuned into exactly what I was thinking. I wondered if he was telepathic, whether he could read everyone he met as if their inner lives were tattooed on their faces. Or was it just me? Was it all those years of struggling to make my inner thoughts match my outward behavior that had made me so transparent?

"I brought you into this, Alice—and I feel responsible." His hand went to the gearshift as he took a sharp bend. "You don't have to put yourself in even more danger." Something in his voice had changed. There was an urgency in it, almost as if he was willing me to pull out.

"The Germans killed three people in Brittany today," I replied. "Anything I can do to help thwart their plans has to be worth it. How could I live with myself if I pulled out now?" I sounded far braver than I felt.

Jack fell silent. We were going more slowly now. I thought we must be nearly home, although I couldn't see anything but the tunnel of hedgerows ahead of us.

"I'm taking you down to the village," he said, turning the car sharply to the left, onto a road that was even narrower than the one we'd left behind. "We'll walk along the beach. The tide won't be in very far yet—and it'll be a lot easier than going through the valley at this time of night."

He parked the car beside the school. Jack had a flashlight, whose thin beam reflected off the cobblestones as we walked. We went along the narrow street that led to the quayside, past houses that betrayed no sign of the people inside. Every window was blacked out. Not even a crack of light was visible. The rancid smell of fish drifted on the breeze as we neared the cellar where the barrels of pilchards were stored. Somewhere in the fields above the village, I heard a donkey braying. The only other sound was the distant lap of the waves breaking on the mudflats out in the estuary.

We both took off our shoes when we reached the beach. Jack rolled up his trousers to his knees, to avoid getting them wet when we negotiated the rock pools. He said it was a mercy I couldn't see what he looked like. It was the first time he'd shown any vestige of self-consciousness. There was something comforting about it—that he cared what I thought of him.

He took my hand when we reached the place where the rocks jutted above the sand. "Try not to step on the seaweed," he said. "It's very slippery." He directed the flashlight beam a couple of yards ahead, then brought it back to our feet. The light made the dark hairs on his legs glisten. To my shame, I had a sudden vision of us lying together on my bed in the boathouse, legs entwined.

When we reached the door, he let go of my hand. He apologized a second time for the evening being cut short. This time I didn't reply. I stood there awkwardly, wondering whether I should offer him a cup of tea or a glass of water, anything to keep him for a moment longer.

"I should go," he said. "The tide won't be long coming in." Then he reached up and patted the side of my head, ruffling my hair with his fingers. "It's growing, isn't it? In a few months' time you'll be a new woman."

Those few careless words were like a slap in the face. They made me think that in his mind, it was Morwenna he was caressing, that he was willing me to become more like her, to bring her back from the dead. Clearly he was still obsessed with her—the girl who had laughed as she dived beneath the waves, who had emerged from the sea with nothing but her hair to cover her, who had made love to him on the deck of his boat. Jack was still here in body, but, like the man in the mermaid legend, his heart was somewhere beneath the ocean.

"You're thinking about Morwenna, aren't you?"

The moment I spoke I regretted it. His hand fell away as if he'd touched a live electric wire.

"Why do you say that?" There was a painful anger in his voice. "Why on earth would I be thinking about her?"

"I . . . I don't know." I writhed inside. "I'm sorry. It was a stupid thing to say."

"You think I'm still in love with her? That I see you as some sort of substitute?"

"No . . . I . . . it's just . . ." The words withered in my throat. He'd said exactly what I was thinking. But if I admitted it, he'd know how I felt about him, that I was jealous.

He huffed out a breath. "I shouldn't have burdened you with it. It wasn't fair." The beam of the flashlight swept the sand as he turned away from me. I was flooded with a sense of what might have been. Would we be kissing now, if I hadn't ruined the moment with my foolish imaginings?

Something swelled inside me, a new determination that made me bold. I grasped his hand. "Please, don't go. I can't bear to think that I've hurt you."

He didn't try to pull away. He took my other hand in his, closing the distance between us. "I don't deserve your sympathy, Alice, or anything else, for that matter," he murmured. "Is it something they taught you in the convent—how to break a man with tenderness?" His lips brushed my forehead. "I'll see you in the morning." A moment later he was gone.

I stayed awake long after Jack had melted into the darkness. I sat on the log pile outside the boathouse, a blanket draped over my shoulders, listening to the breaking waves and the night sounds from the woods behind me. I went over everything he'd said, again and again, trying to make sense of it.

I don't deserve your sympathy. What had he meant by that? He'd left me feeling that there was something he wasn't telling me—something beyond the secret he'd asked me to keep.

You think I'm still in love with her? The contempt in his voice when he'd said that was unforgettable. But he hadn't denied it. Perhaps what had made him sound so incredulous was not that question, but the one that had followed—about him seeing me as some sort of substitute. As if the very idea of him thinking of me in that way was ridiculous.

I wondered if he'd told me the truth about what had happened to Morwenna. Could it be that she was still alive? That he was waiting for the day the war ended to go and reclaim her? But surely he wouldn't have lied about that? To say that someone was dead when they were not would be a wicked thing to do.

I was staring at the sky, at the bright constellation of Orion sinking to the west. The flash of shame that flared inside me was as hot as those stars. Wasn't that exactly what I had done? Pretended to the world that I was dead when I was still alive?

As the whisper of the encroaching waves grew louder, a veil of mist drifted up the beach. I shivered, pulling the blanket up around my neck. The mist swirled about me like a living thing, as if something had come up from beneath the water to grab at my feet and drag me in. I had a fleeting vision of the mermaid in the church, eyes burning as she rose from the sea, her features melting into the face of the girl in the photograph. And the lips mouthing words I could not hear, only feel in my heart: *Keep away from him. He's mine.*

Chapter 19

I had no idea how long I'd been outside. When I dragged myself off to bed, the luminous hands of the little travel clock showed five past two. The alarm went off less than four hours later. I went through the motions of washing and dressing, all the time listening for the barking of Brock as he came tearing out of the trees on the edge of the cove. But there was no sound of the dog. By the time I was ready to go up to the farm, Jack hadn't appeared.

The water in the estuary had an oily, sinister look. I stood for a moment, watching the waves break, relentless and indifferent, lapping at the carcass of a gull and pulling it under. The tide was like a living thing, but immortal, a tireless, ravenous beast that consumed any dead creature in its path, scouring the bones white. I thought of Jack, his head in his hands, as he'd described diving into the murky water, fighting the swell, desperate to save Morwenna. *The lifeboat went out looking for her. They searched for days. But her body was never found.*

I pictured her lying dead on the ocean floor, her hair floating out from her body, swaying in the current like eelgrass. And Ned—darling Ned—crying for his mother, too young to understand that she was gone forever. It struck me, more forcefully than ever, that if Jack cared for me at all, in whatever way, I must try to make him listen to me, somehow persuade him to soften his attitude toward Ned. But how on earth was

I going to do that unless he had a change of heart about the estate and everything that went with it?

I thought I might meet Jack on the path up to the house. But my only companions on that walk were the birds that rustled in the dark recesses of the leafy canopy that enveloped me. The heady scents of the flowers and blossoms were soporific. If I'd sat down, even for a moment, I'm sure I would have fallen asleep.

I trudged into the milking shed, wondering how I was going to summon the energy to get through the day ahead. The Land Girls were already there, chatting away as they bent beneath the dusty bodies of the cows. Edith's head popped up as I plonked down beside one of the waiting animals. Her eyes were bright, her lipstick a perfect purple bow. No one would have guessed what I suspected: that she'd been up all night, cavorting in the field behind Constantine's village hall with an American soldier.

"Shame about the power cut, wasn't it?" She gave me a devious smile. "You looked like you were enjoying yourself."

I nodded and ducked down to grasp the teats. The last thing I wanted was an interrogation.

"Still, at least you got a decent night's sleep," Edith went on. "We didn't bother going to bed, did we, girls?"

Muffled laughter came from beneath the cows farther up the line.

"Did that Yank try it on—the one we saw you dancing with?" This time it was Marjorie, shouting to make herself heard. "Is that why His Lordship came to the rescue?"

"No," I called back, without looking up. "He was just a bit energetic, that's all."

"We thought there was going to be a fight!" This was from Rita. "His Lordship looked fit to throttle him!"

I pulled too hard on the teats, making the poor animal I was milking shift suddenly in the stall. What Rita had said left me feeling even more confused about Jack. I told myself that she was bound to be exaggerating. They loved drama—I knew that well enough by now. The idea of Jack getting into a fight with the soldier I'd danced with would have immense appeal.

"We can get a message to your boyfriend if you want to see him again," Marjorie piped up.

I looked up, startled. Edith must have seen the expression on my face. "I don't think she fancied him that much," she yelled across to Marjorie. "He looked a bit young—and a bit desperate. She wants a fella who's a bit more . . . *mature*."

This produced hoots of laughter from Marjorie and Rita. They started discussing which of the many Americans they'd met at the dance would be suitable for me.

"We're meeting them at the pub in the village tomorrow night," Edith said. "Why don't you come with us?"

I took a breath, inhaling the warm, earthy aroma of the cow whose sturdy haunches were hiding my blushes. "That's very kind of you." I struggled to sound casual. "But I'm tied up for the next few days—they want me over at the hospital in Falmouth."

What an accomplished liar I was becoming. To my relief, they left me alone after that. But the lie had brought the sudden realization that in less than twenty-four hours, I would be on my way to France. I'd allowed myself to become so obsessed with Jack that the looming danger of what lay ahead had been eclipsed. I moved along the row of animals in a trancelike state, my mind hundreds of miles away, back in Brussels, replaying the horror stories the nuns had told about the Great War. How would I cope if it all went wrong? If the Germans caught me out, what would they do to me?

It's not too late to change your mind. I was back in Cornwall, in Jack's car, watching the silhouettes of trees glide past the window.

What a coward you are! Did you leave your spine on that sinking ship, along with your robe and veil? Sister Clare's voice drowned out Jack's. Yes, I had been a coward, not facing up to the order, letting them all think that I had gone down with the *Brabantia*. Too late now to make that right. But not too late to show some courage.

When the milking was done, I made my way back through the valley to the church. I'd only remembered what day it was as I was about to leave the boathouse. I thought how different my Sundays were now. In Africa, by this time of the day, I would have already attended chapel three times.

There was no one else in the church when I arrived. I'd got there early on purpose. I wanted to light candles. One for each of the agents we were taking to France—and one for Miranda, who was still missing. As I placed them in the sand tray near the altar, I prayed for the agents' safety, for Jack's, and for my own.

Then I lit two more, for Kamaria and Kenyada. It was their birthday—two whole years since the day I'd stumbled upon them in the jungle about to have their lives snuffed out before they'd even begun. I gazed at the flames, murmuring prayers for their future health and well-being. It struck me—not for the first time—that I would never know how they were, that in leaving the order in the way I had, I had forfeited any chance of getting news of them. I made a silent vow, as I stood in front of the flickering candles, that if I survived the coming ordeal in France, then somehow, someday, I would find a way of seeing them again.

As I settled into a pew, I realized what a preposterous notion that was. I had no idea how much it would cost to make such a journey, and even if I had the money, I couldn't turn up at the orphanage, because everyone there would have heard that I was dead.

The Lord hates a lying tongue.

How many times had I heard Sister Clare say those words to the young African men who had worked at the mission hospital? In pretending to be dead, I hadn't *told* a lie, but what I'd done amounted to the same thing. Did God hate me for that? Would he turn a deaf ear to my prayers because of it? Would he disapprove of me going to France, pretending to be a nun, when I'd rejected that life?

My eyes traveled across to the choir stalls. I could just pick out the carving of the mermaid. The flickering candlelight made her seem alive, as if she were twisting this way and that, struggling to break free of the wooden waves lapping around her tail. It was impossible to look at her without thinking of Morwenna: the maid from the rectory in Sithney, going for a dip in the sea on her day off, catching sight of a young man fishing on a yacht moored in the bay, and swimming out, curious.

People used to say that if a man followed a mermaid into the sea, she'd take him down to the depths of the ocean and eat him up. Merle's words came back to me as I gazed at the image. It struck me what an apt description of Jack that was: the way he'd suddenly changed when I'd mentioned Morwenna, like a man eaten up by the past.

I heard footsteps behind me. I twisted my head around, hoping it was him, come early for the service to change into his chorister's robes. But it was one of the mothers from the village. I recognized her and her two little girls from the party Merle's children had attended. She gave me a nod of acknowledgment, then shepherded her children into a pew near the back of the church. Other people began to file in after that, but there was no sign of Jack.

Merle was among the last to arrive. The children crowded into my pew, Ned scrambling onto my lap, but Merle made him and the others move along so that we could have a whispered conversation before the service began. She glanced over her shoulder before telling me that Jack had left a message that he'd been called away. The look she gave me made it clear that his sudden absence had to do with the SOE. I wondered if the mission had been called off for some reason.

"Aunt Marie and Uncle Pierre send their regards." She'd anticipated the question I couldn't ask. I nodded. We would be going, then.

"How was the dance?" she whispered.

"Good—while it lasted," I hissed back.

Her mouth turned down when I told her about the power cut. She was about to say something else when the organ struck up. We all stood as the choir came up the aisle, followed by the vicar.

When the service was over, she led me to a quiet spot in the corner of the churchyard. While the children chased each other around the gravestones, she told me that the radio parts I was supposed to be taking to France hadn't arrived, and that Jack had needed to drive to somewhere near London to collect them.

"Will he be back in time?" I knew from what he'd already told me that it took the better part of a day to get to London by car.

"Only just," she replied. "He won't be coming back here. He'll go straight to the mooring place upriver to pick up the motorboat. He left the map for me to give you, though—he wants you to study it before you leave." She opened her handbag and pulled out what looked like a folded silk handkerchief. "Don't look at it now," she whispered. "Just put it in your pocket. There are two things inside that you might need." Her face clouded as she handed it to me. "There's an Irish passport. If the Germans find that on you, then in theory, they can't kill you or imprison you." I knew, before she said it, what else the silk concealed: it was the pill she had told me about—the one an agent could swallow in extremis.

Chapter 20

*L*ess than twenty-four hours later I was lying in a hammock on *La Coquille*, drifting in and out of sleep as the boat bobbed gently at its mooring in New Grimsby harbor. We'd left Cornwall in heavy rain—the conditions far too miserable for anyone who didn't need to be on deck to linger there. I had squeezed into the cabin with the five agents while Jack piloted the motor launch to the Scillies. It had been impossible to lie down in the cabin. One of the men had fallen asleep beside me, his head lolling onto my shoulder as he slipped into unconsciousness. It felt awkward, too intimate—but I didn't want to risk waking him by shifting the other way.

Jack had been pale with exhaustion when we reached the island of Tresco. Despite the bad weather, we'd made it into port before it was fully light. He'd disappeared soon after we transferred to the fishing boat. Now I saw that he was fast asleep in a hammock a few yards from mine. In the dim light I could see his chest rise and fall. His hair, matted by the salt air, clung to his forehead. I thought how young he looked. Sleep had wiped all the tension and fatigue from his face.

I wasn't sure what time it was when I decided to go up on deck. Jack was still comatose, but the men we were taking to France had gone up before me and were drinking coffee from tin mugs. The rainstorm of the previous night had blown itself out. The sun was just visible above the crenellated tower of Cromwell's Castle. If I hadn't known which way the harbor faced, I wouldn't have been able to guess whether it was morning or afternoon.

The men were talking about the progress of the war. They were speculating—or rather arguing—about what the Allied strategy would be following the surrender of the German and Italian armies in Tunisia. I sat with them, drinking coffee, listening to what they believed would happen when the men who had been fighting in North Africa began to push into Italy. Fred Bechélet would almost certainly be part of that invading force, if he was alive. I wondered if Merle had heard anything. I'd been so preoccupied in the past few days that I hadn't asked her.

None of the men spoke about anything personal. Like last time, we used code names when addressing each other. I had no idea where any of them would be heading when we reached France. And I was certain that no one on the boat except Jack knew that my first destination on landing was to be the Ursuline convent in Lannion. As I glanced from one face to another, I couldn't help thinking of Miranda, who had sat with me, like this, just a month ago. I wondered if these men ever thought about death, whether the energetic debate they were engaged in was a way of shutting it out of their minds.

La Coquille got underway a couple of hours before sunset. The agents went below to play poker as we pulled out of the harbor. They invited me to join them—even offered to teach me how to play when I confessed my total ignorance of card games—but I told them how rough the sea had been on the way out of the Scillies last time and said I'd better stay up on deck in case I got seasick. It was an excuse, of course: I hadn't exchanged more than a handful of words with Jack since we'd left Cornwall. I was desperate to talk to him. He'd left me dangling by a thread after the dance. I had to know what was going on in his head.

"I thought you might like some help," I said, as I went into the wheelhouse. "I can take the binoculars if you like—or the wheel for a while, if you prefer."

He handed me the binoculars without a word. I stood beside him, scanning the horizon for anything that might represent a potential threat, wondering all the while why he was so silent, why, now that we had the opportunity at last, he didn't seem to want to speak to me.

"I looked at the radio parts," I said, still peering through the binoculars. "They're small enough to fit under a skullcap, which would be a good hiding place because the wimple sits on top of it. The explosives I'll strap around my waist and across my back. The robe and scapular should camouflage any lumps and bumps."

I heard him draw in a breath. "How long is it since you've ridden a bike?"

"I was seventeen. But they say you never forget."

"Have you studied the map?"

"Yes." I lowered the binoculars. "When I get to the convent, I plan to sew it to the underside of the veil—the part that hangs down at the back. Then I can flip it over if I need to read it."

"It sounds as though you've thought of everything."

I wondered why he didn't sound pleased. I stared into the distance, at the red ball of the sun sinking into the sea. I could hardly believe it was only two nights ago that he'd held me in his arms and whisked me across the dance floor. I told myself I shouldn't be surprised that he was taciturn, cold, even. But I sensed that something was amiss, that I'd done something to make him want to distance himself from me.

"Is something the matter? Have I done something wrong?" I turned to him, but he didn't look at me—just kept his eyes fixed on the horizon.

"No, Alice, you haven't done anything. It's . . ." He hesitated, as if he were weighing his words. "It's not you. Forgive me—I'm not very good at sentimental stuff." The stubble on his jaw caught the light as the muscles tightened. "I don't think you realize how fearful I am of losing you."

The boat shook as a wave caught the bow. Spray spattered the window. I felt as if I were watching a film in slow motion. Had I heard right? Had he really said that?

"If anything were to happen to you, it would be my fault." He turned, looking straight at me for the first time since we'd left Cornwall. His eyes glittered red with the reflection of the dying sun. "That day, when I found you on the beach, I made a very selfish decision. I should have let you go when you recovered—to Falmouth or some other place."

"Selfish?" I stared back at him, bewildered. "Why do you say that? You said I could save more lives doing this than by being a nurse."

"And that's absolutely true—but there was an ulterior motive for persuading you to stay." He held my gaze. "When I saw you lying there on the sand, and realized you were alive, I felt as if I'd been given a second chance." He shook his head slowly. "Remember when you said that all you wanted was to do some good in the world? Well, so did I: I wanted to make up for the person I'd been, for what I did to Morwenna."

The worm of jealousy slid out of the hole it had made in my heart. "Jack, I'm not Morwenna resurrected."

"I know that." His eyes narrowed, the lids clenching as if he were in pain. "I didn't—I *don't*—want you to be her. It was about trying to make amends, about saving a life for the one I'd taken."

"But you didn't *take* her life—it was an accident." I searched his face. There was something there that I hadn't seen before. It was the kind of look I'd seen in the eyes of patients on their way to the operating table.

"I . . . didn't tell you all of it," he said. "I couldn't. Not then." He glanced out to sea, scanning the breaking waves. "I'd been bottling it up—for years—and when I realized that you'd guessed the truth about

Ned, all I could do was give you the bare minimum." He let out a long breath. "You see, she didn't slip on the ladder. There was an argument."

I felt my blood surge. "What happened?"

"We were on board *Firefly*, talking about the money I was going to give her. I was stupid. Lost my head. I think it was the shock of seeing Ned in the flesh. I accused her of trying to trap me. I said I had no way of knowing if Ned was my child. That made her furious. She said she had a birth certificate, that the date would prove it. When she pulled it out of her bag, the wind took it. She tried to grab it as it went over the side. That's when she fell."

I saw it all in my mind's eye: her hair billowing around her face, her body flailing as she went over the side. "But it was still an accident." I breathed. "You didn't push her—did you?"

"I didn't touch her." He pressed his forehead with the heel of his hand. "But the inescapable fact is that it wouldn't have happened if I hadn't doubted her. She would still be alive. Ned would still have a mother."

The torture was etched in his face. I didn't doubt that he was telling the truth that he hadn't pushed her over the side of the boat—but in his mind he'd as good as murdered her. No wonder that brooding, haunted air seemed to follow him like a cloud.

I hardly dared to ask the next question, but I had to know. "Did you really doubt that Ned was yours?"

"When I first opened the letter, it struck me as highly suspicious that she'd waited all that time to tell me of Ned's existence. But some part of me got carried away with the idea of having a child. I decided that the only decent thing to do would be to marry her." His lips disappeared momentarily as he sucked them in over his teeth. "It would have been a secret marriage. My father was very ill by then. I couldn't face trying to explain it to him." He shook his head. "I had it all planned out. The wedding would take place on Guernsey, and Morwenna would stay there with Ned. I was so certain it was the right thing to do that

I ordered a trousseau for her—a set of clothes and a wedding dress. I nearly got caught out, because the housekeeper opened the parcel. I had to cook up a story about them being for a cousin planning an elopement."

I swallowed hard. So, that talk of a secret wife had been closer to the truth than the village gossips had realized. Something else dawned on me then. "Those clothes," I murmured. "The ones you gave me—were they hers?"

He nodded. "They'd lain in a trunk, never worn, for three years. I'd taken them with me on *Firefly* to give to her, but when I got to Guernsey and saw Ned, I was confused. His hair and eyes were brown—like mine, not Morwenna's: she had red hair and her eyes were green. But I had no idea whether Ned was the age he should have been if she'd become pregnant when we were together, in the spring of 1938. I didn't know enough about young children to be able to tell his age. By the time we got onto the boat, I was so worked up I said things I shouldn't have." He rubbed his knuckles against the bristly outline of his jaw. "I can still see her face—that look in her eyes when I challenged her. They seemed to change color, like the sea when a squall blows up, from deep emerald to slate gray. 'I thought you'd say that!' She almost spat the words at me. That was when she produced the birth certificate."

The scene he'd conjured was so vivid. I saw Morwenna, eyes blazing, like the mermaid in the church.

"When they were searching for her—during that week I stayed on Guernsey—I went to the public-records office in St. Peter Port. They had the original certificate there. The dates matched. He was born on the sixth of January 1939—nine months after we started seeing one another." He shook his head. "I suppose you're thinking what I thought, that a certificate doesn't necessarily prove anything, that she could have been carrying on with some other man while she was seeing me. But there was something else." He leaned closer, pushing back the hair that grew above his left ear. "Can you see this?" He moved his finger from the tip of his cheekbone to the place where the ear attached, just below the temple. I saw that there was a tiny puncture in the skin. "Ned has the same thing. It's an extra sinus—quite rare and completely harmless—and it's passed down through families."

My mind flashed back to the time I'd bathed Ned at the boathouse and, seeing what looked like a needle hole in his ear, asked if Louis had been hurting him.

"I didn't realize Ned had it until I was leaving Guernsey. When I went to say goodbye, I ruffled his hair, and there it was." Jack lowered his eyes to the worn wooden boards of the wheelhouse. "I felt this awful, sick feeling when I saw it. I should have believed her. Should have trusted her. Can you imagine, when he's older, what he'd say if he found out what I'd done?" The pain in his voice was palpable.

"But you wouldn't have to tell him what you've told me," I said. "He doesn't need to know all that. Morwenna's death was an accident: Whatever you were saying or thinking when it happened, you didn't mean for her to fall overboard. You didn't *kill* her."

"I might as well have."

I reached out and touched his arm. "You can't let it go on gnawing away at you, Jack. You have to forgive yourself."

"How can I? Ned wouldn't forgive me—I'm certain of that."

"Well, I believe everyone can be forgiven, no matter what they've done." It came out sounding horribly trite.

"How can I be forgiven? If it wasn't for me, she'd still be alive. I killed her."

"You're not a murderer, Jack. It was an accident." My hand was still on his arm. I wanted to pull him closer, to comfort him, but I could feel the tension in his muscles through the woolen jersey. I was afraid that he would recoil. "You said that when you found me on the beach you wanted to make amends—that was why you helped me."

He nodded. "What of it?"

"Well, don't you think that one way you could make amends would be to acknowledge Ned?"

He huffed out a sigh. "I've already told you why I can't do that."

"Yes," I said. "The family honor. But don't you see what it's doing to you? You're at war with yourself. You couldn't tell anyone about Morwenna because of the shame it would have brought, and the same thing has trapped you into denying that Ned is your son: You put the estate and the family name above everything else. Bricks and mortar are more important to you than people." I was aware that I was being blunt, brutal, even. But for his sake and Ned's, I had to say it. "Isn't there more honor in being a father to Ned? Isn't that more important than a house and social standing?"

He pulled away from me. Anger flashed across his face. "Tell me, Alice—how can someone who gave up all worldly possessions at the age of eighteen have any idea what it's like to be in my position?"

"I don't pretend to know that." I tried to sound unruffled. The contempt in his voice had cut me to the heart. "What I do know is that a house can't talk to you when you're feeling lonely. It can't wrap its arms around you when you're unhappy. It can't love you, Jack."

For a while he said nothing, gripping the wheel of the boat as if he were squeezing the breath out of some living thing. When he did speak, he didn't look at me. "You're right, of course." He sounded tight, grudging. "A place like Penheligan can be as much of a curse as a blessing. It broke my father's heart. I'm just trying not to let it break mine."

I wondered what he meant. He'd told me about the financial strain the house had put on his father when the shipping business had failed. Was he talking about money again? Or was it about the hold the house had on him, eclipsing his feelings for Ned?

"It's a kind of love, though, isn't it?" he went on. "Not the sort you read about in the Bible—I grant you that. It's hard to describe, the way it enters your blood, the feeling of indebtedness to all those generations of people who strove to create something beautiful, something lasting."

"But that kind of love can destroy a person," I replied. "Is that what your ancestors would have wanted for you?"

His head whipped round. "Who are you to lecture me about love? You gave your Irish boy up without much of a fight, didn't you?"

"Perhaps I did," I countered. "Don't you think I despised myself for not standing up to my father? For running to a convent when I could have run away with Dan? Perhaps we're very much alike in that respect: we both let down the people we thought we were in love with."

"Touché." His voice was a harsh whisper.

For a while there was silence between us. He was staring into the distance, his face outlined by the glow of the setting sun. I stood there, wretched, beside him, fiddling with the strap of the binoculars. I hadn't intended to make him angry. I hadn't meant to sound so patronizing, so judgmental.

"Why are we doing this, Alice? Why are we fighting?" He turned toward me, one hand still on the wheel. "You're about to go to France—and I wish to God you weren't. All I wanted was to tell you what I've been meaning to say ever since we were standing here, like this, a month ago."

His eyes had a liquid softness, so different from the piercing look he'd given me just moments before. Suddenly he was kissing me. I could taste the sea on his lips, feel the roughness of the stubble peppering his skin. Waves slapped against the bow, rocking my body against his. I closed my eyes. And a moment later the sky above us exploded.

Chapter 21

An earsplitting roar of engines pulled us apart. He pushed me down so hard I caught my arm on the engine housing. I felt the weight of him on top of me as the planes screamed past. When the noise began to subside, I felt his hair brush my cheek as he raised his head.

"Junkers. Six of them. Heading south." He got up and held out his hands to me. "Sorry—I hope I didn't hurt you."

I shook my head as he helped me to my feet. "Why didn't they fire?"

He patted the wheel. "No Luftwaffe pilot would waste ammunition on a bunch of French fishermen."

"What the hell was that?" The shout came from the stern of the boat. Through the glass I saw a head emerge from below. Soon all five men were standing on the deck, craning their necks, shading their eyes against the orange glimmer of the sky. I took the wheel while Jack went to talk to them.

There was no chance for us to be alone again after that. Everyone was on edge, wondering if the planes would come back, afraid that their presence signaled the start of other enemy action. I went belowdecks but it was impossible to sleep. My mouth burned where Jack's lips had touched me. Blood pounded in my ears as if I'd been transported to the bottom of the ocean, beneath the waves that crashed against the boat. The fusion of emotions—elation, agitation, fear, confusion—overwhelmed me.

Images of myself, dressed as a nun, as I would be in a few hours' time, flashed alongside close-ups of Jack's face, one moment angry and contemptuous, the next ardent and tender. Was he angry with me or with himself? Why had he kissed me after dismissing my advice as naïve and hypocritical? Was a man like Jack—so guilt ridden and conflicted—capable of loving someone? Was his heart too poisoned by his inability to forgive himself? I feared that kissing me had been a desperate, meaningless act, a way of escaping from things he couldn't face up to.

It seemed no time at all before I heard the rumble of *La Coquille*'s anchor chain tumbling over the side of the boat. One of the men called down to me. I didn't respond at first. My brain was so befuddled I didn't recognize my code name. The second time he shouted I jumped up. If I was going to be of any use on the mission, I needed to pull myself together. People's lives depended on me being quick thinking and alert. I took a deep breath and went up on deck.

Jack was waiting on the starboard side, ready to release the rope that held the dinghy once I had climbed into it with the others. I had to go first, so that the men who were going to hide under the tarpaulin could position themselves under my feet.

"Good luck." Jack squeezed my arm as I went over the side. "See you tomorrow."

As I scrambled down the ladder, I sent up a silent prayer. Tomorrow seemed an eternity away.

I had a strange sense of déjà vu as the dinghy headed for the shore. It was exactly like the last time: the mackerel line in my hand, four bodies in the belly of the boat, the silhouette of a man pulling on oars. The only difference was that this time, I was the only woman.

The handover was easier than it had been on the previous mission. None of those waiting to be picked up had any injuries. I stayed where I was in the stern while one of them rowed back to *La Coquille*, saving my strength for the next stage of the operation.

There was a moment of panic when what looked like a patrol boat headed in our direction. But it turned out to be a lone fisherman setting lobster pots. I shouted a greeting in French, then wished him more success than we were having with the mackerel. This seemed to satisfy him. He waved as we rowed away.

Jack hadn't gone far from where he'd dropped me off. I could see his silhouette as he helped the escapees aboard. I didn't go up with them. I was to row back as soon as they were safely delivered. It would be a race against the clock because of the shortness of the night. I had to get to the harbor at Lannion under cover of darkness.

I rowed as fast as I could, watching the black shape of *La Coquille* grow smaller and smaller. I felt very vulnerable, very much alone. I did what I'd always done when I was frightened. The prayers were a mixture of the ones I knew by heart and ones I made up: I asked for protection, for courage, and for the ability to look serene, despite my terror.

To find the harbor, I had to go north once I neared the beach where the exchange of men had taken place. I hugged the coastline for a few hundred yards. Jack had said that I would feel the current change as I entered the estuary of the river Léguer, where Lannion was located. A couple of times I stopped rowing to see if I could feel anything. The little boat rocked gently. I put my hand over the side, desperate for some indication that I was going in the right direction. I couldn't have gone the wrong way, could I? I stared at the sky, wishing I knew more about the patterns of stars overhead. I knew Orion, but that was nowhere to be seen. I searched for the North Star, but the sky was already beginning to lighten. Frantic now, I began rowing again. And then, suddenly, I felt it: the pull of the tide. I hardly needed to row—it was taking me into the mouth of the river.

I glided beneath a stone bridge. Soon I saw the shapes of bigger boats than mine at anchor on both sides. I knew that I had to go under a second bridge, then find a mooring place on the north bank of the river. The next bridge came up more quickly than I expected, looming out of a veil of mist that hung over the water. I steered toward a set of stone steps that led down from the quayside to the water. I made a grab for a metal ring embedded in the wall. My fingers almost slipped on the slimy, weed-covered bricks surrounding it. For a moment I thought I was going to lose my balance and topple into the dark water. But I held on tight and after a few seconds the boat stopped wobbling.

I tied the rope securely then climbed out. At the top of the steps I paused, searching for signs of life. The curfew was due to end at sunrise. It was risky to be on the streets, but I wanted to find the convent before it got properly light. In broad daylight it would be less easy to fool anyone into believing I was a man.

I was still wearing the oilskins I'd put on before leaving Cornwall. The radio parts and explosives were in two bags strapped around my waist under my jacket. I'd memorized the layout of the streets around the harbor, so I didn't need to refer to the map. The buildings on the riverbank were half-timbered houses with flowers tumbling from window boxes. Even in the gray twilight the old town looked pretty.

I was about to move away from the quayside when I spotted a beam of light moving toward me, farther up the river. Someone was walking by the boats, shining a flashlight at each vessel. I scrambled back down the steps and crouched under the arch of the bridge. I prayed that the patroller wouldn't come down this way with his flashlight. The dinghy was out of sight and probably not big enough to be of any interest. It was lucky that Jack hadn't brought me all the way to Lannion in *La Coquille*. He'd discussed the idea but been advised that it would be too risky with the escapees on board. Clearly the senior officers of the SOE were very well informed.

I held my breath as the footsteps came closer. The beam of the flashlight glanced off the stonework above my head. Then the patroller was gone. I waited a minute longer, then crept back up the steps and darted across to where the houses were. I set off toward a church spire to the east, taking care to stay in the shadows of the doorways. The Ursuline convent was on Rue Jean Savidan—a long street that ran almost parallel to the river a couple of blocks back. I turned left at the church and made my way around the edge of a square.

I stopped in the entrance to a baker's shop before venturing any farther. The scent of warm bread came wafting under the door, making my stomach rumble. I was just about to step out into the open when two men in uniform appeared around the corner, just yards from where I was standing. The sight of the red armbands with the swastika emblazoned on them paralyzed me. My mouth went dry and my rumbling stomach froze. This was the enemy. The embodiment of the evil I had pledged to fight. Even the way they walked betrayed their arrogance. They were talking to each other as they made their way across the square. I heard one of them chuckle as he glanced my way. For one awful moment I thought they were coming to the bakery. I tried to flatten myself against the wall. To my relief, they passed by without stopping.

When their voices had died away, I crept out of my hiding place. My hands were shaking. I clenched my fists inside the sleeves of my jacket. Minutes later I was on Rue Jean Savidan. The convent was easy to find. The medieval building was an imposing sight, its facade touched by the pink dawn light. I'd been instructed to go down an alley at the side of the building and rap four times on a blue-painted door.

Even though I knew what to expect, it was something of a shock to find myself face-to-face with a nun. Her veil shadowed her face. She let me in without a word and led me down a passageway to a small, bare room containing only a table and a single chair. A wooden crucifix hung on the wall. Beneath were two hooks, on which the clothes they had prepared for me hung.

"Deshabillez-vous, s'il vous plait." She sounded very young. *"Je vais vous montrer comment porter les vêtements."*

"Merci beaucoup."

She was offering to help me dress. She had no idea, of course, that I'd been a nun. And I couldn't tell her. She turned her back while I took off my fisherman's clothes. Before the habit went on, I strapped some of the equipment I was taking to the Resistance to my body. The plastic explosives, each of which was the size and shape of a large cigar, were sewn into webbing that allowed me to wrap them around my torso. When I'd finished doing that, I had to pretend not to know in what order to put on the various items of clothing.

Without looking around, the nun handed me a chemise just like the one I'd been wearing when I washed up in Mermaid's Cove. There was a number stitched into the back of the neck. Two-three-six: lower than the one I'd been given as a novice. As I pulled the chemise over my head, I wondered how many nuns, over the centuries, this number had belonged to. The sleeve of the garment caught on the gun strapped to my left arm. I eased it over the metal barrel, wondering what the sister would say if she knew that she was helping someone who was not only carrying explosives, but a lethal weapon.

The next thing I put on was a pair of black woolen stockings, held up by elasticized garters. Then came an underskirt, and on top of that a wide-sleeved robe. Before the scapular could go over that, the first two layers of headgear had to be in place. I'd begun to tighten the strings of the skullcap when I remembered the transmitters. I needed to sew them inside the cap before the wimple and veil went on.

The nun went off to fetch a needle and thread. I looked down at the long black garments that swathed my body, so familiar and yet so strange, like a long-lost relative. I was glad that there was no mirror in the room. It was hard enough to justify what I was doing without catching sight of myself.

An hour later I was almost ready. I'd secured the radio parts inside the skullcap, and sewn the silk map between the two layers of the veil. My assistant helped me put on the wimple, which covered the skullcap and extended from my head into something like a large white bib over my shoulders and chest. On top of that she placed a stiff circular coif, to which she pinned the veil. Finally, she hooked a large wooden cross and chain around my neck and gave me a rosary to hang from my belt. And one more thing—a silver ring. I couldn't look at it as I pushed it onto my finger. It made me feel the way I imagined someone would if they were married and had taken off their wedding ring to pursue a love affair.

"Comment vous sentez-vous?"

How did I feel? I didn't trust myself to answer that question. I turned my head from side to side, trying to get used to the veil. I wondered how I'd managed all those years in Africa with the restricted vision. I hoped it would come back quickly, that knack of making small, frequent head movements to avoid colliding with people or objects. Doing it while riding a bicycle was going to take some practice.

Luckily there was a large inner courtyard at the convent. I spent a while riding around it, attracting curious glances from nuns on their way to chapel. When I felt confident enough to venture outside, the nun who'd helped me to dress asked me if I'd step inside the chapel because the Mother Superior wanted to give me a blessing.

The office of matins was just coming to an end. I could hear the singing before I reached the great wooden door with its curlicued iron hinges. The sound had a disturbing effect. My nerves were already stretched to the breaking point, and those ethereal harmonies, so sweet and so familiar, brought tears trickling down my face. I wiped them away with the sleeve of my robe. I didn't want the Mother Superior to see me like that.

I waited at the back of the chapel until all the nuns had filed out. Then I was led up to the altar, where the Mother Superior was on her knees, praying. She stood up when she heard me coming—very sprightly for a woman whose face suggested she was in her late seventies. Her eyes were as pale and clear as the sea on a winter's morning. I knelt and bowed my head.

"Que Dieu vous bénisse, ma fille." The blessing transported me back to Belgium, to the day before I'd sailed for Africa, when the head of the order in Brussels had delivered an identical benediction.

The Mother Superior's hand rested on my veil, directly above the radio transmitters. She wouldn't be able to feel them through the stiff coif. And although she had sanctioned my disguise, I doubted that she knew I was carrying explosives under my robes. It seemed to be SOE policy to tell people the bare minimum. I could almost imagine the conversation between Jack and his commanding officer. *Tell the nuns we're taking radio parts to the Resistance—no need to mention the other stuff. We don't want a moral crisis fouling this thing up.*

I kept my eyes lowered as I got up to leave. To look at her would have brought fresh tears, tears of guilt this time. I hadn't realized just how powerful an effect it would have, putting on the habit, hearing the singing, kneeling before the kind of woman I would have had to answer to if I'd gone back to Dublin. The magnitude of my deception made me burn with shame.

The sister who had helped me to dress asked if I would like to come with her to the refectory for breakfast. But I couldn't face the sea of curious faces that would greet me there. I told her that I needed to be on my way. I waited in the courtyard while she went to fetch the medical supplies to put in the bicycle basket. This was to be my cover if I was questioned at any checkpoint: that I was on my way to treat a sick patient who was housebound. When she returned, she tucked a croissant and a couple of apples under the bandages.

My hands trembled as I pushed the bicycle out of the gate into the street. It was still early, but there were more people about now. Women with shopping baskets, elderly men with baguettes in one hand and newspapers in the other, children loitering in shop fronts on their way to school. I thought people would stare at me as I wobbled along, veil flying out behind me. But no one did. To the residents of Lannion, a nun on a bicycle was likely an unremarkable sight. The Ursulines were not an enclosed order. Like the one I had belonged to, this order had sisters working in the community as nurses, midwives, and teachers.

Soon the shops and houses petered out. I gripped the handlebars tight, the fear intensifying with the prospect of encountering a checkpoint. I didn't know exactly where it would be. According to intelligence, the Germans moved them often in a bid to outwit the Resistance.

In an attempt to calm myself, I tried to concentrate on the sights and sounds of the countryside I was passing through. The road had narrowed into a lane with hedges of hazel, hawthorn, and honeysuckle on either side. I could see the landscape through the gaps, where farm gates enclosed fields of ripening wheat and barley. It looked so much like Cornwall. Even the names of the places had a familiar ring. When I'd studied the map of the area around Lannion, I'd come across villages that sounded quite like Cornish ones: Penvern, Trebeurden, Brélidy. I hadn't realized until then that the ancient language of the region, Breton, had the same Celtic roots as Cornish and Irish.

I was heading to a place called Kermaria—five miles northeast of Lannion. Not far on a bicycle, I told myself. I wobbled as I took a tight bend in the road. The long black habit flew out in the breeze, threatening to catch in the spokes of the wheels. I could feel the hard edges of the explosives dig into my ribs as I leaned forward to keep my balance. The thought of falling was terrifying. What might the impact do to those miniature bombs?

Please, help me get through this. Keep me safe.

My whispered prayer was drowned out by the sudden trill of a blackbird in the branches of a sycamore that overhung the road. I went on praying, summoning faces to distract me from the mounting panic. I prayed for Ned, for Merle and her children, and, of course, for Jack. I pictured him on board *La Coquille*, throwing nets over the side as he and the other men played the part of fishermen, whiling away the daylight hours until it was time to drop anchor and lie in wait for me. I told myself that by this time tomorrow, we would be together, heading back to the Isles of Scilly, en route to Cornwall. The memory of his kiss was a powerful antidote to fear. All I had to do was keep calm and play a role I knew by heart.

I heard the German guards before I saw them. A vehicle screeched to a halt on the road ahead, screened from my view by the hedgerow. Doors slammed and greetings were shouted. I didn't speak the language, but *guten morgen* was easy enough to understand. I slowed down and dismounted, pushing the bike slowly toward the checkpoint. There were four of them, leaning against a truck painted in camouflage colors. They were laughing and passing round a flask of something. One of them stepped forward when he caught sight of me.

"*Bonjour!*" I tried to smile with my eyes, not my mouth, remembering what Sister Margarita had drummed into us at the convent in Dublin: *A sister should always have a serene visage and a gracious air.* With every breath I could feel the explosives strapped beneath my robe.

My French identity card was in the bicycle basket, tucked in beside the medical equipment. I reached for it and handed it over. I had my Irish passport, too, but I was only going to show that if they tried to arrest me.

The guard looked at the photograph—one of the ones Jack had taken a month ago. Then he searched my face. In the photo I wore nothing on my head, as regulations required. For one awful moment I thought he was going to ask me to remove my veil and wimple to see if

I truly resembled the image on the card. But after a couple of moments he waved me through.

My legs were trembling as I climbed back onto the bicycle. I almost got tangled up in my long robes. What an idiot I would have looked if I'd fallen flat on my face. My heart was pounding as I rode away. I was terrified that the guard would change his mind and come running after me. But all I could hear was the rise and fall of the men's laughter as they resumed their conversation.

I kept pedaling until I could no longer hear them. A few minutes later I spotted a signpost up ahead. It pointed the way to Kermaria and gave the distance I still had to travel. There were no such signs in Cornwall. All over Britain, they'd been removed in case of an invasion. I'd memorized the route to Kermaria, just in case the same thing had happened in Brittany—but it was reassuring to see the signpost.

I didn't know whether I'd encounter another checkpoint before I reached the farmhouse where the handover of equipment was due to take place. The road took me uphill for a while, and I began to overheat under the layers of cloth on my head and body. I stopped when I reached the brow of the hill. I had no water, but I reached for one of the apples in the basket, thinking that would be better than nothing. I could see a village in the valley below. The sun glinted on the slate roofs of cottages nestled around a church with a spire of honey-colored stone. I knew it must be Kermaria, and that the farmhouse was somewhere to the left of the road I was on, about half a mile short of the village itself. I could see a few lone buildings dotted around. The only clue I had to finding the right one was that it was approached down a lane opposite a field with a timeworn stone obelisk in the middle of it.

The rush of air as I coasted down the hill was a welcome relief. I slowed down when the road leveled out. The hedges were too overgrown to give any view of the fields beyond. The only way I was going to find the obelisk was to dismount and stop at every farm gate until I spotted it.

I'd been walking for about ten minutes when I caught sight of something glistening in the middle of a field of pale golden barley. The sun was lighting up the surface of a jagged slab of pinkish-gray stone that rose above the rippling stalks like a hunchbacked giant. I looked over my shoulder. There was a pathway on the other side of the road—more of a track than a lane. But it had to be the way to the farmhouse the Resistance was using.

I'd only gone a few yards off the road when I heard the crunch of tires behind me. Instinctively I pressed myself into the hedge, pulling the bike against my body. It was useless, of course: the track was too narrow for me to hide from anyone who passed by. My heart hammered as the sound grew louder. I didn't catch sight of the vehicle until it came around the bend. To my utter relief it was a van with the words *"Boulangerie Auffret de Kermaria"* painted on the side—the local bakery's delivery truck. I waited until it had disappeared around another bend, then followed behind.

As I approached the gates of the farmhouse, I heard the van's engine splutter and die. I crouched behind the stone pillar on one side of the gates, cautious about going any farther. Through the gap between the pillar and the hedge, I saw the back door of the van swing open. And then a woman, her hair flying out behind her as she jumped to the ground. My hand went to my mouth. I'd last seen that face grinning up at me from the belly of the dinghy before a tarpaulin covered it over. It was Miranda.

Chapter 22

I wanted to call out to her, but I bit my tongue. Someone else was getting out of the van. A man. He was tall and well built, olive skinned, with a bushy black mustache. He wore a pale blue shirt and loose-fitting corduroy trousers. Was he from the Resistance? The man I was supposed to be meeting? He was in the right place. But why had he brought Miranda here?

He stood by the van, looking around as if he were trying to spot something or someone. It had to be me he was looking for; he must have seen me when he drove past. There was a coded greeting I was supposed to give when I reached the farmhouse. But I was suddenly afraid to reveal myself—no longer sure who to trust.

Suddenly he called out: *"Où êtes-vous? Tante Marie vous attend!"* Where are you? Aunt Marie is waiting!

I clutched the pillar as I raised myself up, trembling with relief. *"Comment va Tante Marie? J'ai apporté quelque chose pour son mal de tête."* How is Aunt Marie? I've brought something for her headache.

He strode toward me, beaming. "Come inside," he said, still speaking in French. He took my bicycle and wheeled it to the front of the farmhouse, propping it against the whitewashed wall. He held the door open for me. Miranda was sitting at a rustic wooden table, tearing at a hunk of bread as if she hadn't eaten for weeks. She looked much thinner than when I'd last seen her. Her skin was very pale—almost translucent—and there were dark smudges under her eyes. She paused between bites, coughing. It was a cough I'd heard many times in the mission hospital: the harbinger of tuberculosis.

"What happened to you?" I sank down in the chair opposite hers.

She looked at me, still chewing, her face blank at first. Then her eyes lit up in recognition. She dropped the bread on the table. The chair scraped the floor as she pulled herself up. "My God! Ariel!" She came around the table and hugged me. "Oh, it's good to see you!"

"We were so worried . . . we thought . . ."

"That I was dead?" She held me at arm's length, her eyes wide as they traveled over my face. "I almost was—but I got away." She nodded at the man, who was pouring something from a jug into three glasses. "Josef found me this morning, hiding in the shed where he keeps his flour."

"She was lucky I got there first." He spoke in English this time, with a strong accent. "The Germans were on their way to take a sack of it for their camp. We had to lock her in the cellar until they'd gone." He put a glass down in front of me.

"What's this?" I lifted it to my mouth.

"Good Breton cider." He smiled. "It's very strong. Before you drink too much, I'd better take what you've brought for me."

There was so much I wanted to ask Miranda: so many questions about what had happened and how she'd survived. But I knew Josef was right. The priority was handing over what I'd smuggled past the Germans under my robe. And it would be a huge relief to shed the rolls of explosives chafing my skin.

I undressed upstairs in one of the bedrooms. There was a woman's nightgown strewn across the patchwork quilt of the double bed. Josef's wife's, I assumed. I wondered if she worked alongside him in the bakery, whether she'd helped to hide Miranda when the Germans came for their flour. The very ordinariness of the room—the rumpled bedclothes, the chamber pot under the chair—belied the remarkable bravery of these people. How much easier, and safer, it would be for them to kowtow to the enemy, accept the occupation, and carry on as best they could. But instead they were risking their lives to free the country they loved.

I went downstairs feeling lighter, freer, boosted by knowing that this part of the job was done. Josef was looking out of the kitchen window. He kept going back to glance across the yard as he produced more bread, along with butter and cheese, to go with the cider. Miranda and I shared it as she told me about the prison camp where she'd been held for the past three weeks.

"They didn't twig that I was an agent, or they would have tortured me." Her voice was as matter-of-fact as if she'd been commenting on the weather.

"Why did they arrest you?" I took another swallow of the cider. It was very bitter but warming as it went down.

"Because I was out after the curfew. I told them I was a history student from Paris, on a field trip to see the Neolithic standing stones of Brittany."

"But if they believed that why didn't they let you go?"

"They . . ." She glanced down at the lump of cheese on her plate. "They found another reason to keep me."

"Les bâtardes," Josef hissed.

Only then did I grasp the chilling reality that she had been raped by her captors, kept prisoner for no other reason than that. There were no words to convey the outrage I felt about what the Germans had done. I got up and went over to her, put my hand on her shoulder. But she shrugged it off.

"I'm all right." She nodded, and kept nodding, as if she were trying to convince herself. "What matters is what *I* took from *them*." She took something from her pocket and laid it on the table. It was a piece of silk, like the one Merle had given me.

"It's a map of the Atlantic Wall," she said, as she unfolded it. "It was passed to me by one of the other prisoners—a woman from the Resistance in Normandy—before she was taken out to be executed." She ran her finger along the blue line that meandered across the fabric from the top right-hand corner to the bottom left. "The Germans are planning to beef up their sea defenses in northern France. Up to now, only the ports have been fortified. But they're going to plant land mines and antitank devices on the beaches of Normandy." She pointed to red crosses dotted along the outline of the coast. "These show where the fortifications will be. Underwater obstacles and naval mines will be placed in waters just offshore. The intention is to destroy the Allied landing craft before they can unload on the beaches."

"She has to get this back to London." Josef glanced at me. "It's too complex to be sent by radio." He went over to the window again, his face grave. "She needs to be on that boat of yours tonight—but I can't take her any farther."

"Why not?"

"The Germans have been watching me. They'd think it very suspicious if they caught me driving to Lannion. They'd want to know why I was taking bread to a town where there are four boulangeries."

"And they'll be looking for me," Miranda said. "The prison camp's only ten miles from here. They're going to be searching any vehicle heading for the coast." She folded the map and put it back in her pocket. "My only chance would be to keep away from the roads: go through the fields and hide in hedges."

The brave smile couldn't conceal the paleness of her skin and the hollow look of her eyes. I wondered how she'd find the strength to walk the five miles to Lannion—more like six or seven miles, probably, if she was going through fields.

"There's another solution, though, isn't there?" She was looking at me intently. "*You* could take it."

I gazed back at her. "Well, yes, I could, but what about you? You can't go on hiding out here. You . . ." I faltered, not wanting to spell out what was on my mind: that she needed medical attention and somewhere safe to recuperate. "You could be putting other people in danger," I said instead. "Anyone who hides you would be at risk of being arrested—or worse." I paused, suddenly seeing another way. "Why don't you pretend to be me? Take these clothes and my identity card, and the bicycle. The Germans won't be surprised when they see the nun that passed through the checkpoint coming back a few hours later." I patted the coif on top of my head. "With this on, they won't even realize it's a different woman."

"But what will *you* do?"

"What you suggested: walk back through the fields. If I run into any trouble, I'll show my Irish passport—they can't detain someone from a neutral country." I sounded full of confidence. I knew that if I showed the slightest trepidation, she wouldn't go along with it. "I'll meet you after dark at the quayside in Lannion," I went on. "We'll row out to *La Coquille* together."

I could see her mind working, weighing it up. "I don't know," she said. She turned to Josef. "What do you think?"

"It's a good plan," he said. "She's right—you need to get back to England. You're a liability to us here." He sounded harsh, but it was what she needed to hear. Clearly she was too dedicated to put her own health first, but she wouldn't want to jeopardize the lives of others.

Miranda blew out a breath. "Okay." She turned back to me. "What about clothes? Mine are filthy and there's no time to wash them. You can't go traipsing across the countryside in your underwear."

"Go back upstairs and see what my wife has," Josef said. "She won't mind—as long as you don't take her Sunday best." He picked up the cloth bag that contained the explosives and transmitters I'd handed over. "I need to go now." He came and shook my hand, then Miranda's. *"Bonne chance."*

"Merci," Miranda replied. Under her breath she murmured: "We're going to need it."

We locked the door when Josef had gone, and ran upstairs. If I was going to walk back to Lannion, there was no time to lose. Miranda started searching through a chest of drawers by the window, looking for something suitable for me to wear. I sat down at the dressing table to unpin my veil. I'd only just started when she let out a cry of alarm.

"The Germans are coming!"

I ran to the window. A truck, like the one I'd seen at the checkpoint, was making its way down the track toward the farmhouse.

"Quick," I said. "Get into bed and lie absolutely still." I grabbed a clean white handkerchief that was lying on top of one of the open drawers.

"What are you going to do?" There was panic in her eyes.

"I'll tell them I'm nursing a TB case and if they come in, they'll catch it. Go on!" I shooed her toward the bed.

I took the stairs two at a time, almost tripping over my robe. I glanced around the kitchen, searching for something sharp. There was a knife hanging from a hook by the sink. I reached for it, my hands shaking. Then I pressed the point of it into the fleshy part of my left ring finger, just hard enough to draw blood. I caught the drops on the handkerchief as they oozed out.

I heard the truck roll into the yard and doors slam as the men jumped out. Then someone hammered on the door. *God help me.* I crossed myself as I went to unlock it. I opened it just a little—enough for the Nazi soldier to see my headdress and the crucifix hanging round my neck.

"Qu'est-ce que vous voulez?" What do you want? I hoped they wouldn't catch the tremor in my voice.

He didn't answer. Just shoved his foot against the door, forcing me back into the kitchen.

"Vous ne pouvez pas entrer." You can't come in. I waved the bloody handkerchief in his face. *"C'est trop dangereux."* Too dangerous. I cocked my head at the stairs. *"Un cas de tuberculose."* I mimed coughing and clutched my chest in case he didn't understand.

He took a step back, turning to the other man, muttering words I didn't know. I thought how young they both looked. So clean-cut. But men like these had raped Miranda.

When he turned back to me, he said, *"Un homme ou une femme?"* A man or a woman? His French was better than I'd anticipated.

"Une jeune fille," I replied. *"La fille du boulanger."* A young girl. The baker's daughter. *"Peut-être les avez-vous croisés sur la route. Lui et sa femme se sont installés à Kermaria."* Perhaps you passed him on the road—he and his wife have gone to stay in Kermaria.

"Nous cherchons une femme." We're looking for a woman. His eyes searched my face. Clear blue, piercing, like ice on the surface of a lake. *"Si vous voyez quelqu'un, vous êtes obligés de nous le dire."* If you see anyone you must tell us.

"Oui, bien sûr." I nodded. I shook out the bloodied handkerchief and said that I must go and see to my patient. The breeze caught it, blowing it within an inch of the man nearest to me. He recoiled, uttering a single word in German: *"Scheisse."* I didn't know what it meant, and I didn't care—all that mattered was that they were leaving.

I waited in the kitchen until the sound of the engine faded away. Then I ran upstairs. Miranda was by the window, watching the truck disappear. She gasped when I showed her the handkerchief.

"You're brilliant! I would never have thought of anything like that."

"You would if you'd worked in a hospital." I smiled with relief at our small victory.

Half an hour later she was ready to go. She looked so different. Almost unrecognizable. The black scapular emphasized the pallor of her skin. But the veil concealed the shadows under her eyes, which was a good thing. In addition to the wooden cross and the rosary beads, I'd given her the sleeve gun to wear beneath the robe. Her foot was on the pedal of the bicycle when I remembered the ring.

"You'd better have this, too." I twisted it off my finger and handed it to her.

"Isn't this a wedding ring?" She looked at me, bewildered. She must have thought it was my own ring, that I was married or a widow.

"Sort of," I replied. "It's what a nun receives when she takes her vows: it makes her a bride of Christ."

"You're very knowledgeable," she said, as she slipped it on.

I opened my mouth, then clamped it shut. There wasn't time to explain why I knew so much, no reason to tell her. She needed to be on her way, as did I.

"How on earth do women cope with this ridiculous getup?" She clicked her tongue as she hoisted the robe to knee height. "It'll be a miracle if I can ride without getting it tangled up in the chain. Honestly, you'd have to be mad to be a nun, wouldn't you?"

I felt my cheeks redden. I looked away, mortified by her honesty. *Mad.* No one had ever said that to my face. But my father had certainly thought it. Dan, too, probably. Perhaps it *was* a kind of madness that had made me join the Sisters of Mary the Virgin. Many aspects of the religious life had certainly seemed irrational, unnatural to me: the twice-weekly self-flagellation and the revolting feet-kissing penances. But did that make everything I'd done as a nun worthless? I thought of all the patients—hundreds over the years—that I'd treated in Africa, the village children I'd inoculated, and, above all, the baby twins I'd saved from certain death. Could I have done those things without being a nun?

Some of them, perhaps, but not in Africa: without the order, I'd never have had the means to get there.

"I feel bad about taking this stuff." Miranda's voice cut through my thoughts. "You needn't have offered it, but you did. That means a lot. I won't forget it. I'll meet you under the bridge. Good luck!" She blew a kiss as she lurched across the yard.

"God bless you." I whispered it under my breath. Saying it out loud might have sounded flippant, given what she was wearing. I watched her grow smaller as she rode off down the track wobbling a little as she got used to the robe flapping around her legs. We'd arranged to meet after the curfew, under cover of darkness. I'd made her promise that if I wasn't there by midnight, she'd leave without me. I warned her not to linger, because the tide would turn soon after that, and she would need the current to be with her, not against her, if she had to row out to *La Coquille* on her own.

I couldn't allow myself to dwell on the implications of that scenario: that Miranda leaving alone would mean that I had got lost, been arrested, or been shot. I went back into the house, up to the bedroom, and checked my reflection in the mirror. I hoped that I looked like a hiker in the woolen trousers and sweater I'd found, with my hair tucked under a scarf. If anyone challenged me, I planned to tell them a similar story to the one she had concocted—that I was an Irish student based in Paris, in Brittany to visit friends.

My reflection blurred as Jack's face flashed in front of me. I pictured him standing at the wheel of *La Coquille*, the wind in his hair as he chugged up and down the coast, waiting for the sun to go down. I kept the image in my head as I shut the bedroom door and made my way downstairs. I could hear his voice whispering, *See you tomorrow.* But what if I didn't make it to Lannion? What if he had to leave without me? The thought of that was not just terrifying—it was unendurable.

I told myself that it was only half a dozen miles or so. Easily walkable in a couple of hours. So long as I kept my head, there was nothing to fear. But no amount of bravado could alter the fact that I was venturing out without the protective cocoon of a nun's habit, without even a French identity card. I knew that if I got caught, there would be no guarantee of merciful treatment.

Please keep me safe. I shot the prayer like an arrow into the sky as I stepped outside.

Chapter 23

The afternoon air was hot and humid. I scrambled through a gap in the hedge when I reached the end of the farm track. Beyond it was rough pastureland. A herd of chestnut-colored cows eyed me curiously, then went back to chewing. I started walking, sending clouds of flies into the air as I dodged around the plate-sized piles of dung strewn across the grass.

I thought that if I kept close to the road, I wouldn't lose my way. But when I reached the boundary of the field, I saw that walking across farmland wasn't going to be as simple as I'd imagined. A stone wall surrounded the meadow I was in. Sharp edges of granite protruded at angles from the top of it. When I put my foot on the lower part, it felt as if it were about to give way.

I went farther along, testing it until I found a section that seemed more solid. The wall was higher than my head. When at last I managed to scale it, I caught a glimpse of a vehicle over the top of the hedge to my left. It was coming toward me. I could only see the roof and part of the windshield, but I was terrified that the driver would see me perched on top of the wall. In my panic I dropped down over the wall, catching my sweater on a jagged point of stone. I hung there for a moment, only one foot in contact with the ground, trying to unhook myself. The fabric ripped as it came away, and I fell in a heap onto the grass.

I breathed in the scent of damp earth and the sharp stink of fox. The side of my face was resting on a patch of nettles. When I lifted my head, my cheek felt as if it had been pricked by a dozen needles. The sleeve of my sweater was sticky with cow dung. Rolling over, I saw that it was all down the legs of my trousers, too. But I knew I was lucky to have got away with nothing worse than smelly clothes and a few stings. Looking up at the wall, I realized I could easily have sprained an ankle when I fell. I was going to have to be much more careful if I was going to reach Lannion in one piece. I heard the truck rumble by, the sound of the engine fading into the distance. That, at least, was one danger averted.

The time it took me to get safely over walls and through hedges made my progress far slower than I'd anticipated. I tried to keep to the edges of the fields, thinking that I'd be less likely to be spotted than if I was out in the open. It wasn't just the Germans I was afraid of. I knew I'd be in trouble if any farmer caught me tramping across his land: in Ireland it wasn't unheard of for them to take potshots at trespassers.

At one point, I threw myself to the ground in a field of barley when I caught sight of what I thought was a man standing between the rows of golden stalks. I don't know how long I lay there before I dared to raise my head, only to discover that what I'd seen was a scarecrow in the distance.

I kept looking at the sky, using the sun to check that I was going in the right direction. I could no longer see nor hear the road, and I was afraid I'd somehow veered away from the route I needed to follow. My map was still sewn inside the veil that Miranda was wearing, but I'd studied it well enough to know that I must keep going in a south-westerly direction to reach Lannion. Thankfully it was well past midday, which made it easier to figure out which way was west.

After what felt like many hours, I caught a glimpse of the river. I was so relieved to see it that I broke into a run across a field of cabbages. I could smell the bitter green scent of the leaves as my boots trampled them. I was so intent on reaching the boundary, on scaling the wall and seeing the harbor down below, that I didn't spot the gate set in the hedge to the left of me, or the three German soldiers perched on top of it, smoking cigarettes.

It was no wonder that they didn't believe my story. I was running through a field, with torn, dirty clothes, and nettle welts on my face that must have made me look as if I'd been in a fight. They took my passport and frog-marched me to a hut across the road. I was shaking and retching as they shoved me inside. When they locked the door, I was in total darkness. Panic seized me, making my heart thump so hard I thought I might pass out. There was nowhere to sit but the floor. I slumped in a corner, breathless, trying to recite the Hail Mary. I'd done the same thing when the *Brabantia* was torpedoed, whispering it over and over to quell the terror as I clung to life in the freezing water. I told myself I'd survived that and I'd survive this, that God wouldn't have saved me from death only to abandon me now.

But you've abandoned him. Sister Clare's face loomed out of the darkness.

"I *haven't*," I whispered. "I've never stopped praying, never stopped saying the rosary. Just because I don't wear the habit anymore doesn't mean I don't believe."

You've gone your own way, though, haven't you? Allowed that man to take God's place in your heart. A man who got a girl pregnant and drove her to her death.

"Yes, he did wrong. But he's not evil."

Isn't he? What about the boy? Isn't that wicked, deceiving a child?

The door of the hut flew open. I blinked, blinded by the orange rays of the sinking sun. A man stood, silhouetted against the light.

"You come from Ireland? But you are living in Paris?" He spoke in English, very loudly.

"Yes." I stood up, my legs tingling with pins and needles. I clutched the rough wooden wall beside me, firing prayers into the space between us. *Please, God, make him let me go. Don't let him hurt me. Help me get back to Jack.*

"Why were you running?" He started moving toward me.

"I . . . I disturbed a wasps' nest—when I climbed over a wall. They were stinging me." I touched the nettle rash on my face. This was the story I'd stuttered out when the men on the gate had pounced on me. I could smell the rancid cow dung on the cuff of my sleeve. He must have smelled it, too. He stopped. Took a step back.

"Your passport is being checked. You will stay here." He turned away, slamming the door behind him.

Once again, I was plunged into darkness. I sank onto the floor, hugging myself, glad of the reek of my clothes, because it was a kind of protection. Surely no man would want to touch me, smelling as I did. I told myself that it was still light outside, that if they let me go in the next couple of hours, I could still make it to Lannion before midnight. I groped around the hut, trying to find something other than the floor to sit on. My fingers found a pile of canvas—possibly tents—that I'd glimpsed when they'd thrown me into the hut. The texture reminded me of the sailcloth bed I'd made in the boathouse back in Cornwall. I sank down onto it and closed my eyes, conjuring precious images of Mermaid's Cove. How I longed to wake up to the lapping waves and the cries of seabirds, to walk through those enchanted gardens to the house, to read bedtime stories to Ned and the others, to sit in the library, chatting to Merle. And—what I'd never done but ached for most of all—to lie on a blanket under the stars with Jack.

I must have fallen asleep. The rattle of the key in the lock woke me. I scrambled to my feet, heart pounding.

"You can go now." It was the same voice as before. Not quite as loud. I could see his face this time, because he was standing outside the door, in the light. *The light.* It was still light. I could do it. Get back to the harbor in time to meet Miranda.

"Thank you." I took my passport from his outstretched hand as I stumbled out of the hut. There was another man, leaning against a truck, watching me. I nodded toward him and started walking. Down the road. Downhill to the river. I'd gone a few yards when I sensed that something wasn't right. The sun was behind me, not in front of me. It wasn't setting—it was rising.

Chapter 24

The bell woke me before dawn. I scrambled out of bed, onto my knees. For a few sleep-befuddled moments I thought I was back in Africa.

It was my second morning at the Ursuline convent at Lannion. I was in a dormitory of thirty other women. I could hear their murmured prayers, see the shapes of bodies behind the curtains that separated our beds as they rose from their knees to get dressed. I pulled the familiar calico shift over my head. The only thing that differed from my old life at the mission house in Africa was the number stitched inside the neck: 236 instead of 937.

I'd turned up at the door of the convent, filthy and near hysterical, on the day the Germans had let me go. They'd fed me, run a bath for me, and given me clean clothes. The Mother Superior herself, Mère de Saint-Philippe, had come to hear what had happened to me. She told me that I could stay at the convent for as long as I needed to. The only condition was that I must live as the nuns did, with no special treatment. It wouldn't be wise, she said, to draw attention to the fact that I was there. She didn't say the word *Resistance*, but it was clear that there must be no hint to the outside world of the nuns' sympathy for freedom fighters.

I was given the clothes a novice would wear: a short robe, just below knee length, and a white scarf, pinned at the nape of my neck. It was like being back in Dublin, when, a month before my eighteenth birthday, I'd made that fateful decision to join the Sisters of Mary the Virgin.

The kindness of the French nuns shamed me, intensified the guilt that had never gone away. But those feelings didn't eclipse what dominated my thoughts: my desperation to get a message to Jack.

Mère de Saint-Philippe had told me that Miranda had come to the convent to exchange the nun's habit for the fisherman's clothes I'd left behind. I'd gone to the harbor as soon as I reached Lannion, to make sure that the dinghy had gone. I'd stood staring at the metal ring the boat had been tied to, picturing Miranda waiting in the dark before finally giving up hope of me coming. I'd imagined Jack leaning over the side of *La Coquille*, bewilderment on his face when he realized that the woman climbing up the rope ladder wasn't me.

He would have had no choice but to return home: he had a boatload of escapees on board, and Miranda would have told him about the map. The urgency of getting that to London was paramount and would have to override any fears he had for my safety. I wondered what he would have been thinking as he set a course for the Isles of Scilly. It must have crossed his mind that I might be dead. I had to find a way of letting him know that I was alive.

I knew that the Mother Superior must be in communication with the Resistance. My first impulse was to ask if she could get word to England that I'd made it back to Lannion and was living at the convent. But I realized what a selfish request that would be. Any sister who undertook it would be putting herself at risk. I had to work out a way to do it myself.

After matins on my third day at the convent, I asked permission to write a letter. I knew it would be useless to try to mail anything to Jack in England—no letters were permitted to be sent from occupied France. There was only one person I knew who could get a message to him. I didn't know the exact address. I hoped that "Monsieur Josef Auffret, La Boulangerie, Kermaria" would suffice. This is what I wrote:

> *Cher Monsieur Auffret,*
> *Merci de dire à votre livreur que je dois annuler ma*
> *commande de baguettes car je déménage à Lannion. Ma*
> *facture doit être envoyée à ma soeur, Madame Antoine.*
> *Très amicalement, Mademoiselle Ariel*

The Mother Superior agreed that it sounded innocent enough: a woman canceling her bread order because she was moving to another town and giving instructions for her outstanding bill to be sent to her sister. Josef would know there was a hidden message as soon as he saw who it was from. *Votre livreur* meant "your deliveryman"—an obvious enough reference to Jack. Josef probably wouldn't grasp the significance of *"ma soeur, Madame Antoine,"* but Merle would when it came in via Morse code. Not "my sister, Mrs. Anthony" but "Sister Anthony"—my nun's name. It would convey the message that I'd found my way back to the convent.

Josef wouldn't be able to reply to my letter, of course. I would just have to trust that on the next new moon, arrangements would be put in place for me to join whoever was being picked up from the beach south of Lannion.

To wait a whole month to see Jack again seemed like an eternity. I told myself I was lucky to be in a place that was safe and familiar. In the meantime, I tried to make myself useful at the convent. Part of the building housed an infirmary, where twenty-five elderly invalids who had no family were cared for by the nuns. I asked if I could help with the work there.

My days began to fall into the same pattern they had followed in the Congo, rising early to go to chapel, eating a silent meal in the

refectory, then going to the infirmary. The passing hours were punctuated by the bell summoning me to prayers at regular intervals.

At the end of my first full week at the convent, Mère de Saint-
Philippe summoned me to her office. Her pale blue eyes had a *Mona
Lisa* look about them.

"Vous vous êtes très bien intégrée ici, ma fille." You have fit in very
well here, my daughter.

I was glad she thought so.

"The sisters have told me what a lovely singing voice you have," she
went on in French. "You sing with such confidence—even in Latin."
She was looking straight into my eyes. I felt as if she could see inside my
head, see me squirming. I knew then that I couldn't go on pretending.
She had guessed my secret.

I dropped my head, unable to bear the searchlight gaze. *"J'aurais dû
vous le dire. J'ai été nonne."* I should have told you. I used to be a nun.

She murmured something I didn't catch. Then she asked me why
I hadn't wanted to tell her.

"I . . . I was ashamed," I mumbled in French. "You've been so
kind . . ." Suddenly it all came tumbling out. The row with my
father over Dan, the dream of nursing in Africa, the pain of rescuing the twins and then being separated from them, the attack on the
Brabantia and the chance of a new life in Cornwall.

"You were on your way back to Ireland, to your motherhouse?"

"Yes. But I didn't want to go—I knew that, even before the ship
was hit."

"Do they know what happened to you?"

I stared at my feet. There was no hint of accusation in her voice,
nothing judgmental in what she had said. But under her gaze I felt like
an utter hypocrite. I thought about the things I'd said to Jack—how I'd
berated him for not owning up to being Ned's father. How could I have
done that when I hadn't even had the guts to tell the nuns in Dublin
that I'd survived the shipwreck?

"I accuse myself of dishonesty, Reverend Mother." Even in French, the words had such familiarity. I had slipped back into the discipline of the mea culpa without even realizing it. My face burned with humiliation. I was expecting a penance to be pronounced—foolish, as I was no longer a nun. But what she said to me was quite different from that. She asked me if I'd lost my faith.

I tried to swallow down the choking feeling in my throat. "N . . . no—I've never stopped believing."

"Do you think that God sent you to Cornwall?"

"I . . . I don't know . . ." I faltered. "I told myself that he wouldn't have saved me from drowning unless he had some other purpose for me. I prayed for guidance. And . . . then I was asked to do this secret work."

She was silent for a moment. I wondered if she was praying, too: for the right words for someone who had rejected everything she represented. "You have many fine qualities," she said at last. "You are courageous. You put your own life at risk to keep that young woman safe. And you are kind and caring—the sisters at the infirmary have seen that. But you will never be at peace with yourself until you put right the wrong you have done."

Tears pricked the back of my eyes. "How can I do that? They think I'm dead." I knew in my heart that even if it had been physically possible—if a ship had magically appeared in Lannion harbor, willing and able to transport me to Ireland—I would have said no. I would have begged them to take me to Cornwall instead.

"If you wish, I will write to the Mother Superior in Dublin when you have left us. I will lay out the facts as you have related them to me. I'll tell her to expect a letter from you in due course."

"Th . . . that would be . . ." My voice died, overcome by her compassion.

"It would be the first step," she said. "What happens after that will be up to you."

I nodded, coughing to clear my throat. "But is it possible for you to send a letter? I thought . . ."

"To a neutral country, yes. It might be opened, of course, but I'll be careful not to include any information that would put you or the work you do at risk."

She stood up and came around the desk to where I was sitting. She laid her hand on my head and said: *"Seigneur Dieu, bénis ta fille et donne la paix."* Lord God, bless your daughter and give her peace.

I couldn't help myself then: the words released all the pent-up emotion of the past weeks and months. Tears streamed down my face.

In the days that followed I worked in the infirmary, went to chapel, ate my meals with the nuns, and behaved, in every respect, as if I'd never left the religious life. But often, as I was washing one of the elderly patients or reciting the familiar words of a psalm or a prayer, I would be hundreds of miles away, walking beneath towering stands of bamboo, ducking under the clustered blossoms of rhododendrons, and running my fingers over the furry trunks of tree ferns. I would be chasing Ned through the churchyard, or walking alongside Jack, with Brock sniffing at my heels. Sometimes it would be early morning, and I would be sitting alone outside the boathouse, throwing crumbs to the tame robin and listening to the whisper of the waves. And other times it would be dark, with stars pricking the sky like pins in purple velvet, and Jack would be lying beside me on a blanket on the sand.

Each night, on my way to bed, I would glance out of the dormitory window, searching for the moon. I watched it wax to full, then lost sight of it as it waned to a quarter, rising too late to be visible at bedtime. I was counting the days—only a week now—until it disappeared completely. I pictured Jack piloting the motor launch from its hiding place in one of the creeks along the Helford River, bringing it round to the jetty where the agents would be waiting, and blind George Retallack standing in the shadows of the schoolhouse, listening for the signal to untie the rope.

I'd hoped for a communication of some kind—confirmation that Jack had received my message. But as the days wore on and nothing came, I told myself that he would have thought it too dangerous for the Resistance to make direct contact with the convent. I knew the window of time when *La Coquille* would be able to return to Brittany, and where the dinghy would come ashore. All I had to do was be there.

Two days before the new moon, Mère de Saint-Philippe summoned me to her office. This time there was no hint of a smile on her face: her eyes were glacial. She motioned me to sit down. Then she reached into a drawer and pulled out a sheet of newsprint. Without a word she pushed it across the desk.

It was the front page of *L'Heure Bretonne*—the regional newspaper. There was a grainy image of a boat beneath the headline: *"La voie d'évacuation secrète."* Secret Escape Route Exposed.

My mouth went dry as I read the report. Someone had betrayed us. The Germans knew all about the clandestine runs between Cornwall and Brittany. Not only did they know, they had taken drastic action to destroy the escape route: "Following the information received, a bombing raid was carried out yesterday in the Isles of Scilly, and much damage was done to boats in New Grimsby harbor." Frantically I searched for the date the newspaper had come out. Monday, June 28—two days ago.

My heart hammered as I saw it in my mind's eye. The peace of New Grimsby Sound shattered as German planes screamed overhead raining destruction, fire ripping through the hull of *La Coquille*, her engine exploding in a plume of black smoke. He wouldn't have been there, would he? Not *four* days before the new moon?

"C'est un coup terrible, je sais." It's a terrible blow, I know.

I couldn't reply. My throat was paralyzed.

She told me not to be afraid, that all the nuns were praying for me and for the safety of the brave souls who had risked their lives to save others. As she spoke, I felt as if I were hovering above my own body, looking down at myself, nodding like an automaton. She was saying that I could stay on at the convent—that as I had never formally left the Sisters of Mary the Virgin, I could resume the religious life in Brittany, if I chose—and that to try to get back to England now would be impossible.

I stared, stupefied, into her pale, kind eyes. Was this God's judgment? For going my own way and telling myself it was what he wanted? A voice inside me screamed. *Punish me, then! But just let Jack be alive.*

Chapter 25

That night I lay awake, watching the curtains surrounding my bed fade to gray with the dying light. No matter how many times I told myself that Jack wouldn't have been aboard *La Coquille* when it was bombed, I couldn't help fearing the worst. The times of our departure had varied, depending on the tide and the weather conditions: on our first mission, we'd reached the Scillies two days before the new moon, but the second time it had been a whole day earlier. If a storm had been predicted for that crucial time of darkness, Jack might have headed for New Grimsby in advance of it. I prayed with all my heart that he hadn't.

The worst thing was not knowing. There was no way of finding out unless I risked a journey to Kermaria to find Josef Auffret—and that would put him in danger as well as myself. The thought of going on living at the convent, agonizing over Jack, was unbearable. I knew with absolute certainty that I couldn't return to my old life. The person I had been before the shipwreck was gone forever. It wasn't only Jack that I yearned for. I longed for Mermaid's Cove—for the salt tang of the breeze and the sound of the waves, for the lush valley and the warbling of birds in the green canopy of leaves, for Ned's laughter as he stamped through snowdrifts of fallen petals, for cozy evenings chatting with Merle in the library. Cornwall called to me like a siren. I had to get back. But how?

The next morning, I asked to see Mère de Saint-Philippe. I had to tell her that I couldn't stay at the convent—that no matter what the danger, I had to find a way of getting back to England. During the night I'd come up with a plan. If I could go south to Spain, a neutral country, I could find a boat that would take me back to England. But for that I would need money. The only option was to beg for a loan, to be repaid on my return. I knew it was a lot to ask: the money they had was meant for much more worthy purposes, and if anything happened to me along the way, they might never get the loan back. But I was desperate.

The Mother Superior listened to my request without interruption. When I'd finished explaining she sat silently contemplating for a moment before she spoke.

"Cet homme—êtes-vous amoureux de lui?"

My breath caught in my throat. She wanted to know if I was in love with Jack. Was I so transparent? "I . . ." I dropped my head. She must think me very weak—and that I had strayed very far from the vows I'd taken. I looked up at her, shamefaced. But before I could frame any reply, she said something equally unexpected: that being in love with Jack didn't mean that I loved God less.

"L'amour entre un homme et une femme est sacré aussi," she said. The love between a man and a woman is holy, too.

It felt as though she were giving us her blessing, as if she somehow knew that Jack was alive and that, with her help, I could reach him. She said that she would have to discuss the question of a loan with the senior sister who dealt with the finances. I kissed her hand as I left the room, not knowing what was about to unfold: that within hours I would be leaving the convent without so much as a centime in my pocket.

I was feeding supper to one of the elderly ladies in the infirmary when Sister Thérèse, the nun who had helped me dress for my mission with the Resistance, came to find me. She told me that someone was waiting to see me in the nuns' recreation room. When I asked her who it was, she put her finger to her lips. She took the spoon from my hand and motioned for me to go.

I made my way along the passageway that connected the infirmary to the main part of the convent, wondering if the Mother Superior had somehow already got word to the Resistance that I needed to get to Spain. Merle had told me that there was a whole network of teams operating across occupied France, with established escape routes overland, as well as by sea. Perhaps the person waiting for me would be able to tell me how to find a courier who was heading south.

I had the shock of my life when I opened the door to the recreation room.

"George?"

"Miss Alice? Is that you?"

I ran and hugged him, almost knocking his white stick from his hand. "I can't believe it! How on earth did you get here?"

"In Leo Badger's boat." He smiled. "Didn't reckon 'e'd be needin' it for a while yet, so me an' 'Is Lordship painted out the name an' turned her Froggy like. *La Patelle*, she's called now: that means limpet in French, 'e tells me. Anyway, 'e sent me to tell you 'e's waitin' for you down at the 'arbor."

Frantic with joy, I was barely coherent when Mère de Saint-Philippe came to say goodbye. George and I walked out of the convent arm in arm. What could have looked more natural, more normal, than a nun helping a blind man along the streets of the town?

On the way to the harbor he told me how the plan to rescue me had evolved. He was careful not to raise his voice above a whisper—he seemed to sense when people were about to pass by, even when they were still yards away. It had been his idea, he said, to use Leo's boat. Jack had contemplated taking the motor launch across the Channel, but it would have attracted too much attention. It had been a rough crossing in such a small boat, but they knew she could make it to France because Leo had done it before: he'd been one of dozens of fishermen who had answered the call to rescue retreating British troops from Dunkirk in 1940.

"When we got 'ere 'Is Lordship was all for going to fetch you 'imself," George went on. "But I told 'im 'e was more likely to be rumbled than me, if anyone spotted 'im trying to get inside a convent. 'E asked me 'ow I'd find my way, an' 'ow I'd make the nuns understand when I got there, not 'avin' a word of French. So, I got 'im to write me two messages in French, one on card an' one on paper, so's I could tell the difference. The first one said: 'Where is the convent?' An' the second said: 'I need to speak to the Irish sister.'"

"But weren't you afraid of being stopped? What would have happened if someone had started asking questions?"

He made a muffled, mumbling sound, raising his white stick and waving it in front of his face. "When folks see that you're blind, it's easy to fool them into believing there's other things wrong with you." He chuckled. "Piece of cake, it was."

I squeezed his arm. "Thank you for being so brave."

"It's nothing, miss," he replied. "I 'aven't 'ad this much fun in a long time. An' anyway, one good turn deserves another. You saved Leo's life, remember."

We soon reached the riverbank. The boats were lined up along the quayside. Men were sitting or standing on the decks, smoking, mending nets. Cooking smells wafted from some of the boats—mussels steaming in wine, fish frying with garlic and onions. We attracted a few curious glances as we walked along, me scanning the side of each vessel for the right name. I was talking in French as I walked, and George nodded away as if he understood every word. We kept up the act until I spotted the magic words: *La Patelle. The Limpet.* I thought my heart would burst out of my rib cage.

"Bonsoir, Soeur Antoine!" There he was, pushing his dark hair back from his forehead as he emerged from belowdecks. My legs threatened to give way as I helped George onto the gangplank.

"Merci pour votre aide." Somehow Jack managed to sound completely natural. *"Voulez-vous prendre un verre de vin avec nous?"*

I felt a bubble of hysterical laughter rise in my chest. He was thanking me for my assistance, asking me if I would stay for a glass of wine. It was insane, having to go through this charade when all I wanted was to throw my arms around his neck. Struggling to keep my face straight and my French suitably formal, I thanked him for his invitation and said that I would prefer a glass of mineral water, if he had some. With a little nod he took my hand, ushering me toward the steps to the galley while George tactfully settled himself down on a coil of rope. I almost tripped over my robe in my haste to get down there.

"Oh, Alice! I thought I'd lost you!" He pulled me to him, laughing as my coif bumped against his forehead.

"And I thought I'd never . . ." The words died away as my mouth found his. We stood there in the galley, wrapped in each other's arms—a ridiculous sight, no doubt, if anyone could have seen us, me in my nun's habit and him in clothes smeared with fish guts and engine oil. His skin still had that fragrant Christmas-tree smell, despite two days at sea. It flooded my senses as we clung together, devouring each other.

When at last we broke away he brought his hand up to my face, stroking my cheek as he gazed into my eyes. "I wish we had more time—but we've got to get going." He glanced toward the steps up to the deck. "The other fishing boats will be heading out at dusk, and we need to be among them. The Germans have got gun emplacements at the mouth of the estuary. They've been on high alert ever since they found out what we've been up to."

He had fisherman's clothes for me to change into. As I unpinned my veil and removed the various layers of the headdress, I heard the chug of engines as the boats moored nearby began to pull away from the harbor. If there had been more time, I might have lingered over the sight of the nun's habit, neatly folded, now lying on the bench seat: my old life, discarded not with guilt this time, but with a new sense of hope and anticipation.

I pulled on the corduroy trousers and the baggy shirt. The identity card I'd carried on the first trip to France was in the pocket of the trousers. I was Jean-Luc Piquemal, fisherman, from Saint-Brieuc, a few miles to the south of Lannion. Tucked inside the identity card was a note, handwritten in French:

> *Dear friend,*
> *I heard this morning that you are coming home. There*
> *are no words to describe what that news meant to me.*
> *Thanks to you, my precious package arrived, the contents*
> *of which were received with immense gratitude, and are*
> *already being put to good use. I wish you a safe journey.*
> *Miranda*

I smiled as I read it. She had chosen the words carefully, not compromising my identity, nor giving any clue to what she and I had done. It simply sounded like the message of one close friend to another. I pictured her going into the SOE office in London, unfolding the map of the Atlantic Wall in front of eager, astonished faces. What a prize that was. I hoped that now they would give Miranda a rest—make sure she got the medical treatment she needed.

I tucked the note back in my pocket, then tied a bandanna around my head. There was no mirror in the tiny space belowdecks, so I couldn't check whether I'd made a decent job of concealing my hair. I shrugged as I tucked in a stray tuft, telling myself it didn't much matter, because soon I would be away from here, free from all the pretense, free to be my new self.

When I got up on deck the light was fading. The boats on either side of us had already gone. Jack called to me in French from the wheelhouse. "I'm going to get her started. Will you cast off? Just jump back on before she starts to move."

As I headed for the gangplank I glanced at George, who was sitting in the stern, playing a harmonica. The haunting melody reminded me of Irish folk songs I'd learned at school. His face was in shadow. From this distance it was impossible to tell that he was blind. I thought of how heroic he'd been, setting out alone to find me at the convent.

The gangplank wobbled as I stepped onto it. I was going to have to be careful getting back aboard after I'd untied the ropes—otherwise I'd end up in the river. I went to the first of the two mooring posts and bent over it.

"Arrêtez!" The voice loomed out of the twilight. Twisting my head, I saw a thickset man in uniform coming toward me, a gun holster silhouetted against his body. *"Quel est votre nom?"* His French was heavily accented, his tone brusque.

"Je m'appelle Jean-Luc Piquemal," I mumbled, praying that the pitch of my voice wouldn't give me away.

"Montrez-moi votre carte d'identité." Show me your identity card.

He shone a flashlight onto the fake document. Then he barked out more questions: the name of the boat and what we were doing in Lannion. I kept my voice as low as I could. Inside I was trembling, terrified that he'd see through my disguise. I wondered if he'd been watching when I boarded the boat—seen a nun get on but not get off.

"This boat is not registered. Stay there!" He stepped onto the gangplank, then boarded the boat. It creaked with his weight. My heart lurched as I remembered my convent clothes, lying in the galley. What if he went down there? I craned my neck, desperate to alert Jack. But he was in the wheelhouse. He wouldn't see anything. And with the noise of the engine, he wouldn't hear a thing.

I could see the top of George's head at the other end of the boat. I saw it jerk backward, as if he'd been shoved. The German was shouting at him. I heard the words *stupid* and *pig* barked out in French. He was trying to interrogate George in the same way he'd done to me, but of course, George couldn't reply—if he opened his mouth, he would give away that he couldn't speak the language.

Panic rose like bile in my chest. I heard a crash and a yell. I couldn't stand the thought of George, blind and defenseless, at the mercy of a man wielding a gun. I leapt onto the gangplank with no idea what to do other than to put myself between them. But as I reached the top, I saw that Jack was already there. He'd grappled the German from behind, one hand over his mouth and the other on his right arm, pinning it to his side. The gun had dropped onto the deck. I ran over and grabbed it. But as I looked up, I saw Jack stagger backward. He landed with a sickening thud on the deck. The German lurched at me, yanking my arm to get the gun. I don't remember my finger finding the trigger, don't remember squeezing it; all I can recall is the crack as it went off, like a branch giving way in a storm. And the weight of his body as he collapsed onto me.

Chapter 26

I lay on the deck, unable to move. I could smell the blood oozing from his body. I called to George to help me—in such a state of shock that I forgot to speak in French. George pulled the German off me, then helped me to sit up.

"Are you all right, Miss Alice?"

"Y . . . yes, I think so." I rubbed my arm where it had been pinned to the deck. "Is he . . . ?"

"No, miss—'e's still breathing."

"Oh . . . thank God . . . I . . . but what about . . ." I went to move but my legs buckled under me. I couldn't see Jack. I thought he'd fallen a few feet from where I was lying. Then I caught sight of something moving. Jack's hand, feeling his head. He was across the deck, on the starboard side. Before I could call out to him, he was on his feet.

"Oh, darling . . ." He was beside me, cradling me in his arms. "Are you hurt?"

I shook my head. "I . . . I shot him . . . I . . . I didn't m . . . mean to . . . I . . . th . . . thought I'd . . ." I began to shake uncontrollably.

He drew me closer and kissed my mouth, stilling the rattle of my teeth. "Please, don't get upset; we'll sort him out. We need to get going now—quickly, before anyone else comes. Can you just hold on while I cast off?"

I nodded. *I* should have done it, but I was paralyzed by a mixture of horror and revulsion. It was only when the man that I had shot let out a grunt of pain that I snapped out of it. The wound was at the top of his left arm. The sleeve of his jacket was bloody, but if an artery had been severed, it would have been completely soaked by now. I asked George if there was a knife up on deck that I could use to cut the jacket off.

"I know what 'Is Lordship would say," George muttered. "Finish the bugger off! The only good German's a dead German."

"This war's taken enough lives already, George," I said. "He might be the enemy, but he's a human being, just like us."

It was fully dark by the time we reached the open sea. The German was tethered by his ankles to the bunk bed he was lying on, and his good arm was bound to his body. Jack had insisted on this. If, as George had suggested, Jack would have preferred to shoot the man dead or dump him over the side of the boat, he didn't say so. He hadn't protested when I'd asked him to help me. He'd simply said that we needed to wait to get him belowdecks until *La Patelle* was far enough up the estuary to be safe from any harbor patrol. So, I'd covered the man with a blanket and sat beside him, ready to clamp my hand over his mouth if any boat approached us.

Once we got the German down to the galley, I swapped the bandanna I'd used as a bandage for the nun's skullcap I'd taken off when I boarded the boat—the strings on the cap made it easier to tighten, to stem the loss of blood.

"*Quel est votre nom?*" I asked him as I screwed the top back onto the bottle of iodine I'd found.

"Gunter," he breathed. "*Qu'est-ce que vous allez faire de moi?*" What are you going to do with me?

I told him that we would take him back to England; that he would be treated in a hospital and then would go to a prison camp. I asked him if he had a family in Germany, and he told me that he was married with a son and a daughter. I said that I would make sure that the Red Cross sent word to them that he was okay. Later, when I went up on deck to retrieve the jacket I'd had to cut off him, I found a wallet with a photograph of his wife and children tucked inside. The little boy was about the same age as Ned, the girl a year or two older than Jacqueline. Tears stung my eyes as I held it up to the hurricane lamp I was carrying. I'd almost killed their father. In the end, we were just the same: ordinary people dragged into terrible situations.

I took it to show Jack in the wheelhouse. He bit his lip as he stared at it. "I'm thankful, for their sake, that he's alive," he said. He took one hand off the wheel and slipped it around my waist. "You know, when I thought you might be dead . . . the . . . the sense of loss . . ." He pulled me closer. "It was . . . overpowering. I kept thinking about what you'd said that last night we were together, that bricks and mortar were more important to me than people." I felt him draw in a long breath. "One day Ned came to me, crying. He'd fallen down and cut his knee. He wanted you, Alice. He wanted to know where you were and why you hadn't come back. It struck me then, like a body blow, what it was going to be like for him growing up without a mother or a father. I suddenly saw what you'd tried so hard to tell me: that a grand house and a noble name have no real value if they cause pain."

I stretched up and kissed the side of his face. "That's good to hear," I murmured. "I'm sorry I was so heavy handed about it—but you know I had to say it."

He nodded. "I realized something else that day Ned hurt his knee. I took him fishing in the rock pools to try to cheer him up. When we passed the boathouse, he said he wished he could live there, instead of at Penheligan. When I asked him why, he said: 'Because it's a happy place.' That cut me to the quick. But he was quite right. Penheligan has never been a happy place—not in all the time I've lived there." His hand slid up my back, stroking the hair at the nape of my neck. "I've been happier these past few months, visiting you at the boathouse, than I've been in years. I didn't want to see it, didn't want to believe that someone so steeped in the beliefs I'd turned away from could be a better person than me. But you are. You offer your love with no strings attached; you always put other people first. What you did for Miranda was amazing: you sacrificed your own safety to ensure hers."

I kissed him again. I was going to tell him how much I'd missed him when we were apart, that what I'd longed for more than anything was to be back there with him, lying on a blanket on the sand, under the stars. But his lips were on my ear, nuzzling the skin, sending shivers of rapture down inside.

"We don't get many chances to be happy, do we?" he murmured. Then, with one hand still on the wheel, he dropped down on one knee. "Alice, will you marry me?"

Chapter 27

The sea was the color of the jacaranda flowers that heralded spring in the Congo, lilac blue in the twilight of a September evening. Our ship was gliding through the English Channel, heading south. We could see the lights of France twinkling across the water. By midnight, we would be off the coast of Brittany, passing close to the place where things could have turned out so very differently for Jack and me.

"Isn't that a wonderful sight?" I leaned over the rail of the liner, craning my neck.

"It is." Jack's hand was on my shoulder. "Hard to believe it's more than a year since the place was liberated. Even harder to believe that we played a part in bringing it about."

Another, smaller hand tugged at my skirt. "Mummy, is it dinner-time yet? I'm hungry."

I bent down to straighten the captain's cap that had slipped so far back on Ned's head that it was about to fall off. Merle and Fred had given it to him on his birthday, and he insisted on wearing it all the time, even at the table. "I'm sorry, sweetheart, it won't be long now. I promise." I glanced at Jack. "We'll have to ask if he can have his meals earlier in future."

Jack dropped to his knees, his head level with Ned's. "Tonight's a special occasion," he said. "That's why you're allowed to stay up late, with all the grown-ups. It's Mummy and Daddy's wedding anniversary. Do you remember that day?"

Ned nodded. "I was hiding behind the door with Auntie Merle. And when you came out of the church, we throwed those things at you."

"Rose petals." Jack smiled up at me. "They stuck in Mummy's hair, didn't they? She looked like the fairy queen."

"And then we had currant cake—and Louis was sick on Danny's dress."

"It's funny, what kids remember, isn't it?" Jack murmured as we made our way down to the dining room. "What sticks in my mind is all the faces. The smiles. People like Leo Badger and George Retallack—the whole village, crammed into the church, singing their hearts out."

"Is that *all* you remember?" I nudged him in the ribs with my elbow.

"Well, of course, I couldn't wait for it to get dark." He gave me a sidelong glance. "We were lucky it was so warm, weren't we? And thank heaven for the blackout . . ."

The memory of our wedding night was as vivid as if it had happened days ago, not two whole years before. Jack had laughed when I'd asked if we could spend it at the boathouse. He said he'd thought of taking me to London—to somewhere fancy, like the Ritz. But it had been magical, lying outside on a blanket, listening to the lap of the waves and the piping cries of the seabirds, watching the sky turn scarlet in the west as the sun disappeared, counting the stars as they began to appear. And then, when it was dark enough to know that no one could possibly see us, we'd begun undressing each other.

In the morning we'd found rose petals everywhere. They must have tumbled out of our clothes. I'd even found some in my underwear. The tide was in and we'd run into the waves, wading out as far as the barricade across the cove before wrapping arms and legs around each other and making love again, right there, in the water.

There hadn't been time for a proper honeymoon. Although we could no longer make the clandestine runs across to Brittany, there was plenty for us to do. As well as intercepting messages and training the agents who were still being parachuted in, we had two hundred American soldiers camping in the cow pastures beyond the walled garden. They were building a road through the valley to the beach, preparing for the tanks that would soon be on their way to France for the D-Day landings.

"Mummy, will there be ice cream?" Ned's voice brought me back to reality.

"We'll have to wait and see," I replied. "You'll have to eat up all your dinner first."

Later, when he was tucked up in bed, we sat outside the cabin in deck chairs, sipping champagne. I reminded Jack of the day, eight months after the wedding, when we'd sat on the rocks above the cove watching hundreds of American troops massing at the water's edge, about to embark for the Normandy beaches.

"Yes, I remember," he said. "We'd just been to see the stone, hadn't we? We counted all the tanks and jeeps as they came down the valley. It was never ending—and we watched them all being loaded onto the landing ship."

I nodded. On that day, June 1, 1944, Jack had erected a granite tombstone in the churchyard in memory of Morwenna. It gave the dates of her birth and death, and the fact that she was the mother of Edward John Trewella. It had been Jack's final act of contrition, his way of making peace with the past. We'd taken Ned with us to see the stone put in place and explained to him that his real mummy had died when he was a baby—just like Jack's mother, whose gravestone was just yards away. We'd been worried about Ned's reaction, but he didn't cry. He stared at the inscription for a while, then heard the shouting in the cove below. Half an hour later he was so engrossed in watching the American troops he seemed to have forgotten everything else.

Jack reached for my hand. "I wish they hadn't had to blow up the boathouse. That upset you terribly, I know."

The memory of seeing the shattered ruins of my old home brought a lump to my throat. They'd had to dynamite it to make way for the tanks they were transporting to France.

"We'll rebuild it, I promise, when we open the place up to the public," he said. "The War Office has a fund to help put things back to how they used to be."

"I'm looking forward to that," I replied. "To working with you on the house and the gardens." That was how we planned to live: inviting the outside world in to experience the history and beauty of the Penheligan estate. Merle and Fred were already hard at work, converting one of the barns into a tearoom, which Merle was going to run while Fred helped us restore the lush tranquility of the tropical groves Jack's ancestors had created.

We'd had to sell off some of the farmland to raise the extra cash, which had been a hard decision for Jack. He hadn't liked the idea of people invading what had always been his family's private sanctuary. But when I told him what a healing place the valley had been for me, how simply walking among the towering trees and fragrant shrubs had felt like a spiritual experience, he'd been persuaded that others should share that.

"I couldn't even have contemplated it without you." He squeezed my hand. "I was like a bird in a gilded cage. You opened the door, Alice."

I smiled and leaned in close, brushing his cheek with my lips. If I had opened a door for Jack, then he had opened one for me—the day he'd gathered me up from where the sea had swept me, seen past the flotsam of my life, and given me the chance to be the person I was meant to be.

It took us ten days to reach our destination. We stopped at Lisbon, then the island of Tenerife, and at various ports down the west coast of Africa before docking at Lobito in the Portuguese territory of Angola. It gave me a dizzy sense of déjà vu, stepping off the gangplank, as I had eleven years ago. Like a reluctant host, the smell rose up to greet me—the odor of decay mixed with engine oil and the tang of spices. Women dressed in brilliant colors stared out from behind market stalls stacked with swordfish, bushmeat, cigarettes, and soap. Men milled around, loading cargo, piling suitcases. Mangy dogs and skinny cats lurked in the shadows, hiding from the burning sun.

We faced a long and dusty train ride east, across the border to the Belgian Congo, but I didn't mind and neither did Jack—especially when the motion of the wheels lulled Ned to sleep and I broke the news I'd been longing to reveal.

"A baby?" Jack stared at me, a bewildered smile on his face. "How long have you known?"

"Well, I wasn't sure, but I suspected before we left Cornwall."

"Why didn't you tell me?" The smile stretched into a beaming grin.

"I . . . I was afraid you might change your mind. That if you knew there was a baby on the way, you might think it was too much, taking on the twins as well." I felt ashamed, looking into those liquid eyes. I knew I shouldn't have doubted him. "I'm sorry—it was underhanded of me. But I—"

"Alice!" He put his arm around my shoulders and pulled me to him. "I know how much it means to you. The house is big enough for a dozen children, if that's what you want."

"Hmm—I think four's enough to be going on with, don't you?" With a wry smile I glanced at Ned, whose head had shifted sideways in my lap. His mouth was opening and closing, as if he were catching flies in his sleep.

With his free hand, Jack reached across to stroke Ned's hair. "He's going to be a busy little fellow, isn't he, with a new brother and sister to take home and another one on the way?"

I put my hand on top of his. "Did you ever imagine, in your wildest dreams, that you'd marry an ex-nun who'd drag you halfway across the world to adopt a couple of orphans?"

"Did you ever imagine you'd fall in love with a man who'd send you into a war zone with enough dynamite strapped to your body to blow up ten bridges?"

We both started laughing then, covering our mouths, trying not to wake Ned.

By the time the border guard came to check our documents, Jack had fallen asleep, too. I put my finger to my lips as the carriage door opened. I had the passports in my handbag.

"Thank you, Lady Trewella," the guard whispered as he handed them back.

It still sounded strange, that new name. But I'd had so many names since the day the sea had washed away the trappings of my old life: Sister Anthony had given way to Alice; Alice had turned into Jean-Luc; Jean-Luc had doubled as Ariel; and Ariel had become Soeur Antoine, before reverting to Alice again. Now I was Lady Alice, Viscountess Trewella.

I looked out of the window, at the great African sky studded with a million glittering stars. My hand went to the silver chain that hung around my neck—a gift from Jack, to hold the ring that I'd worn as a nun. It was a symbol of my old life and I had not wanted to part with it.

A song drifted through my head as I ran my fingers over the curve of the ring, my eyes still on the stars: *"Regina Caeli."* "The Queen of Heaven." Those Latin words had been the first I'd heard while lying on the sand, hovering between life and death. Jack's voice, singing me home.

Afterword

The idea for *The House at Mermaid's Cove* came to me in an ancient church on Cornwall's northwest coast. Saint Senara's, in the village of Zennor, contains a medieval bench end, carved more than five hundred years ago, with the image of a mermaid. The carving is said to have been made as a warning to the congregation. According to legend, a chorister, Matthew Trewella, was lured into the sea at Pendour Cove by a mermaid who came to the church in disguise to hear his beautiful singing.

The church's name echoes the centuries-old link between Cornwall and the region of Brittany on France's northwest coast. Saint Senara is thought to have been the sixth-century Irish princess Asenora, who was married to a Breton king. Folklore has it that the king's mother disliked her because of her Christian faith, and when Asenora became pregnant, persuaded her son that his wife had been unfaithful. Asenora was nailed to a barrel and cast adrift but was visited by an angel while floating in the sea and washed ashore in Cornwall, where her baby was born—a son with whom she eventually founded Christian communities in Cornwall. The idea of an anguished woman being washed onto a Cornish beach mingled in my mind with the mermaid legend and grew into the opening chapter of the novel.

The character of Alice was inspired by Marie Louise Habets (1905–1986), whose life was the subject of Kathryn Hulme's book

The Nun's Story (published by Frederick Muller Ltd., 1956), which was made into a film starring Audrey Hepburn. Marie Louise was a Belgian nun who served as a nurse in the Congo but left the religious life because of a crisis of conscience during World War II. The story of Alice is purely fictional, but many of the challenges she faces mirror those experienced by Marie Louise.

The description of the twin babies Alice discovers about to be buried alive with their dead mother is based on a real incident related by Charles F. Hayward in his book *Women Missionaries* (Collins, 1906), in which the father-in-law of the explorer David Livingstone came upon a group of native men digging a grave for a dead woman and her two living children and begged the men to let him take the boy and girl.

The setting for *The House at Mermaid's Cove* is based on the Trebah estate and the tiny fishing village of Durgan on Cornwall's south coast, between Falmouth and the Helford River. Warmed by the Gulf Stream and indented by steep, narrow valleys running down to the sea, this part of Cornwall is home to some of the most beautiful gardens in the world. The unique microclimate means that plants and trees often grow faster and stronger here than in their own countries of origin.

Jack Trewella's ancestral home, Penheligan, is a hybrid of two historic Cornish mansions, Cotehele, near the border with Devon, and Lanhydrock, near Bodmin. Both houses are more than four centuries old, and both contain depictions of the pelican symbol mentioned in the novel.

During World War Two the Secret Operations Executive ran missions between Cornwall and Brittany from a base in the Helford estuary. The route described—via the Isles of Scilly—and the strategy for getting British agents and Allied escapees to and from France is true to what really happened.

Trebah's tropical gardens and the cove itself are now open to the public, the gardens having been restored after the war. Durgan village is owned by the National Trust. The visitor center, housed in the old fish cellar, contains stories and photographs of village characters such as Leo Badger and George Retallack, who lived and worked there during the dark days of the early 1940s.

Farther along the estuary is the boathouse, rebuilt after it was blown up to make way for the US Army vehicles preparing to invade France. Prior to the D-Day landings, more than four hundred American troops, along with eighty tanks and jeeps, embarked from Trebah for the assault landing on Omaha Beach in June 1944. The cove is still known by local people as "Yankee Beach."

Acknowledgments

I'm grateful to the National Trust volunteers at Glendurgan in Cornwall for taking the time to explain some of the history of the area that became the setting for the novel. I'm also indebted to the late Major Tony Hibbert and his wife, Eira, who spent a quarter of a century restoring the subtropical garden at neighboring Trebah—a truly inspirational place that took root in my imagination.

Thank you to Jodi Warshaw, Erin Calligan Mooney, and everyone at Lake Union for the brilliant job they do, and to Christina Henry de Tessan for her very perceptive editorial input.

My friend Janet Thomas has been a great source of encouragement and support. She has always been there when I've needed to talk things through. I'm also grateful to Canon Stuart Bell and his wife, Pru, for their advice on some of the Christian themes in the novel. Mary Jones gave me guidance on aspects of life in Ireland, and Cathy Piquemal advised on French translations of the phrases used by SOE agents during World War II.

Last but by no means least, thanks to my family for their unfailing enthusiasm—and, in particular, to my husband, Steve, for all the early morning cups of coffee, for being my sounding board during the writing process, and for the fun we've had exploring Cornwall together.